Baldur's Gate II

Throne of Bhaal

Drew Karpyshyn

BALDUR'S GATE II
THRONE OF BHAAL
©2001 Wizards of the Coast, Inc.

Distributed in the United States by Holtzbrinck Publishing. Distributed in Canada by Fenn Ltd.

Distributed to the hobby, toy, and comic trade in the United States and Canada by regional distributors.

Distributed worldwide by Wizards of the Coast, Inc. and regional distributors.

Cover art by Todd Grenier
First Printing: September 2001
Library of Congress Catalog Card Number: 00-191029

9 8 7 6 5 4 3 2 1

UK ISBN: 0-7869-2630-9
US ISBN: 0-7869-1985-X
620-T21985

U.S., CANADA,
ASIA, PACIFIC, & LATIN AMERICA
Wizards of the Coast, Inc.
P.O. Box 707
Renton, WA 98057-0707
+1-800-324-6496

EUROPEAN HEADQUARTERS
Wizards of the Coast, Belgium
P.B. 2031
2600 Berchem
Belgium
+32-70-23-32-77

Visit our web site at **www.wizards.com/forgottenrealms**

Mom & dad, this one's for you.

Acknowledgments

This novel would not have been possible without the creative contributions of James Ohlen, Kevin Martens, David Gaider and the rest of the BioWare Throne of Bhaal design team. Thanks, guys.

Prologue

Marpenoth, 1368 DR

"Hush, Ravia," Gerdon warned his wife. "You'll wake the child. You'll scare him."

"He should be scared, Gerdon. I'm scared," Ravia replied, her voice on the verge of a sob. "You know what people are saying. Executions, public burnings . . ."

"No, Ravia!" Gerdon slammed his fist down hard on the heavy table in the middle of the small room his family used as their kitchen. He had crafted the table with his own two hands, just as he had made the chairs around it, just as he had made the bed in the next room. Gerdon had even built the wooden walls around them and the thatch roof overhead. "I will not be driven from my land—my home—by this madness!"

Ravia shook her head, and her voice was soft as she addressed her husband. "Would you rather die, Gerdon? You and your son? The tainted blood runs in Terrel's veins, too."

Gerdon didn't answer right away, but paced the floor of their tiny home. He was sick of having this argument with his wife night after night. He was angry—with Ravia, with the world, even with himself. But more than that, he was afraid. Afraid she might be right. Part of him, however, refused to give in to her desire to flee.

"Those stories come from the north, from Amn. They are barbarians there! The Amnish would kill their neighbors for a handful of coins. They are just looking for any excuse."

Drew Karpyshyn

Rising from where she sat at the table, Ravia crossed the room and blocked the path of her husband's frantic pacing, forcing him to acknowledge her, forcing him to carefully weigh her words, rather than dismiss them out of hand.

"Each week we hear more tales, husband. Each week we hear rumors from towns and villages that grow ever closer to our own land. Not just Amn anymore. You know it is happening in Tethyr and Calimshan now, too. You cannot ignore this, Gerdon!"

"This town is not like that," Gerdon protested, reaching out and pulling his wife close to give her a reassuring hug—though who he was trying to reassure Gerdon could not truly say. "They are simple farmers, like ourselves. Our neighbors would never harm us. We know them."

Ravia made no reply. Uncomfortable with the oppressive silence, Gerdon continued to try and ease the fears of his wife. "Anyway, they would never believe it if anyone told them. Nobody knows but us. Even Terrel does not know."

In a soft whisper Ravia replied, "Maybe he should."

* * * * *

Run. No questions, no answers. No hesitation, no explanation. Run. Just run.

His father had drilled the lesson into Terrel's head every night for the past month. Terrel was only ten. He did not fully understand many of the words his father used—persecution, lynching, genocide, legacy, Bhaalspawn. Terrel *was* old enough to understand what was most important in his father's words.

"If you see strangers at the farm, Terrel, you run. As fast and as far as you can. Just run."

Coming back from his chores in the field, Terrel heard them long before he saw them. Angry shouts of many voices carried far on the evening wind. The mob was marching straight through the fields, heedlessly trampling the crops of Terrel's father under foot. Their torches blazed in the darkening gloom of evening twilight, bathing the crowd in an orange glow. They didn't seem to have noticed Terrel yet. Their attention was focused on the tiny farmhouse in the distance, not on the small figure barely visible in the darkness on the far side of the fields.

But Terrel could see them, illuminated by the flames they held aloft. Even at this distance the young boy recognized many of the men who periodically came to the farm to do business with his father. Only when he saw the unfamiliar uniforms of soldiers amidst the throng did Terrel heed his father's instructions. He ran.

* * * * *

The small house was surrounded. The wall of soldiers and mercenaries encircling the tiny farm slowly closed ranks, drawing the noose ever tighter around the neck of the foul Child of Bhaal. An eager crowd of townsfolk hovered just outside the edges of the circle—anxious to see, but fearful of being seen. The leader of the soldiers, hidden by dark shadows and a heavy hooded cloak, oversaw the entire scene from a safe distance.

The house was quiet as the armored men approached, but a light from within shone through small cracks in the walls. The soldiers stopped, and from the crowd of civilians behind them the mayor was reluctantly pushed to the fore.

Shifting uncomfortably from one foot to the other, the mayor looked around, seeking some comfort or reassurance in the faces of the people he represented. The townsfolk hung back beyond the circle of soldiers, staring at the ground. Their downcast faces were blurred by flickering torchlight and shadows, their true feelings inscrutable.

3

The mayor could clearly see the expression on the faces of the nearby soldiers. Or rather, he could see that their faces held no expression at all. Each of the armored men surrounding the small farmhouse returned the mayor's searching gaze with a look of apathy, devoid of all thought or compassion. They were highly trained not to feel anything but a fanatical obedience to duty and to the will of their cowled leader, almost completely hidden in the shadows.

The mayor cleared his throat, and when he spoke his voice projected clear and loud, despite his reservations—the voice of a man used to making public speeches.

"Gerdon, for the safety of the community you are to be taken into custody, lest your unholy taint bring destruction down on us all! If you surrender without bloodshed, you will be arrested and given a fair trial!"

There was no reply from within the house. The only sound was the occasional crackle or sputter from one of the burning torches. The mayor waited a suitable length of time before speaking again.

"Ravia, your wife, will be allowed to go free if you surrender to us. If you resist, I cannot guarantee her safety."

Again, the only reply was silence. The mayor continued.

"Your son, Terrel, must also be surrendered to us of course. The foul blood of Bhaal runs in his veins as well."

This time the mayor allowed the silence to drag for many minutes before he resumed speaking. He had delivered the carefully composed speech as the hooded figure had instructed him to do. Now he was left with only his own words. When he spoke again, his voice no longer held the deep timbre of an official proclamation.

"Gerdon, please . . . be reasonable. This is unpleasant for us all. For the safety of our families, and yours, you must turn yourself and your son over to the auth—"

The arrow embedded itself in the mayor's chest, the metal point biting deep into the flesh, penetrating

4

between the tough bone of the ribcage and puncturing a lung. The pleas of the mayor were lost in a choking froth of blood. The mayor clutched feebly at the shaft protruding from his torso and slowly collapsed to the ground, dead. Cries of alarm and horror rose up from the mob of townspeople still gathered tightly behind the wall of soldiers surrounding the farmhouse.

As one, the ring of armored men advanced on the building, their faces registering neither shock nor surprise, as if they had expected this result all along. A volley of arrows arced out from the small window of the cabin to thwart their approach, but the deadly projectiles bounced harmlessly off the large, heavy shields of the soldiers as they marched in perfect formation. They closed their ranks until they formed a tight circle less than a dozen feet from the walls of the townhouse.

A familiar voice came from the house. "A curse upon this traitorous town!" Gerdon screamed, "May your souls burn in the Abyss!"

The leader of the soldiers, responding to a sign from the barely visible figure of their cloaked leader in the distant gloom, raised his hand. In unison every second soldier encircling the cabin raised his torch and hurled it at the thatched roof. The flames caught quickly, and the violet night sky was smeared with a plume of thick black smoke.

Half the soldiers still held torches. The other half methodically drew their scimitars and waited. They all kept their shields up high to guard against another assault of arrows.

From within the cabin there was only defiant silence as the thatched roof caught flame, and the fire spread. Soon orange tongues licked their way down the walls, crawling from the roof of the tiny home to scorch the foundations and earth below. The smoke curled up before it was finally thinned and dispersed by the faint wind blowing across the fields.

Gerdon screamed a wail of anguish and grief, an inhuman keening that made the townsfolk cover their ears in terror and shame.

The door to the cabin flew open, wrenched from its hinges as Gerdon burst forth. Armed only with the iron scythe he used to thresh grain, the heavy-set farmer recklessly charged the captain of the soldiers. The armored captain calmly stepped forward to meet the charge, his shield and scimitar prepared to meet the assault.

Wielding his makeshift weapon with the expertise of a master thresher, Gerdon brought the curved blade in low, at the unprotected legs of his opponent. The captain parried the scythe with his own blade and redirected the blow so that it struck harmlessly on the ground by his feet.

In one quick motion Gerdon reversed the direction of his attack, sliding his hands along the long shaft to change the center of balance while twisting his waist and wrenching his shoulders to reverse the momentum of the heavy implement. His opponent was caught off balance by the quick counterstrike, and barely managed to get his shield in the way to take the brunt of the blow.

Driven by the fury of madness and desperation, the force of Gerdon's attack dented the iron shield, knocking the captain back. The soldier lurched awkwardly, struggling to regain his balance even as Gerdon brought the scythe around for the final, fatal swing at the captain's now-exposed flank.

The tool slipped out of Gerdon's suddenly paralyzed hands and the farmer dropped to his knees, the victim of a single well placed slash of a scimitar across his unprotected back. Blinded by his grief and rage, Gerdon hadn't noticed the soldier who had calmly moved into position behind him during his battle with the captain.

Gerdon crumpled to the ground, his legs and arms twitching spastically from the wound that had all but severed his spine. He tried to call for help, a final appeal to his neighbors still standing just out of sight beyond the wall of armored soldiers. But a seizure gripped Gerdon's body, and only animal grunts and moans escaped his throat.

The captain sheathed his weapon and stepped over to kick the scythe out of reach of Gerdon's uncontrollably flailing hands. He jerked his head in the direction of his men, and four of them rushed up, each grabbing hold of one of Gerdon's thrashing limbs. They lifted the convulsing man from the ground, carried him over to the burning cabin in which his wife's smoldering corpse lay, and threw him on the inferno.

As Gerdon's body struck the blazing walls of his home, the fire-weakened framework gave way and collapsed, burying the paralyzed man beneath the flaming wreckage.

"Captain!" a stern voice called out from the crowd a second later. "I found this one running through the fields, trying to escape."

Half a dozen soldiers pushed their way through the mob of horrified civilians to join their fellows impassively watching the burning remains of the building. One of the new arrivals dragged a boy behind him, his fist firmly clenching a knot of the child's hair.

The captain followed their progress with a dispassionate gaze as the boy was forced into the center of the circle and his arms pinned behind his back by one of the soldiers. Bathed in the light from the mounting flames the boy was clearly visible to the entire assemblage.

"What is your name, boy?" the captain demanded.

The boy was silent.

The captain turned to the crowd. "What is this child's name?"

For several seconds there was silence, and then an anonymous voice called out, "Terrel. Gerdon's son."

With a single, fluid motion the captain drew his scimitar. Voices cried out in protest. One exclaimed, "But he's only a child!"

"A child of Bhaal," the captain clarified, drawing his blade across the helpless lad's exposed throat.

7

Chapter One

"I want to go home . . . to Candlekeep."

Abdel had never uttered truer words than those he had spoken at the foot of the Tree of Life. But there was one thing Abdel had learned from the recent events of his life—he rarely got what he wanted.

He should have been a hero many times over. First he had slain his evil half brother Sarevok and saved the city of Baldur's Gate from a bloody and senseless war. Then, with Jaheira by his side, Abdel had defeated the sorcerer Jon Irenicus and saved the life and soul of his childhood friend and half sister, Imoen. Abdel had died, ventured into the Abyss, and finally been reborn at the foot of the Tree of Life. In the process he had liberated the elven city of Suldanessellar, thwarted the plot of the mad mage Irenicus to become an immortal, and prevented the destruction of the Tree of Life—the source of all existence on Faerûn.

After all that, the only thing Abdel wanted was to return to his childhood home, but there was no hero's welcome awaiting Abdel when he left the safety of Suldanessellar, and the walls of Candlekeep were farther away than ever.

"Abdel, we need to rest." The exhausted voice of Jaheira, Abdel's lover, cut through the brooding thoughts of the big sellsword as he blazed a path through the thick undergrowth beneath the towering trees of Tethir Forest. "We cannot go on tonight. As soon as we find a clearing we should stop."

8

Glancing over at the beautiful half-elf who had stood beside him throughout all his trials, Abdel saw her fine features were drawn and haggard. Her normally olive skin was almost black with the dust and dirt of their seemingly endless journey. Her long, thick, black hair was matted and tangled, its lustrous copper streaks now dull and dingy. In the shards of light from the full moon streaming through the thick ceiling of branches above them, her violet eyes still burned with energy and intensity. Jaheira would follow him to the end of Faerûn without complaint. Abdel realized it was not for herself that she demanded they stop.

Imoen, the young woman who had shared Abdel's youth, hopes, and dreams during his upbringing at Candlekeep, was lagging behind. Barely five feet tall, she was forced to take twice as many steps as Abdel to keep the pace he set. The toll was clearly evident. Her normally bright and mischievous eyes were half closed, her head drooped to her chest, her chestnut bangs fell down across her pale, freckled brow. The sprightly bounce in her step was gone. She marched with the heavy, stiff-legged tread of one forced far beyond the limits of endurance. Like Abdel, Imoen had the blood of a god coursing through her veins. However, the tainted essence of their father had been largely purged from her body and soul by the mad experiments of the mage Irenicus, and she lacked the superhuman fortitude of her half brother.

The semiconscious young woman stumbled on a gnarled root jutting up from the floor of the dark woods, but Abdel was there to catch her before she hit the ground. He moved with the unnatural speed of a being who was more than a man and only slightly less than a god. He scooped her up without a word and cradled her in his gigantic arms. They pressed onward through the thick trees, Jaheira now leading the way, until they found a small clearing. Abdel gently lowered his half sister to the forest floor and turned a concerned face up to Jaheira.

"She'll be all right," the half-elf assured him. "She just needs to rest. As do I."

"How long?"

The question itself was simple, yet Jaheira hesitated before answering. Abdel understood. Living as fugitives was taking a steep toll on each of the trio, but Imoen suffered most of all. Hunted like animals, the three of them had spent the past few weeks on the run. Their pursuers—mercenaries, soldiers, bounty hunters, and religious fanatics—were relentless, driving Abdel and his companions ever southward through the inhospitable wilderness. Jaheira had to balance their need for rest against the urgency of their perpetual flight.

"We need a few hours, Abdel. At least." Jaheira sighed before continuing. "That should be enough for Imoen to get back on her feet, but she won't last long, even then. A week of bed rest wouldn't be enough to get her back to full strength at this stage. Imoen is not like you Abdel. . . not anymore. Not since Irenicus stole your father's essence from her soul."

Abdel nodded. "A few hours then." Jaheira might be stronger than Imoen, but Abdel could tell she too was suffering from sleep deprivation and exhaustion. The large warrior felt only the faintest hint of fatigue in his own massive muscles, but the life force of a god dwelt within him. "You rest, my love. I'll stand watch."

Jaheira shook her head slightly, too tired to give a more emphatic response. "Not yet. I think I can find something to revive us a little bit. Some mint, or some ginseng root, maybe. Not much, but it will help."

There was no point in arguing with her, Abdel realized. Despite her exhaustion, Jaheira's will was as adamant as ever. She was determined to seek out some beneficial plant or herb in the undergrowth of the surrounding forest, and nothing he said would change her mind. Offering to explore the bushes himself would be pointless—Jaheira was a druid, a servant of the balance and of nature. She might recognize the medicinal and recuperative value of the nearby flora, but Abdel himself would have no clue. During his years as a mercenary and hired blade, the sellsword had picked up some basic survival knowledge. Here in the southern tip of Tethir Forest the plants were completely alien to Abdel's eyes.

"Don't go far," Abdel warned.

Jaheira gave a slight nod in response and vanished into the thick darkness of the woods.

Imoen rested fitfully, mumbling and twitching often as she lay on the cold ground. Abdel could do little but watch and curse those who hunted them. If he was alone, he could stand and fight. For anyone but Abdel, such a thought would have been ludicrous, and until recently, even he would not have considered the idea.

As a teenager Abdel had been bigger and stronger than most of the grown men he had encountered, and as an adult Abdel was perhaps the largest, most imposing human on the face of Faerûn. Standing seven feet tall, the heavily muscled young man had carved out a reputation for himself as a blade for hire, mercenary, bodyguard, warrior—as a sellsword, Abdel had done it all. Then he had learned the truth that would forever change his life.

Abdel was the son of the Lord of Murder, the offspring of the god Bhaal. A dead god, true, but a god nonetheless. The identity of his father had turned Abdel into a fugitive on the run, pursued by enemies and bounty hunters wherever he went. His lineage had also changed Abdel's life in even more astonishing ways. He was evolving, physically changing. He still looked like a normal, if remarkably large, human man, but he wasn't human. Not anymore. Jaheira called him an avatar—a physical manifestation of his immortal father.

Drew Karpyshyn

Being an avatar had its share of advantages. Abdel's body had become a vessel for the essence of Bhaal. Even for his enormous size he was freakishly strong. Somehow his body was now able to draw on the immortal essence contained within to replenish itself, healing grievous and even fatal injuries at an astounding rate. Abdel's endurance, strength, and physical prowess were unmatched throughout the lands of Faerûn. His power was growing. Every day Abdel felt himself becoming stronger, felt his abilities passing further and further beyond the limiting thresholds of mortality.

His remarkable regenerative powers could now render the arrows and blades of his enemies all but useless. The wounds inflicted would heal almost instantly. Virtually invincible, Abdel believed he could single-handedly slaughter an entire company and walk away unharmed. Imoen and Jaheira were not blessed with his extraordinary constitution. They would be vulnerable, and in the chaos of a full-scale battle Abdel didn't know if he could protect them.

There was something else: Immune to all physical weaponry, Abdel was vulnerable in another way. The big sellsword was no stranger to violence. His chosen profession had nurtured and honed his bloodlust, feeding the evil part of him that was the legacy of Bhaal to all his children. Only Jaheira's love had prevented Abdel from succumbing to the taint of the dead Lord of Murder and becoming a soulless killing machine like his half brother Sarevok had been.

The support and guidance of the woman he loved had enabled Abdel to fight against his own impulses. With Jaheira's patient and understanding hand on his shoulder, he had learned to control the hate and the rage within him, to suppress the terrible transformation that threatened to overwhelm him. But that control was fragile. The wholesale slaughter of his pursuers might unleash the terrible monster he had learned to cage within himself.

12

It had happened before—to both himself and Imoen, though Abdel had purged the beast from Imoen's spirit in a vicious, bloody battle at the foot of the Tree of Life. But the potential for Abdel to turn into a mindless abomination bent only on killing every living being within reach was still very real. In victory over his enemies Abdel's very identity could be consumed by the foul essence of his unholy father and his body would transform into the four-armed demon that was the physical manifestation of Bhaal's evil on Faerûn. If he wasn't careful, Abdel knew, he might become the Ravager again.

The slightest whisper of leaves caused Abdel to spin around and drop into a low crouch, drawing his heavy broadsword from the sheath on his back in a single, fluid motion. He stood with the blade poised to strike at the first appearance of the unseen intruder, his powerful hands clenching at the hilt of his weapon so hard his knuckles were white. The enormous muscles of his arms and shoulders rippled and twitched in anticipation, then relaxed when Jaheira emerged from the forest and stepped into the clearing.

The attractive druid held up a handful of small, three-cornered leaves, then popped one into her own mouth. "These will help, but we still need to sleep. Even you, Abdel." She handed him one of the leaves. "For Imoen. Just place it under her tongue if she's too tired to chew."

Abdel did as he was told, dropping to his knees and setting his sword on the ground as he tenderly lifted the head of his exhausted half sister. She didn't respond to his voice when he urged her to take the leaf, so Abdel gently tilted her face back and opened her tiny mouth. He slipped the leaf beneath her tongue and lowered her head back to the cold ground. Jaheira handed him a blanket from the pack she carried on her back, and he carefully arranged it over the winsome body of the sleeping young woman.

Drew Karpyshyn

Jaheira lay down a few feet away, and Abdel crawled over beside her. She snuggled up close, resting her head in the crook of his massive arm and pressing herself against him to try and draw warmth from his well-muscled body.

"I spoke to the animals of the forest," the druid whispered in a groggy voice, already succumbing to the welcome embrace of sleep. "They will warn us if anyone approaches."

Reassured by Jaheira's words, Abdel shifted slightly on the cold ground, trying to get comfortable without disturbing the already sleeping druid. He had full confidence in Jaheira's ability to commune with the birds and beasts of the forest. He knew they would be well watched over while they slept, but for some reason Abdel could not will himself to close his eyes.

He struggled with the dilemma of their situation. The hunters were close, and with both Imoen and Jaheira able to travel less and less each day it was only a matter of time until the three were found. Abdel would be forced to fight, forced into a confrontation he desperately wanted to avoid.

Not for the first time, Abdel considered slipping away while Imoen and Jaheira slept. He could lure their pursuers away from the two women. Let them live in peace while he lived the never-ending life of a fugitive. Abdel sighed and closed his eyes, dismissing the option as he always did. Even if he could bring himself to leave Jaheira's side, even if he could force himself to abandon Imoen and the woman he loved, he had no way to be certain the hunters would follow him.

They chased Abdel for his blood—the tainted blood of a dead god. They persecuted him for the sins of his father, Bhaal. Rumors of sudden arrests, senseless tortures, and immediate executions were too frequent and too widespread to be discounted. Like all the Bhaalspawn, Abdel was on the run—sentenced to incarceration or death not because of anything he had done, but simply because of who he was.

14

Imoen was a Bhaalspawn, too. Even though the taint of the dead god had been all but purged from her soul, her life would be forfeit if they were captured, just as surely as Abdel's. Imoen was not strong enough to survive without Abdel and Jaheira helping her.

Overwhelmed by the hopelessness of his situation, Abdel at last gave in to sleep.

* * * * *

He was standing in a void, a dead world of gray nothingness. Abdel felt for the great blade he normally kept strapped to his back and was reassured when his hand brushed against the cold metal of the hilt.

"There is no need for that here—though if it comforts you, so be it."

The voice was neither male nor female. It seemed to be the sound of a great host speaking in perfect, harmonious unison. Resisting the instinctive impulse to draw his sword, Abdel spun around. His head snapped from side to side, seeking out the unknown speaker or speakers. He saw nothing but empty gray on every side.

"Show yourself!" His voice echoed in the emptiness, drawing his attention momentarily back to his strange surroundings. Abdel glanced up and saw there was no sky above him, he glanced down and realized there was no earth below. He didn't even feel as if he was standing on anything.

"There is nothing to fear, Abdel Adrian. You will not fall."

Obviously, the disembodied voice could read his thoughts, wherever—or whatever—it was. Abdel was surprised to notice that the words of the voice did not echo like his.

"Show yourself," Abdel said again. This time it was more of a request than a command.

"Prepare thyself, Child of Bhaal."

Suddenly, Abdel was not alone in the void. The entity did not slowly materialize from the gray as Abdel had expected. It didn't flash or magically shimmer into being as if from a wizard's spell. One moment there was nothing, the next the entity was there—as real and permanent as if it had existed in this strange nether realm for an eternity before Abdel's own appearance.

The being was male, with white hair and a beard. Though it resembled a human in form the features were neither handsome nor ugly and were unremarkable. It was not mortal. No mortal could compare to such a divine creation. It was clad in a black flowing robe, in contrast to its flawless alabaster skin. The material seemed to meld with the being that wore it, flowing together so that Abdel could not tell where the apparel ended and the entity began. His eyes swam with the dark depths of eternity, pierced with blazing points of purest light—like the starry sky on a clear, bright night. The face was both young and old, both omnipotent and innocent.

The creature towered over Abdel's own seven-foot frame, and the robe encompassed all of the celestial patterns of the moons and stars. Bathed in the glorious presence, Abdel could only stand in speechless awe for several seconds.

When he at last found his voice, he could only utter, "I must be dreaming."

"A dream can be no less true than that what you call the real world," the entity assured him.

"Are you a god?" Abdel asked, unaware he had even formed the question in his head until he heard his own voice echoing in the surrounding void.

"Not a god, but a servant of the Divine Will. There are greater powers than the gods, Abdel Adrian."

Abdel shook his head to try and dispel the fog of wonder that seemed to envelop his thoughts. His mind cleared somewhat.

"Where am I?" Abdel was certain the magnificent specimen before him knew the answer to his question. Perhaps it knew the answer to all questions.

"We are between, Abdel Adrian," the being responded in its harmonious multitude of voices. "That which was, that which is, and that which may be. All things are possible here, yet none truly exist."

"I . . . don't understand." A part of Abdel felt ashamed to admit his ignorance to this glorious creature. But another part, a small, hard ember at the core of Abdel's being, felt resentment toward the entity before him.

"No, you are not yet ready to truly understand." The creature seemed to be momentarily speaking to itself before turning its responses back toward Abdel. "This was once the realm of Bhaal—a piece of the Abyss blighted and scarred by the hate and evil of your father's existence. But Bhaal is dead, and he no longer holds sway here."

Abdel pondered the being's reply for a long time. The creature stood motionless before him, radiant and stunning. When the entity first appeared, Abdel had felt his own identity all but crushed beneath the creature's splendor. Now, however, Abdel no longer felt overwhelmed by the entity's mere presence.

"You brought me here, didn't you? Why?"

"Your presence here is as much your own will as mine, Abdel Adrian—though you do not yet know it. You are here to prepare."

"Prepare for what?" Abdel asked, already certain he knew what the answer would be.

"Your destiny. The legacy of your father. You are a Child of Bhaal, Abdel Adrian. Know this, and you shall know thyself."

The small ember of resentment briefly flared up in the sellsword's breast. Destiny, the legacy of Bhaal; in his entire life, in all he had seen and done, Abdel had never encountered anything remotely resembling the creature now before him. Yet this spectacular being was repeating the same refrain Abdel had been hearing ever since the night his half brother Sarevok's minions had killed Gorion, Abdel's foster father.

17

Drew Karpyshyn

With a weary sigh Abdel asked a series of all-too-familiar questions.

"What of my legacy, then? What future does my destiny hold? And what do you want from me?"

The entity, physically perfect in its statuesque motionlessness up until this point, shifted its head slightly. The illusion was shattered. For all the spectacle of this seemingly omniscient, omnipotent creature, Abdel realized, the entity was uncertain. Again, the ember of resentment flared up within the muscular chest of the giant warrior.

"I have watched you closely, Abdel Adrian," the man informed him. "The Immortal is strong within you. There are many paths for the Children of Bhaal yet to walk, and you shall be one at the forefront of the journey."

"Children?" Abdel asked in surprise. "You mean Imoen is involved, too?"

"You and Imoen are not alone. Your destiny is entwined with that of many, many others."

"And just what is this destiny you speak of? What future awaits me?"

"Your destiny is yet unclear," the being admitted. "But know that the time of prophecy is near. There are those who seek to destroy you and your kin, Abdel. Betrayal awaits at every turn, and hidden enemies plot to kill you."

"Hidden enemies? Who? Why can't you just tell me?"

"There are secrets I cannot divulge. My actions are bound by forces mortals cannot fathom. I can only guide you to the answers you seek, Abdel Adrian. I cannot give the answers to you.

"Seek those who share the taint of your blood and you shall find the answers I cannot give."

Abdel woke to Jaheira's screams.

Chapter Two

Illasera sensed the hunt was near an end. She licked her lips in anticipation as she slung her bow from her taut, muscular shoulder. Without breaking her long, graceful stride she silently notched a single black arrow from the quiver on her slim hip. The trampled undergrowth, snapped twigs, and broken branches marking the path of her quarry's passing were fresh—a few hours old at most. The faint footprints on the hard forest floor, all but invisible to those unfamiliar with the ways of the hunter, revealed a steadily decreasing stride length—an obvious sign of fatigue. Illasera was certain the trio she stalked would have to stop for the night to rest, but the Huntress was still going. She would catch them soon.

She paused, her finely honed predator's senses picking up yet another indication of her targets' nearby presence. Illasera could smell her prey. The scent of musky sweat hung heavy on the still air trapped within the densely wooded Tethir Forest. It was more than that though, Illasera was one of the Five. She could *feel* them. The blood of the Bhaalspawn called out to her, like calling to like, urging her on. She set off again, quickening her pace with every eager step, slipping through the trees, silent as a shadow.

A flicker of movement caught the corner of her eye. She unleashed a single arrow, pinning the small bird that had just flown by to a tree. As she marched past, Illasera glanced down at the tiny feathered body impaled on the point, still twitching feebly in a hopeless effort to escape. The creature had been trying to warn her prey.

The Huntress brushed a strand of long hair back from her face and laughed softly to herself as she pressed on. One of the three she stalked could speak with the animals of the forest, commune with them in ways most people could not fathom. One of her prey was a child of the grove, a servant of nature, a druid.

They were foolish if they believed such feathered sentinels could protect them. Each of the Five was blessed with unholy power. The legacy of their tainted, immortal father manifested itself in them in different ways. Illasera's power linked her to the earth. Like the druid, Illasera could touch the creatures of the forest. She could use her power to influence the natural order. However, hers was not a symbiotic relationship. When Illasera used her power, nature was bent to serve her tainted will.

Illasera hesitated, considering the consequences of her actions. She could send out a call to the darker spirits that dwelt within the wood—a call that would surely be heard by the nearby druid. But if the Bhaalspawn were as close as Illasera suspected, as close as they *felt*, the advance warning of her presence would not be enough to allow them to escape.

Standing still, she tilted her head back and raised her arms to the black sky. Her eyes blazed with a dark fire. Overhead the leaves rustled and branches shook as Illasera gathered her power in a chill wind. The nearby animals fled in silent terror at the touch of the icy air or cowered in the cover of the forest undergrowth, paralyzed with fear.

The ground trembled with the mounting magic of the dark archer. A great flock of fowl burst from the shelter of the nearby branches, blotting out the moon as they arced toward the sky. The sound of a thousand beating wings couldn't hide the harsh screams of terror from their feathered throats. The Huntress echoed their cries with a scream of her own, unleashing a wave of malevolent magic that rumbled across the forest's floor as Illasera sent forth an unholy summons none could deny.

The denizens of the forest—fowl, beasts, even the trees themselves—were touched by the unholy call as the dark magic enveloped them. Leaves withered and died instantly, branches became twisted and gnarled, roots rotted and tangled, even the trunks of the great oaks warped and bent into an abomination of their natural form. The smaller creatures of the forest fell dead, their existence obliterated by Illasera's necromancy. Those that were stronger began to change—metamorphosing into mutated, diseased versions of their true form. Corrupted by the evil taint of one of the Five, the helpless creatures' minds were dominated and consumed by Illasera's own evil consciousness.

They gathered around Illasera's form. A pack of what had once been wolves circled their fell mistress. With a single silent command Illasera sent her minions off as advance scouts to lead the Huntress to her prey.

Nearby, a woman screamed.

* * * * *

Jaheira's anguished cry woke Abdel instantly, ripping him from the strange dream. A heartbeat later he was on his feet with his heavy sword drawn as his eyes scoured the surrounding foliage for signs of danger.

He saw nothing, unable to pierce the darkness of the night. "Jaheira," he whispered, "What is it, my love?"

A single, arcane word from fell from Jaheira's lips, and the grove was bathed in a soft, warm light. The magical illumination allowed Abdel to see clearly. Jaheira was already on her feet, the familiar quarterstaff she used as a weapon clenched tightly in her fists as she stood beside Abdel. Imoen was still on the ground, slowly struggling to raise her weary form to a standing position, fumbling with the tiny dagger she kept tucked inside her belt.

Abdel barely noticed his two female companions. Instead, his attention was drawn to the unfamiliar surroundings, and he understood the horrified reaction of his druid companion. What had been a lush, vibrant forest when he had fallen asleep had become a moribund grove of decay. Towering trees were now rotting dead wood, their trunks twisted and malformed. All around them dead leaves tumbled slowly to the ground, falling from dead branches to cover the clearing like a sickly yellow blanket.

The pungent smell of decomposing vegetation assailed Abdel's nostrils. Beneath the sickly sweet odor he half imagined he could smell something else—something foul and unclean.

"What is this?" Imoen asked in a harsh, uneasy whisper.

"Fell magic," Jaheira replied, "an abomination of the natural order."

"Get into a defensive position," Abdel ordered, taking charge of the situation. He was certain an attack was imminent, and he had no desire to let something spring at his unprotected back from the surrounding trees. The three companions moved into a tight circle, standing back to back near the center of the small clearing.

The brush of Jaheira's hair against Abdel's bare arm sent an electric shiver of longing along the big man's spine, but he shook off the effect of his lover's touch. He needed to focus on the impenetrable wall of gray and twisted trees ahead of him.

He did not have long to wait.

The attack came from all sides simultaneously, as Abdel knew it would and hoped it wouldn't. A pack of five creatures familiar in form yet somehow alien and altered launched themselves from the cover of the forest, hurling their bodies with reckless abandon at the three defenders.

One great wolf leaped at Abdel's throat, and a part of the sellsword's mind instinctively recoiled at what he saw. The beast's eyes were milky white, the pupils lost in the murky pus that wept from the half-blind orbs leaving a sticky, glistening trail of slime oozing down the creature's snout. Great flecks of gray foam flew from the wolf's open jaws. Its teeth were barely visible beneath the thick froth welling up from its throat. The wolf's heavy coat was matted and tangled. The flesh showing through the many patches of mange was discolored and covered with festering lesions. The fur of the creature pulsated, as if millions of maggots wriggled just beneath the surface. Worst of all was the smell, the sickly sweet stench of gangrenous flesh that threatened to overwhelm Abdel's gag reflex and drop him retching to his knees.

Only a small part of Abdel's mind was refined enough to feel any revulsion at the abhorrent lupine form. The majority of his brain operated on a more basic, primal level. Abdel's sword moved with the speed of thought, slicing through the chest of the diseased wolf. The blade ripped through fur and ribcage, covering the sellsword in a spray of warm blood.

Abdel let the momentum of his blow spin him around to face the creatures converging on Jaheira and Imoen. By the time the corpse of the first wolf had hit the ground, Abdel's sword was already disemboweling a second that had leaped toward Imoen.

From the corner of his eye, Abdel noticed Jaheira had met the charge of a third wolf by cracking her staff down on its brow, caving in its skull with a single stroke, but the momentum of the brain-dead beast was unabated. The disease-ridden body bowled Jaheira over, burying her beneath a tumbling mass of filthy, vermin-ridden fur and flesh.

Unable to immediately aid Jaheira, Abdel kicked Imoen in the back with a heavy boot, sending her stumbling back off balance and pushing her out of the way of the snapping jaws of a fourth attacker. The wolf, deprived of its initial target, spun to face the new threat, its powerful hind legs propelling it up at Abdel's unprotected throat. Its teeth sank deep into the warrior's windpipe, and the creature wrenched its head hard to the side, ripping his throat open.

The weight of the wolf attack knocked the big man over, sending him toppling backward to the hard earth. As he fell, Abdel brought the point of his weapon up, wedging it into the fold of skin between two of the beast's ribs. The creature was too close for Abdel to get any leverage into his thrusting attack, but when the combatants struck the ground the force of their momentum and the wolf's own mass impaled the beast on Abdel's blade.

The injury to Abdel would have been instantly fatal to any mortal on Abeir-toril—but Abdel had ceased being a mortal long ago. Even as he worked the point of his sword deeper into his foe, Abdel could feel the flesh of his savaged throat regenerating. Momentarily trapped beneath the weight of the wolf, the warrior twisted his blade, tearing cartilage and snapping bone as he opened a fist-size hole in the chest of his opponent. The diseased wolf died instantly, and in the scant second it took Abdel to roll the corpse off to one side, Abdel's own wound had completely healed.

Drenched in gore, Abdel jumped up to meet the next attacker, only to find the fifth and final wolf feebly twitching on the ground. The hilt of Imoen's dagger protruded from between its haunches. The beast had been killed by a single well-placed strike at the base of its brain.

Beside him Jaheira had already managed to crawl out from under the foul corpse of the wolf she had killed. The druid was on her knees retching uncontrollably, physically sickened by her close contact with the unnatural monstrosity that had attacked her. Apart from her obvious discomfort and embarrassment, Abdel could tell she was unharmed.

Then he noticed Imoen, curled up near the corpse of the first wolf and clutching at her arm, feebly trying to staunch the flow of blood. Abdel crossed the clearing in a single bounding stride, and dropped to his knees beside his half sister. He glanced at Jaheira as he did so.

"I'm all right, Abdel," Imoen said, trying to give him a brave smile, but she could only manage to grit her teeth in pain. Abdel gently took her wrist and turned her arm so he could examine her injury. The underside of her arm was torn open from the wrist to the elbow. Sinew and muscle spilled out from the wound.

Imoen winced and paled at the sight. In a shaky voice she whispered, "Guess I don't heal as fast as you, big brother."

Jaheira dropped down beside them, still wiping away the last vestiges of vomit from her lips. "Horrible," she said simply. "Those things were once animals, and something turned them into those . . . *perversions* of nature. We should burn the corpses of those abominations."

Neither Abdel nor Imoen replied, and Jaheira suddenly seemed to notice the vicious gash in Imoen's arm. "I am sorry, child," she said as she quickly examined the damage. "I did not mean to let my outrage over nature's defilement interfere with my attending to your suffering."

From a pouch at her belt Jaheira pulled a handful of small, blood-red berries. She held them in a fist above Imoen's torn flesh and squeezed, letting the crimson juice dribble down into the wound. Imoen grunted in shock and tried to jerk her arm away, but Jaheira's sure grip kept the girl's limb immobilized.

"Does it hurt, child?"

Imoen nodded, but she was gritting her teeth too tight to reply.

"There is infection and disease setting in already. I shudder to even imagine what foul afflictions could result from the touch of those beasts. This will cleanse the wound."

Now that he was certain Jaheira had attended to Imoen, Abdel was able to return his attention to the unseen threats that might still linger within the forest. Something was still out there, watching them.

* * * * *

Illasera arrived at the edge of the small clearing shortly after her scouts, but the battle was already over. Not that she was surprised. She fully expected two Bhaal-spawn to be more than a match for the wolves—even wolves touched and transformed by Illasera's own powerful magic. But her minions had done their job—the Huntress now had her quarry in sight.

Still unnoticed by the three people in the clearing, the archer took a silent half-step back, willing herself to vanish among the dead and leafless gray branches. From her well-camouflaged position, Illasera surveyed the situation.

As she had been told, and as the tracks indicated, there were indeed three—two females, and a very large, very muscular male. Illasera knew only two were children of the Lord of Murder. Bhaal's Anointed, the leader of the Five, had been quite clear on that point: two tainted by the divine essence, and one mortal companion. Of course, all three would die beneath the hand of the Huntress.

The man, Illasera guessed, was one of the Bhaalspawn. His great size, his immense, rippling muscles, the natural, predatory grace with which he moved—these signs alone would have been enough to give him away. When she looked at the amazing physical specimen, Illasera could almost see the man's body as a physical representation of Bhaal's divine fury.

The females, however, were not so simply identified. Not all the Bhaalspawn were as easy to spot as the male warrior had been. Many were humble, unremarkable folk like peasants, farmers, and merchants. Insignificant in their lives, they were important only because of what their deaths would mean to the Five.

Illasera hesitated, carefully pondering her next move. She had a good supply of ordinary, reliable arrows. She could unleash a volley at her targets, virtually drowning them beneath a rain of feathered fletches, but the leader of the Five had warned Illasera that such mundane weaponry would be all but useless against these particular Bhaalspawn.

The manifestation of their immortal father's legacy varied greatly with each of the god's progeny. Miraculous invulnerabilities were uncommon but not unheard of among a select few of the most powerful children of Bhaal. The Five had long ago learned how to counter the powerful immunities that blessed some of the Lord of Murder's offspring.

Noiselessly, the Huntress pulled an arrow from her quiver, taking care to choose one of her specially prepared weapons. The magically runed arrows were precious, she had only a few. Unable to determine exactly which two were the offspring of a god, Illasera had to assume they all possessed the tainted blood. She took careful, deliberate aim at the woman tending to the injured girl. Illasera understood death, she understood killing. She knew to eliminate the healers first.

* * * * *

Abdel never saw the camouflaged female form of Illasera as she raised her bow, but his eyes were drawn to the movement of the arrow she loosed. Abdel thrust his bare arm out and into the path of the projectile, intercepting it as it flew through the air on a line toward Jaheira's throat. His action was one of pure instinct—an instinct based on the innate understanding that because of his tainted blood he was impervious to all physical harm.

27

The missile pierced his left forearm, ripping through the sinew and muscle until the metal tip protruded out several inches on the other side. Imoen shrieked in surprise and fear, and Jaheira threw herself over the vulnerable girl's body. Abdel stepped into the unseen archer's line of fire, offering himself up as a human shield, confident in his superhuman recuperative powers to protect him from the deadly projectiles.

With his companions safely guarded by his own body, Abdel seized the black shaft of the weapon embedded in his left arm with his free hand. He barely noticed the strange red runes intricately painted onto the dark wood as he yanked the missile out from his flesh, further damaging his already wounded arm. Agonizing white pain seared his soul, momentarily blinding Abdel. The big man grunted and tried to shake off the effect.

Pain for Abdel was meaningless, a useless byproduct of his mortal life, an evolutionary mechanism lesser organisms relied on to warn them of potentially lethal damage to their bodies. For Abdel, that warning could serve no purpose. All pain was transitory, all damage inflicted only temporary.

Abdel stared down at his wound to watch the regenerative process. Occasionally, his mind was still fascinated by the instantaneous healing abilities of his own body. But something strange happened, or rather, didn't happen. The thick blood welling up from the ragged hole in Abdel's arm didn't abate. The tattered fragments of hanging skin around the edges of the gaping hole had not begun to mend themselves, the severed muscle tissue was still severed. Staring down at his hemorrhaging wound, Abdel was momentarily stunned by the dawning realization of his own vulnerability.

He heard the faint, unmistakable twang of a bowstring, and he spun his body to the right as he ducked down. The arrow that would have pierced his eye whizzed past his ear, and the arrow that would have buried itself in his heart struck him in the meat of his left shoulder.

Only the soft voice of Imoen kept Abdel from charging blindly into the undergrowth in pursuit of the invisible assailant, the arrow still dangling from his shoulder. "Wait, Abdel."

The confidence in her voice surprised Abdel, and he hesitated a split second—a hesitation that saved his life. The sharp hiss of another arrow split the air, the missile arcing toward the dried blood on Abdel's unprotected throat. A foot away from where the big warrior stood, the arrow changed direction, and landed harmlessly on the surrounding undergrowth.

Amazed, Abdel turned to stare down at his younger sibling. Jaheira had bound Imoen's arm with a tight wrap, and the slim girl was now sitting up. She flashed him a smile.

"A minor enchantment I learned while studying at Candlekeep. If we stay close, the arrows can't harm us."

Abdel nodded and raised his blade. Jaheira was up beside him an instant later, gently working the shaft of the arrow free from his shoulder. The sellsword flinched as another feathered shaft ricocheted off mere inches from his face, then laughed at his own reaction.

"If you want me," he called out, "you'll have to come out and face me!"

There was the sound of a blade being unsheathed, and a tall, dark-haired woman clad all in gray stepped into the clearing. In each hand she artfully balanced a rapier. Abdel noticed the thin blades did not reflect the magical illumination Jaheira had cast over the clearing, but seemed to absorb the light. Flecks of red on the twin blades merely confirmed what he already knew: Like the strange arrows, these weapons could do permanent damage to his body.

"I've killed greater Bhaalspawn than you," the woman hissed as she slowly advanced. "I am one of the Five, and your blood is mine!"

From the way the woman held her blades—spread wide before her, one high, the other low—Abdel could tell she was skilled in more than just wielding a bow. Anxious to keep Jaheira and Imoen out of danger, and no longer needing Imoen's magical shield to guard against incoming arrows, Abdel stepped forward to meet his foe.

His left arm dangled uselessly by his side. The blood still pouring out made Abdel feel sluggish and weak. The woman flicked her wrist, and one of her blades sliced a deep cut across Abdel's cheek.

The warrior swore to himself. Caught completely off guard by the quickness of her attack, he had barely been able to lean back far enough to avoid losing an eye. He brought his own heavy sword to bear, carving a wide arc through the air. His long, black hair was now soaking wet with sweat and stuck to his face. His lithe opponent leaped nimbly out of the way and rewarded his effort by carving a pair of deep incisions across the back of his sword arm.

Abdel grunted in surprise and pain and chopped down with another blow. The woman dodged out of the way again, but this time Abdel was expecting it. His move had been a feint, and when she spun to avoid his sword, he lashed out with his leg, sweeping her off her feet.

His heavy broadsword stabbed down to finish off his prone opponent, but she managed to roll out of the way, and Abdel struck only the hard ground, the shockwave sending a jarring bolt of pain up through his injured arm.

The woman was on her feet again, blades poised to deliver another series of razor quick slashes to Abdel's bare skin. If he had been whole, Abdel knew, he would have easily dispatched the woman. She was fast, but Abdel was faster, but only when he wasn't hampered by a useless arm. Unable to grip his massive sword with both hands, Abdel couldn't deliver the lightning-quick counter-strikes he often used to overwhelm his opponents.

Instead, he was forced to take a defensive approach, delivering several wide, sweeping passes of his blade to force his opponent back. The woman moved out of range easily each time, and despite her retreat, her hungry eyes constantly sought the slightest hint of an opening that would allow her to finish the battle.

Weary from blood loss, the warrior stumbled, and the woman was on him. Abdel managed to parry the first blade as it flashed toward his eyes, but the point of the second struck unimpeded, piercing his side just above the belt. Abdel screamed in frustrated rage and pain, dropped his weapon to the ground, and unleashed the wrath of Bhaal.

The unholy taint that pulsed within the sellsword's veins erupted in an explosion of insane fury, overwhelming Abdel's mind and soul. Although there was no change in Abdel's physical appearance, the part of him that was Abdel nearly ceased to exist, all but consumed by the raging inferno of hate and bloodlust. The Lord of Murder walked the land again.

Mindlessly Abdel seized the woman with both hands, heedless of his mangled left arm. The horrified female was pulled into a lethal bear hug, Abdel's massive, muscled limbs wrapping around her body and pinning her arms to her sides. He squeezed, and the sound of cracking, snapping bones echoed through the clearing.

Tilting back her head to scream, the woman could only manage a choking gurgle. Her eyes rolled back into her head, blood bubbled up from her mouth and nose, and crimson tears rolled down her cheeks.

Trapped within his own consciousness, Abdel fought to regain his sense of self, fought to cage the part of him he had unwittingly unleashed. He was powerless to do anything but watch as Bhaal's avatar leaned his head forward and tore a piece of flesh from the dying woman's neck, feasting on his vanquished foe. The struggles of the woman grew weaker, and Abdel disdainfully let her drop to the ground in a quivering mass of pulpy flesh.

The monster turned its attention to the two women standing only a few yards away. The essence of Bhaal tried to advance the body it now possessed, but through sheer force of will Abdel refused to let it take a single step. It stood with one foot raised as Abdel struggled to regain control of his physical being, struggled to douse the unquenchable fire of Bhaal within his own soul.

"Abdel," Jaheira asked, a concerned look on her face. "Abdel, what's happening?"

He wanted to scream out a warning to her, but all of his focus was on preventing his own possessed body from taking that first, fateful step. Then he felt the transformation begin. Despite all his efforts, his body was beginning to change. He was becoming the four-armed demon known to mortals as the Ravager.

"Abdel!" Imoen shrieked, her own expression mirroring that of Jaheira's. "No, Abdel!"

Chapter Three

The faces of Imoen and Jaheira seemed to melt into the gray nothing that suddenly surrounded him, and the entity threatening to take over his body and soul vanished with them. Abdel Adrian had returned to the void, and the Ravager was no more.

Instinctively, his hand reached over his shoulder to feel the reassuring touch of his broadsword's hilt, strapped to his back as it had been in his dream. This time, however, the Abyssal plane was somehow different. For one thing, this was no dream. Abdel had been conscious and fully awake when he felt the mortal world slipping away—or was it he who had slipped away? And his left arm still dripped blood from the ragged wounds inflicted by the arrows of the huntress in the clearing. But it was more than the awareness that this was no dream that differentiated the void from the last time he had been here.

He felt ground beneath his feet. At least, he felt as if he was standing on something solid, though when he looked down there was nothing there. The endless gray surrounding him was altered as well. Instead of a bleak plane of nonexistent nothingness, Abdel felt himself to be lost within obscuring mist. There was something in this plane, something concealed by the fog. Unlike his dream world, this place was not an empty void, it was a place of secrets.

As if responding to his inner realization, the mists parted slightly to reveal the outlines of several doors standing upright within the clouds. Abdel hesitated, then approached. The words of the cloaked being from his dream came back to Abdel—this place was Bhaal's realm, a plane in the Abyss once ruled by the Lord of Murder, shaped by the will of Abdel's evil, immortal father.

Despite this, Abdel still felt he had little to fear from simply examining a door. Actually opening the portal, Abdel noted to himself, was another matter entirely.

How could he open a door that wasn't attached to anything? Each of the portals just hung in the air with no frame, no walls, no hinges. Just the doors, five in all. Built from solid, stout oak they were remarkable in neither size nor shape. They bore no ornamentation save for a simple, functional handle. In fact, there was nothing unusual about the doors at all—except for their surroundings, or lack of surroundings, to be more precise.

Abdel drew his great sword and cautiously circled the free-standing portals, looking for something. He didn't find it.

"Hello?" he called out at last, not sure whether he expected the being from his dream to appear and answer him. His voice echoed back at him from the gray mists.

"Is anybody here?" Abdel called again.

The voice that came back to him from the mist was not the chorus of the creature that he expected, but it was a voice Abdel recognized all too well.

"I am here, brother. As are you."

A figure emerged from the mist, a man from Abdel's past. He was clad from head to toe in black, metal armor. Many of the heavy iron plates were adorned with razor-sharp blades, making the suit both a defensive and offensive instrument of war. The fierce warrior stood well over seven feet tall, one of the few humans who had ever been able to look Abdel directly in the eye. Their similarity of stature was not surprising, given that the man was Abdel's half brother whom Abdel had killed in the town of Baldur's Gate—Sarevok.

34

Sarevok had not stepped out from the cover of the obscuring mist into view as Abdel might have expected. He had coalesced into view, solidifying into existence not ten feet in front of Abdel's disbelieving eyes.

Abdel shook his head and tightened his grip on his sword, ignoring the flare of pain that shot up through his injured left arm and into his shoulder. "I killed you," he said, half to himself. "You're dead."

His half brother laughed in a deep, joyless rumble. "And was not your lover, Jaheira, once dead as well, my brother? Yet the priests of Gond brought her back. Death is not always the end."

At least he wasn't armed, Abdel noticed. The dark blade Sarevok had wielded during their duel beneath Baldur's Gate was nowhere to be seen. Still, the big sellsword didn't drop his guard. If Abdel was careless enough to let his half brother get in too close, the vicious metal blades fashioned into the iron plates of Sarevok's armor were capable of inflicting horrendous injuries. Abdel was once again very conscious of his ability to be harmed.

"What are you doing here?" Abdel demanded.

"Waiting for you. I knew you would return to this empty plane of our father, Abdel, and so I waited."

Sarevok's words were intriguing, but Abdel knew all too well the deceitful nature of his half brother. Sarevok was evil incarnate. The blood of countless innocents was on his massive hands. He had plotted Abdel's own demise, once. He had been responsible for the death of Jaheira's husband. He had even nearly killed Jaheira herself.

The dark-armored warrior had masterminded a campaign of slaughter and terror up and down the Sword Coast. His machinations had nearly caused a senseless war between the towns of Nashkel and Baldur's Gate—a war of sacrifice and blood that Sarevok had hoped would bring their father back to life.

Drew Karpyshyn

All this was nothing to Abdel. Death, war, attempts on his life and the lives of his companions—Abdel's entire life had centered around such things. Sarevok, however, had other blood on his hands. Sarevok had arranged the murder of Gorion, Abdel's mentor and adopted father, the one person in Abdel's life who had sought to steer him away from the violence and atrocities that accompanied his birthright. Despite all his other crimes, it was for Gorion's death that Abdel had killed Sarevok.

Abdel wasn't about to let a second chance to avenge Gorion's death pass by.

"You waited a long time just so I could kill you again," he said, taking a quick step toward Sarevok and bringing his broadsword to bear. Abdel was nothing but a blur of furious movement, but Sarevok simply stepped out of range, slapping the blade down with a heavy mailed fist.

The cold, emotionless laugh of Sarevok caused Abdel to stumble back, anticipating a counterattack, but Sarevok made no move toward him.

"I see your impulsive nature has not changed, Abdel. You may vent your rage on me yet again, if you wish . . . though your efforts will be for naught." Sarevok's voice still had the deep resonance Abdel remembered, it still carried an ominous undercurrent of implied violence in every word. Yet somehow the voice had changed. It lacked the malevolent chill, the hiss of pure evil that had sent shivers of loathing down Abdel's spine in the past.

Using his sword to cut tight circles in the air in front of him, Abdel moved warily forward. All he needed was one opportunity, a single opening he could use to drive his sword between the iron plates of his brother's armor.

"You cannot kill me here, Abdel," Sarevok assured him, seemingly oblivious of Abdel's approach. "When you slew me in the mortal realm, I became a part of you. I became part of this empty world. Even if you chop me into a million pieces, I will still be here."

Abdel let his weapon speak for him, hacking savagely at his half brother's waist. Sarevok made no move to defend himself, but stood in place and welcomed the attack. The blade slashed into the dark armor, carved effortlessly through Sarevok's torso, and emerged from the other side.

Abdel stepped back to avoid the geyser of blood that would erupt from his dismembered foe's lower extremities, but there was no blood. The upper half of Sarevok's body did not topple over and collapse twitching on the gray ground. Abdel's opponent simply dissolved, vanishing from existence in the same manner he had appeared.

"When you are done with this foolery, I have an offer for you, Abdel."

The voice came from behind him this time. Abdel dropped and rolled forward, away from an anticipated attack at his unprotected back. Coming out of his roll, he twisted his body so that he was now facing his opponent as he sprang to his feet.

Sarevok stood motionless, looking exactly as he had before Abdel had tried to cut him in two.

Abdel considered attacking again. He had yet to meet an opponent he couldn't beat down with sheer brute force. He had never fought an incorporeal spirit in the abandoned nether plane of a dead god before. Reluctantly, Abdel had to face the possibility that this was a situation he couldn't solve with his sword. Slowly, his eyes focused warily on the motionless form of his half brother, and Abdel lowered his sword.

"There is no point in fighting a ghost."

"Ghost?" Sarevok seemed amused by the word, though his voice reflected no change in its cold monotone. "Yes, I suppose I am a ghost, though not in the common sense of the word. We can help each other, Abdel. We each have something the other needs."

Now it was Abdel's turn to laugh—a harsh, bitter

sound. "I will never help you, Sarevok. You can offer me nothing I might need."

"Rash as ever, Abdel, that is the fire of our father burning within you. Unlike you, my brother, I am no longer consumed by the flames of hate and bloodlust. You purged me of Bhaal's taint. For that, I thank you."

Uncertain of how to react to the unexpected, though somewhat emotionless, gratitude of the man he had killed, Abdel remained silent.

"Do not dismiss my offer out of passion and recklessness, Abdel. I have information you need. And in the end, I assure you, my offer will benefit you much more than it will me."

"Information?" Abdel asked, his curiosity piqued. "What kind of information?"

"How you may escape this dead world of our father, for one thing. But there is more, Abdel, much more."

Abdel scowled, knowing Sarevok had made a point he could not easily dismiss. Abdel had no idea how he had come to this gray, empty plane. He had no clue how to return to Jaheira and Imoen in the mortal world. Part of him was still leery about striking a bargain with this mortal enemy from his past.

"And what do you need of me?" Abdel asked.

Sarevok took a half step forward. The metal plates of his armor shrieked as he brought his arms up. Instinctively, Abdel brought his sword into a defensive position and dropped into a fighting crouch.

Sarevok mimicked the movement, stiffly dropping to one knee, his arms still outstretched, the palms facing upward. It took a second before Abdel realized his half brother wasn't taking an aggressive stance—he was making an offer of supplication. Sarevok was begging him.

"I need you, Abdel Adrian," the big man implored, "to restore me to life."

The words struck Abdel like a stiff slap. His massive

head snapped back in shock. The request was ludicrous, offensive.

"Never!" he shouted. "You are a monster, Sarevok. A creature of pure death and evil. Only a fool would restore you to life so you could resume your slaughtering."

"Please, Abdel," Sarevok replied without any noticeable change in the inflection of his voice, though his arms were still outstretched in a pathetic effort to win sympathy from the half brother he had so greatly wronged. "I am not the being I was. When you knew me, I had ceased to be a man. I was but a vessel, a conduit for the horror of Bhaal. The taint of our dark father had overwhelmed me. My very identity had been consumed by the inferno of hate, bloodlust, and madness. I was not Sarevok, I was a demon in human form."

"You're lying! You just want to avoid responsibility for all the death and destruction you brought about!"

Sarevok shook his head, rose wearily from his knee and lowered his arms before resuming his pleas in his deep, passionless monotone. "I knew the joy of killing long before Bhaal's taint utterly consumed me," he admitted. "I am, and always will be, an instrument of violence. During all my days, during all my travels, death ever followed in my wake. Yet could not the same be said of you, Abdel Adrian? Were we really so different?"

Abdel took an involuntary step back, physically rejecting Sarevok's accusation. Despite his reaction, Abdel knew Sarevok spoke the truth. Many times the sellsword had felt the blinding fury of his father's essence touch his own soul. Many times he had felt the claws of the Lord of Murder's spirit wrap themselves around his own heart. He understood the eternal struggle to resist the evil within himself, the war to maintain his own identity when he unleashed the rage within and allowed the crimson ocean of Bhaal's taint to drown his mind.

Abdel had emerged from each struggle against his inner evil victorious so far. Was it possible Sarevok had once been like himself but had succumbed to Bhaal's taint? Had Sarevok become a mortal manifestation of Bhaal himself, a creature no longer responsible for its actions?

Taking advantage of Abdel's prolonged silence, Sarevok continued pleading his case. "When you ended my mortal existence, Abdel, you released my spirit from the hells. But instead of freedom, I found myself here—trapped in this limbo that was once Bhaal's realm.

"Since the day of my death I have waited here, knowing you too would one day come to this place. My soul is linked to yours, Abdel, joined by our shared heritage and my death by your hand. I knew you would return, and I have waited here for you, for another chance. A chance to live not as a vessel for Bhaal's hate and desire, but as myself."

"I . . . I don't know if I can believe you." To his own surprise, Abdel said the words almost with regret.

Sarevok nodded. "I understand. You have no reason to trust me. So I will give you a sign of my good faith. I will tell you how to leave this realm so that you may return to the mortal world and those you left behind."

Jaheira! Imoen. The mention of his companions sparked a sudden urgency in Abdel. How long had he been here, in this void? What if the woman he had killed was not the only one hunting them? What if there were more of those mutated wolf creatures lurking in the forest?

"Tell me how to get back!"

Sensing his brother's anxiousness, Sarevok offered reassurance. "Your companions are safe, Abdel. They are in no immediate danger. I will tell you how to go back. Then, if you wish, you may simply leave, and I will not try to stop you. I only ask that you listen to the rest of my offer before you go."

"It's a deal," Abdel answered immediately, eager to say anything to expedite his return to Jaheira's side.

"The doors are the key, Abdel," Sarevok explained. "Merely approach them and concentrate. Will yourself to be back in the mortal realm."

"Which door?" Abdel asked.

"It does not matter. The doors themselves are symbols. They represent the possibilities and the potential of this realm—and of yourself."

Abdel never even hesitated. He simply turned his back on Sarevok and marched toward the nearest door, consciously trying to envision himself stepping through and re-appearing in the clearing where he had left Jaheira and Imoen.

"You made a promise, Abdel," Sarevok called out, making him pause.

He owed Sarevok nothing. Gorion's death was, to Abdel, the worst of his half brother's crimes, but it was not the only one. There was no reason to stay, he should keep walking and leave Sarevok to rot in the void.

"Do you remember my last words to you beneath Baldur's Gate, Abdel? Do you remember what I said as you drove your sword into my heart?" Sarevok asked. "I told you there were others like us, Abdel, other Children of Bhaal who walk the world. You must seek them out if you want answers, Abdel."

The words of Sarevok, so similar to those of the great being in his dream, caused Abdel to turn and face his half brother.

"I can help you find these other Bhaalspawn," Sarevok said. "I can lead you to answers, but you must listen to my offer before you go."

The memory of how Bhaal's taint had nearly overwhelmed him in the clearing came back to Abdel's consciousness. The sick, helpless feeling as his own body became a vessel for the evil taint that had once been a part of the Lord of Murder's immortal essence. Would the answers Sarevok offered finally purge him of his father's legacy? Jaheira's face flashed through Abdel's thoughts,

Drew Karpyshyn

and he cast a glance over his shoulder at the door floating in the gray mists.

"Abdel, the choice is yours."

Chapter Four

"Thank the gods!"

Abdel heard Jaheira's voice a split second before the face of his lover rematerialized before him. The fear and concern in her violet eyes was quickly washed away by tears of relief.

"Abdel," she cried out, rushing across the clearing to embrace him.

In response, Abdel wrapped his mighty right arm around her shoulders, pulling her tight against his muscled chest, his fingers burrowing into her thick, dark hair. His injured left arm dangled uselessly by his side.

"Jaheira," he breathed, saying nothing more but allowing the soft scent of the half-elf to envelop him.

A second later Imoen was there too, leaping up to wrap her own slender arms around Abdel's broad shoulders and sturdy neck.

"Welcome back, big brother!" she exclaimed, literally hanging from his back in her joyous relief.

Abdel held Jaheira against his own body a moment longer before releasing her. He shrugged slightly, and Imoen let go of her grip on his neck, dropping to the ground and landing lightly on her tiny feet.

Seeing them brought back the chilling memory of how he had been on the verge of slaying them both, how he had nearly succumbed to the essence of Bhaal within

43

himself during the last battle and transformed into the Ravager. Abdel vowed he would do everything humanly possible to avoid unleashing his father's fury again. He would only resort to violence as a desperate last resort. If necessary, he would let himself die rather than allow himself to morph into the Ravager again.

Confident now that both Jaheira and Imoen were unharmed, Abdel took quick stock of his environment. The clearing was still bathed in the light of Jaheira's incantation, but glancing up Abdel could see the night above was still dark. The dead, twisted trees still surrounded them, and the decaying leaves still carpeted the clearing floor. The reeking bodies of the foul wolves lay scattered about. Abdel's gaze merely skimmed over their mangled forms, and he quickly averted his eyes when they wandered across to the broken, bloody corpse of the Huntress crumpled near the edge of the clearing.

"How long was I gone?" he asked.

Jaheira took a step back and tilted her head so that she could look directly up into the eyes of her man. His question seemed to momentarily catch her off guard. "A few seconds, Abdel. You were here one second, the next you were gone. What happened?"

Abdel didn't answer right away. He took a second to collect his thoughts.

"I . . . I was taken to another plane. I think. I think I was in the Abyss."

The half-elf looked at him with curious eyes, but it was Imoen who voiced the question. "The Abyss? Who or what could possibly have summoned you there?"

Taking a deep breath, Abdel replied, "Sarevok."

Jaheira gasped and brought her hand up to cover her mouth.

"Sarevok?" Imoen asked. "Why do I recognize that name?"

There was a brief silence. Neither Abdel nor Jaheira was anxious to speak of Sarevok's crimes and open old emotional scars. It was Jaheira who finally spoke.

"He was also a Child of Bhaal, Imoen. He had Gorion killed, and Khalid, my husband. Sarevok tried to start a war in Baldur's Gate. Hundreds of innocent people suffered horribly from his actions. Abdel killed him in the end."

"He's the one who murdered Gorion?" Imoen whispered, not trying to mask the shock and sympathy in her voice. "How horrible it must have been, Abdel, meeting him again."

It was Jaheira who asked the next question, the one Abdel had been dreading.

"What did he want?"

Abdel shuffled his feet, struggling to make himself say the words. "He wanted me to bring him back to life."

Imoen actually laughed. "That's impossible! You're no cleric, Abdel!"

The big sellsword fixed his gaze on Jaheira, trying to read her face as he spoke the next words. "No, it is possible. He told me how, in exchange for the knowledge of how to return to this world. Jaheira would have to help me."

"No!" The half-elf turned her head and spat contemptuously on the ground. "No! I would never do such a thing. To release such a vile evil upon the world is unthinkable. Leave his soul trapped there for all eternity. He deserves no better!"

Gently, Abdel placed his uninjured hand on Jaheira's shoulder. He understood her feelings—his own reaction had initially been the same. Abdel had listened to Sarevok's offer, and he had to share it with her.

"He claims he has changed. He claims the taint of Bhaal has been purged from his soul. I think . . ." Abdel had to pause, and collect his breath before he could continue. "I think he could show me how to do the same."

Lowering her eyes to the ground, Jaheira shook her head in a mute rejection of Abdel's request. Abdel reached out and cupped her chin in his enormous palm and brought her head up until he could look into her eyes. She was crying.

The death of Khalid had brought Abdel and Jaheira together, and the big man knew the guilt and grief over the circumstances of her husband's death still ached in Jaheira's mind. He had always been careful never to press her, never to force her to try and reconcile the contradiction of their love being the result of such a tragedy. Now he was asking Jaheira to forgive the man who had killed her husband for the sake of the man that had taken Khalid's place in her heart. No matter how intensely Abdel longed to free himself from Bhaal's taint, he had no right to put the woman he loved in this position.

Disgusted at his own selfishness, Abdel released her chin and turned away. "I'm sorry, Jaheira. I should never have asked. I will not speak of this again."

* * * * *

Jaheira knew the fight with the wolves and the archer had drained the energy of the three companions. Once the rush of the battle had worn off they would be even more exhausted than they had been when she had demanded they stop to rest earlier in the night. Despite the unease the druid felt within the now-corrupted nature of the clearing, it would be foolish to travel onward.

Abdel might have slain the archer, but they all knew there were many, many more enemies hunting them down. Their days of running were far from over. She would have to send Imoen to seek out more of the mint leaves she had gathered earlier—the ones in her pouch had been spoiled by the spell.

"You must venture beyond the edges of the dead trees," Jaheira explained to the younger woman. "You will need to find fresh, living vegetation." She pressed a single dead leaf into the small hand of the girl. "Like this, but bright green."

Imoen nodded, her eyes still bright with the rush of the recent encounter. "Don't worry, I'll make sure I stay well hidden."

With Abdel's half sister gone, Jaheira could now turn her attention to her lover's wounded arm. She had seen the remarkable regenerative powers of Abdel's body many times over the past months. Injuries that would have crippled or even killed a normal man had barely even slowed the giant warrior down. Even during the fight with the wolves he had sustained grave wounds that had vanished almost instantly. For some reason the arrows of the archer had torn his flesh, rending it in such a way that it would not heal.

"Those arrows," she explained to Abdel as she bandaged his arm and whispered a simple spell to aid the healing process, "were marked with powerful runes and sigils. It is almost as if this woman knew of your ability and knew how to counteract it."

Abdel winced slightly at the touch of her soft hands on the sensitive under-layer of his flesh. "Perhaps there are other Bhaalspawn like me, ones with special powers because of Bhaal's blood. Maybe some of them were captured and experimented on until a weakness was found."

Jaheira nodded. "That may be true, my love. There may indeed be others who share your lineage who have been blessed with similar regenerative powers."

"Blessed?" Abdel muttered in soft surprise. "Nothing of Bhaal's taint is a blessing."

She finished wrapping his arm in silence, mulling over his words. What right did she have to deny him a chance to free himself from the curse of his blood? If there was a chance for Abdel and Imoen, she reminded herself, to escape the awful legacy of the Lord of Murder, how could she stand in their way?

"How must it be done?" she whispered, knowing Abdel would understand her meaning.

The big man shifted his position to gaze in her eyes. Jaheira hoped he could see her steadfast resolution in them. In Abdel's own eyes she could see hesitation, then gratitude and relief.

Drew Karpyshyn

"It must be done in the first light of dawn," he said. "We should wait for Imoen to get back."

* * * * *

Dawn was approaching. Abdel stood with Jaheira by his side, the half-elf's slender, elegant fingers clenched tightly around his own meaty digits. The pair stood at the center of a circle inscribed on the ground. In accordance with the instructions of Sarevok, Imoen had traced the circle with the blade of a knife dipped in Abdel's own blood.

Around the circle were a number of other elaborate and arcane symbols. Each of the intricate patterns had been similarly drawn on the hard ground with painstaking precision by the edge of Imoen's bloody dagger. The girl now stood at a distance, anxiously watching her two friends.

Abdel cast a questioning glance at Jaheira, and she gave him a reassuring nod. The druid began to chant. The words meant nothing to Abdel, of course. He had never learned the language of enchantments. But he could feel the power of the surrounding forest being drawn together by Jaheira's incantation.

The dead branches around them began to sprout green buds, the trees reborn in the gathering elemental energy Jaheira was drawing forth from the natural elements around her.

The first rays of morning light glimmered on the horizon, and Abdel stared directly into the rising sun as it crested the edge of the world. Blinded by the light, Abdel suddenly felt himself floating high above the land— though he could still feel the hard ground of the clearing beneath his feet.

He could no longer feel Jaheira's hand in his grip. He couldn't even feel his own hand anymore. But he could still hear the mantra of words spilling from her lips, calling on Mielikki, the Lady of the Forest, to grant her boon.

Clenching his eyes shut against the glare, Abdel opened himself to the touch of Jaheira's spell. He felt a tug within his body, then was nearly jerked from his feet by a second pull. He felt a warmth in his loins, then a searing in his breast.

He opened his mouth to cry out in pain as his blood began to boil, but his voice was mute, silenced by the awful power of the magic coursing through his veins. Then Abdel felt something rip as a piece of his very soul, his *essence*, was torn away.

The frozen scream was at last unleashed to echo through the surrounding trees, and Abdel collapsed to his hands and knees.

Slowly, his vision returned. From the corner of his eye he caught a glimpse of Jaheira collapsed on the ground beside him, though she, too, was stirring. Still on his knees, Abdel let his weight sink back onto his heels and looked across the clearing.

Sarevok stood there in all his glory. The Bhaalspawn's dark metal armor reflected the bright rays of the sun as they struck the black iron. The keen edges of the blades protruding from the plates on Sarevok's back, shoulders, forearms, and lower legs reflected the light of the dawn, giving testament to their sharpness.

Here in the clearing, as in Bhaal's Abyssal plane, Sarevok was weaponless except for the armor he wore. Abdel scrambled to his feet and drew his sword.

"You still do not trust me, brother," Sarevok noted, the faintest hint of wry amusement detectable in his otherwise monotone speech.

Jaheira reached up and set her hand on Abdel's massive thigh. Abdel glanced down at her weary, pleading face and sheathed his sword so that he might help her up.

"You must be Imoen," Sarevok said, just noticing the slim young woman still hovering on the farthest edge of the clearing. "Abdel did not mention our sister was such an attractive lady."

Imoen sneered at the armor clad figure. "Save your flattery—I'm no sister of yours!"

There was a deep sigh from behind the visor of Sarevok's helmet. "So be it. I was only attempting to be polite. In any case, there is little left that ties us together. I sense much of our father's power has been purged from your soul."

"Abdel rescued me from Bhaal's evil," Imoen declared, shuddering at the memory of how she had herself been, for a short time, the Lord of Murder's avatar on Faerûn.

"As he rescued me," Sarevok replied. "Abdel carries the weight of our taint on his own soul now. For that we both owe him our thanks."

The enormous figure slowly turned to face Jaheira. "I must thank you as well, druid, for your part in my resurrection."

Jaheira glared at Sarevok, and her reply came from between clenched teeth. "I did it for Abdel, not for you."

Sarevok shrugged, the heavy plates of his armor grating against each other as he did so. "I shall thank you, nevertheless."

The four figures stood in silence for several seconds until Jaheira blurted out, "Is that all, Sarevok? Have you nothing else to say? Will you not even apologize for the deaths of our loved ones?"

"Will an apology make any difference?" Sarevok challenged. "It will not bring them back, and I doubt it will make you think any more of me."

The half-elf spun on her heel and stalked off to stand beside Imoen, placing as much distance between herself and Sarevok as was possible. Abdel momentarily considered following her lead but held his ground.

"I have done my part, Sarevok," he said, trying to keep the anger and bitterness from his voice. "You are free to walk the mortal world again. I have restored you to life, as promised. Now tell me what I want to know."

"I walk the land again," Sarevok admitted, "though I do not truly live. Not in any real sense of the word. I have

50

substance, I have form. I can feel and inflict pain. But I am not a creature of flesh and blood as you are, Abdel. I am but an apparition made solid. This armor is my body, the cold scrape of metal is the closest I will ever get to the touch of warm flesh."

"That is not my concern, Sarevok. I have done what you asked. Now you must fulfill your promise. Tell me about the other Bhaalspawn. Tell me how I may purge myself of this taint."

"I do not know how you may free yourself from the Lord of Murder's blood, Abdel," Sarevok replied. "I never promised you that."

"I knew he was not to be trusted!" Jaheira's shrill voice cut through the still air of the early morning. "He has lied to you, Abdel. He has tricked us again!"

Sarevok held up his hand, the palm of the black gauntlet facing outward, a sign for Jaheira to halt her outburst.

"I spoke the truth Abdel, I will deliver what I promised. I told you your destiny was tied to that of the other Children of Bhaal who still walk the land. I told you I could help you find them. I promised to lead you to your destiny."

Abdel stood motionless in front of Sarevok, straining to prevent his muscles from instinctively grabbing for the sword on his back. "And what is this destiny, Sarevok?"

Again there was the grating shriek of metal on metal as Sarevok shrugged his mighty shoulders. "That I cannot say. Perhaps it is to rid yourself of Bhaal's foul essence. Perhaps not. Maybe Melissan knows."

"Melissan?" Abdel asked. "Who is she?"

"She is one who knows more about the Bhaalspawn then I do, Abdel Adrian. If anyone can remove the taint from your soul, it is she. And I know how to find her."

"Then tell us where to find her and be on your way!" Jaheira cried out from the far side of the clearing.

The deep rumble of Sarevok's mirthless laugh filled the forest. "Tell you? No, druid. I will do better than that. I will take you to her. My path is tied with that of your lover. I will be by his side every step of the way."

Abdel took a step toward his half brother, his hand moving unconsciously to the hilt of his sword. "That wasn't the deal, Sarevok!"

The armored man made no move to protect himself. "Strike me down if you wish, Abdel. I will not defend myself. But know if you do that you will never learn the secrets I can show you."

The big sellsword's hand slid slowly off the handle of his weapon. He turned and shared a look with Jaheira. There was anger in the half-elf's violet eyes, but Abdel could tell she had come to the same realization he had. They had brought Sarevok back to life, and now they were stuck with him.

It was Imoen who finally broke the uncomfortable silence that was hanging over the clearing. "So now what?"

"Now we go to meet Melissan," Sarevok replied. "In Saradush."

Chapter Five

The flames from the pit in the center of the temple burned low, casting an eerie red radiance around the room. In the faint light of the ebbing fire it was almost impossible to see the symbol carved into each of the six walls that made up the central chamber of the small building—a grinning gray skull with glowing eyes against a background of tears. The symbol of Bhaal.

Two shrouded figures stood waiting in the room, neither speaking. Although their robes hid their identities from view, the heavy cloaks did not cover them entirely. Fleeting glimpses of their true forms occasionally came into view with each subtle movement. The larger of the two shifted impatiently, revealing a glimpse of rough, scaly skin just barely visible beneath the shadows of his hood. There was the rasping sound of a slithering snake as he took a shuffling step, and his long, forked tongue flicked out once to taste the air to seek the presence of the others who had not yet arrived.

The second figure, slender and smaller than her companion, held up her hand to still his nervous fidgeting, her arm moving in a languid, graceful manner. The fingers were long and slender, delicate as those of any elf on the face of Faerûn, but the complexion of her elf hand was the color of burnt ash. Only skin that had never seen the light of the surface world could look as pale and as dark, the skin of a creature from the Underdark, the skin of a drow.

The larger figure turned his cowled head quickly to the only door. A single reptilian eye reflected the dying embers of the fire as he did so.

A third cloaked figure strode into view, his hood pulled far down to cover his face. He was not as large as the first, but not as slender as the second. Like the drow, his powerful hands were visible beyond the edges of his long sleeves—though they were covered so completely with intricate tattoos and detailed markings it was impossible to even guess what the original color of this man's skin had once been.

"I summoned you because events are moving quickly," the new arrival announced once he had taken his place by the others.

The large one hissed, then pointed an accusatory clawed finger at the late comer. "You are not the leader of the Five! Why did Bhaal's Anointed not summon us?"

"And where are the others?" the female added, her voice a smoky whisper in the flickering twilight.

"One is leading the siege of Saradush. Our fifth is dead, slain by Gorion's ward."

"Illasera?" There was a hint of regret in the reptilian voice.

The tattooed man nodded. "But revenge is soon at hand. Even now Abdel Adrian's fate is sealed. Our trap has been set."

Such veiled speech came naturally to all of the Five. Bhaal's Anointed had trained them well; all their discussions were shrouded in cryptic phrasing and obscure syntax. For a cult born in the secrecy and shadows surrounding Bhaal's death, vague references were more than mere idiosyncratic habit—they were a tool of survival. In the beginning the Five had been unknown, ignored by the outside world. With the spreading slaughter of the Bhaalspawn, the most powerful eyes in the kingdoms of the South were being focused on their plans.

The Five were not yet ready to accept such scrutiny. Their mission was still newborn, a frail infant easily slain. The prying eyes and ears of spies were a constant threat to the continued existence of both the Five and the achievement of their ultimate goal. They were ever conscious of the risk of scrying mages and clairvoyant wizards, even when gathered in their inner sanctum. There was no place that was truly safe, no place that could not be infiltrated by a cunning operative or pierced by the powerful divinations of a meddlesome spellcaster. Even here, in this long-abandoned temple of the Lord of Murder, a single false word, a name carelessly revealed or a plan foolishly exposed could give the enemies of the Five enough information to destroy them.

Illasera was dead, her name now meant nothing to the cause. But the identities of the Five who still lived—and of Bhaal's Anointed, their leader—would not be spoken.

"One of our own has fallen," the tattooed man announced. "We cannot wait for the others. We must perform the ritual before Illasera's essence is lost."

In perfect unison the three lifted their arms to the crumbling roof of Bhaal's abandoned temple. Eyes locked on the floor, and their voices rose up in an ancient chant muffled by the hoods still drawn over their faces and the heavy, dank air of Bhaal's shrine. Words of power tumbled from their lips, and the sputtering flames of the pit in the center of the room flared, arcing to the ceiling in response to the spell.

Heat erupted from the sudden inferno as leaping tongues of fire touched the corners of the room, bathing the gloomy temple in a blazing orange light. Insects and vermin foolish enough to have crept into the deserted ruin were incinerated, consumed by the burning intensity of a dead god's magic unleashed by the Five.

Yet amidst the conflagration the three figures stood unharmed, protected by the sacred words of their dark litany. Oblivious to the heat and flame, they continued the ancient ritual that had been passed down to them by the Anointed One—and passed down to the Anointed One by Bhaal himself.

The stench of death rolled out from the pit at the center of the room. Beneath the shooting flames the embers began to broil and churn. A banshee's wail split the night, the tortured shriek of spirits drawn to the accursed shrine of Bhaal by the irresistible necromancy of the Five. Like wisps of smoke, the souls of the newly dead rose up from the pit.

At first they were but a few, wafting to the ceiling singly or in pairs, but as the incantation deepened, their numbers became legion. Ghosts who had not yet passed to the realms beyond the material world, apparitions of those who were barred from their promised afterlife, phantoms of people so recently deceased they were not even aware of their own demise. The fire in the pit—the fire of Bhaal, the fire of the Abyss—consumed them all, obliterating their existence, incinerating them, feeding itself on their essence until only the echo of their agonized screams remained.

As suddenly as the ritual had begun, it was over. The scorching heat and blazing light vanished, replaced once more by the damp cold and oppressive shadows of the abandoned Temple. The rising flames sputtered and winked out, leaving only the embers burning as feebly as the last vestiges of a dead god's presence on the world.

"Illasera was not there." Despite her efforts, the drow could not keep her voice from betraying her surprise and confusion.

"The Huntress had slain many of Bhaal's children," the reptilian one ventured. "Without the others, without the Anointed One, we may lack the strength to summon the essence of one as powerful as Illasera."

"No, the ritual had power, the failure is not ours. Illasera's essence is . . . gone." The tattooed man spoke slowly, as if he was still pondering the implications of the statement he was making. "Someone else has swallowed her soul."

"Gorion'sss ward hasss grown too ssstrong!" The voice of the scaled man was barely intelligible. His tongue flickered in and out with suppressed rage, and his words were nearly lost in an angry hiss.

"We should have dealt with him long ago," the drow replied, her own voice husky with anger and fear.

"That fool's fate is sealed," the tattooed man assured them, though his own voice was shaky. "The Anointed One is leading him into certain death. We will seize the taint of Bhaal from the dying soul of Gorion's ward and reclaim the essence of Illasera for our immortal master."

The failed ritual had shaken the tattooed man. Like the Five, he was angry, confused, and afraid. He spoke with an explicit recklessness he would have shunned under normal circumstances. "Bhaal's Anointed has assured me that Abdel Adrian will meet his end at Saradush!"

* * * * *

Bhaal's Anointed, favored servant of the Lord of Murder, awoke from the nightmare bathed in sweat, biting back screams of torment at the last possible second.

The dream was always the same. Fire. Not the sweet sacrificial flames that devoured victims during the glory of Bhaal's reign, though the perfume scent of boiling blood and the aroma of roasting flesh were ever present in the dream.

No, the conflagration within the nightmare was a blaze of unbearable agony, of eternal pain that even now did not abate. The flames of the anointing, the inescapable memory of the agonizing baptism of mutilating, disfiguring fire. With each recurrence of the vivid nightmare, Bhaal's Anointed had to relive once more the torment of the ritual that had changed the favored worshiper of the

Lord of Murder from mere follower to Bhaal's Anointed, to serve as guardian of the terrible ceremonies that could lead to a dead god's rebirth.

The Anointed One drew a shuddering breath but otherwise stayed motionless as the terrible dream slowly faded back into the mists of repressed trauma. Those who slept or stood guard nearby, the fools who had no idea of the true identity of the dark figure within their midst, had not noticed their companion's reaction.

Bhaal was dead, his followers lost and scattered, or swallowed up into the ranks of Cyric's rapidly expanding flock. Though the Lord of Murder was dead, Bhaal's Anointed knew he was also very much still alive in the world. Soon the ritual of ascension would begin, and the Lord of Murder would be born anew. And all Faerûn would pay for the suffering Bhaal's Anointed had been forced to endure.

The early years after Bhaal's demise had been the most difficult. Hunted by the fanatical followers of mad Cyric, the mortal who had supplanted the dead god's position in the pantheon, those still faithful to Bhaal had been forced to flee. Their own servants and followers turned on them, throwing their allegiance behind Cyric in a pathetic attempt to save their own lives and salvage their positions within the new order. Bereft of allies, Bhaal's Anointed and the rest of the faithful were forced to abandon their castles and slaves and live like fugitives as the might and power of Bhaal's worshipers was obliterated from the face of Faerûn.

Many went into hiding, reinventing their identities as a shield against their god's numerous enemies. Clerics who once counted on the protection and might of the priestly magic granted by their dark god were forced to turn to other methods for their survival. Even though Bhaal's worshipers could no longer call down the wrath of their god upon their enemies, the worshipers were not without power.

The true believers had learned much at Bhaal's feet. They knew how to survive. They studied the arts of sorcery, replacing divine spells with arcane magics. They sought out the leaders and rulers of the Southlands under false pretenses, sowing the seeds of future alliances. Always working from within the shadows, the faithful cultivated their own political power by learning the darkest secrets of the influential few who shaped the events of Faerûn, then using those secrets without conscience to further their own goals.

None were so skilled in these dark lessons as Bhaal's Anointed. Deception. Lies. Manipulation. Ruthless cunning. In many ways these abilities surpassed that which had been lost: the fierce power of a dark god's unholy magic.

Inevitably, the fortunes of Bhaal's Anointed had risen once more—though few, if any, knew the true identity of the Anointed One. During this time the fortunes of the Bhaalspawn also rose. Driven by the divine essence within, the Bhaalspawn began to rise to prominence up and down the Sword Coast. They attained positions of power and influence in Amn and Tethyr. They attracted followers throughout Calimshan. The first step of Bhaal's return had begun.

The Anointed One shivered as the terror sweat of the nightmare was cooled by an invisible draft. The dreams of the anointing were more frequent now, just one more sign that the time of ascension was approaching. Soon Bhaal's Anointed would receive the ultimate reward for years of faithful service.

It had fallen to Bhaal's Anointed to identify the most powerful of the immortal offspring and approach them one by one in an effort to recruit them to the cause. Promises of the immortal gratitude that would follow in the wake of Bhaal's resurrection inevitably brought visions of incomprehensible wealth and power, and those Bhaalspawn the Anointed One approached were always quick to accept the offer. Thus were born the Five, a secret alliance of the Lord of Murder's progeny, organized and led by Bhaal's Anointed.

The Five were taught to operate as their leader had done for so many years. They learned to work patiently from the deepest shadows. Secrecy was their weapon, anonymity their shield. Bhaal may have been dead but his many, many enemies still lived.

Over time the Five solidified their positions and power, spreading their invisible web of influence throughout the country, always careful to keep their very existence a secret. Throughout it all the guiding hand of Bhaal's Anointed directed their sinister actions.

They were instructed in the ancient rituals of the Lord of Murder. The mysteries of how to capture the fleeing essence of the dying Bhaalspawn were revealed to them. They were taught how to nurse the embers of the unholy fire in the temple so that it might one day be fuelled by the spirits of their dying kin. And the genocide of the Bhaalspawn had begun.

But the wholesale slaughter of the other Bhaalspawn had brought consequences even Bhaal's Anointed had not foreseen. The Five were becoming more independent, less willing to follow the orders of their evil mentor, growing ever stronger as they feasted on the essence of their fallen kin.

Some of them acted rashly and openly now, exposing themselves before the time was right. Illasera had been the most headstrong of the Five. Bhaal's Anointed had sent her to slay Abdel Adrian, knowing full well it would be the Huntress who perished in the encounter. A lesson for the rest of the Five, a warning to curb their growing ambition and recklessness. A lesson that had gone unheeded.

The gray light of approaching dawn was just visible on the horizon. The new day was almost here. The day, Bhaal's Anointed knew, when Abdel Adrian would be brought to Saradush.

Chapter Six

"That's Saradush?" It was Imoen who voiced the questions they all were thinking. "How are we supposed to get inside there?"

Sarevok shrugged. "I only promised to bring you here to meet Melissan. She is inside. If Abdel wants answers to his questions, he must speak with her."

For nearly a week Abdel and his companions had been following Sarevok. Emerging from the shelter of the Tethir Forest they had covered a grueling distance on foot, driven by the enemies behind them and the former enemy who now guided them. Sarevok led them ever east and south, crossing the Sulduskoon river. He led them within a day's march of the legendary Gorge of the Fallen Idol. Finally he had brought them to the northwestern edge of the Omlarandin Mountains, though the rounded, grass covered mounds were little more than oversized foothills.

Saradush itself was located just beyond the western edge of the small range, and after a day's journey south through the rolling hills Abdel and his companions finally got their first glimpse of their destination. They didn't like what they saw.

Saradush was under siege.

The scene was a familiar one to Abdel. The city itself was nearly a mile away, it looked like a small town surrounded by high stone walls that appeared more white than gray. From his vantage point atop the hills overlooking the fields and plains leading to the city gates, he counted nearly a hundred large tents. The sun was just nearing its apex so the glow of campfires was difficult to make out, but Abdel could see thousands of thin smoke trails crawling up through the still air, joining together in a heavy ashen cloud above the plains. Countless tiny figures milled around—soldiers looking to breach the walls. There was no sense of urgency in their actions, but rather a grim, relentless determination. Many of the soldiers clustered together around larger objects.

At this distance Abdel couldn't make the details of the objects out, but he knew what they were. Huge wooden towers, with platforms fifty feet high so that the invaders could see over the walls and analyze their opponent's defenses. Trebuchets and catapults capable of hurling flaming barrels of pitch over the walls stood ready for use. Heavy battering rams with steel coverings extending out and up from the sides to provide some limited protection against the burning oil and flaming arrows were also in a ready position.

Many of the men were lined up row upon row, and even though he couldn't see the flight of their arrows Abdel knew these were the archers, releasing volley after volley of arrows to keep the soldiers inside the walls occupied. With the unending hail of feathered shafts raining down on the defenders from above, the attackers outside were free to position their siege engines and war machines without fear of reprisal. Abdel had been on both sides of sieges many times during his years as a sword for hire. He knew most sieges were bloody, costly—yet inevitably successful—exercises.

Inside the defenders would be whittled down by the unending barrage of missile fire and weakened by starvation and the spread of disease amid the accumulating filth and refuse within. The invaders would keep up the attack, grinding the will of their enemy down and occasionally sending a suicidal rush of ladders and grappling hooks against the walls in the vain hope that their own soldiers would somehow be able to scale the walls and unseat the defenders from the battlements. Of course, the hooks and ladders would be easily dispatched by those inside, and most of the would-be invaders would come crashing to their deaths. The few lucky enough to reach the top would be butchered by the overwhelming number of enemy soldiers gathered against them, their corpses tossed back over the walls in wordless defiance to the attackers.

Eventually, Abdel knew, the town would be forced to surrender because of famine or pestilence. Or a boulder from one of the trebuchets would collapse a large section of the wall and the enemy would pour in through the breach. Or a battering ram would smash the front gates, tearing the wood from its hinges and leaving a gaping hole too large to be defended for long. In rare circumstances the reckless efforts to scale the wall would actually result in victory, if enough soldiers miraculously reached the top of the battlements and were able to hold their position long enough for reinforcements from their own army outside to scramble up and join them.

In the end, Abdel knew, it was always the same. Without outside aid, Saradush would fall.

"You lied to me, Sarevok," Abdel said angrily. "Or you're leading us into a trap."

In the week they had spent traveling to Saradush, Abdel had not said above a dozen words to his half brother. Wisely, Sarevok had not tried to make conversation with either the big sellsword or his half-elf companion. Occasionally he would speak to Imoen, but the cold stares of Jaheira and Abdel kept the young woman's answers brief, and eventually Sarevok had ceased his efforts and continued on in silence.

At night Abdel, Jaheira and Imoen alternated shifts watching over the other two as they slept. None of them trusted Sarevok enough to go to sleep in his presence without having a vigilant guard on duty. For his own part, Sarevok would pass the entire night standing motionless in one place, his face invisible behind his dark visor. Abdel often wondered if the big man's armor supported him in that position, allowing him to sleep standing up—or if the physical form Sarevok had been resurrected in didn't need to sleep at all. He didn't eat, at least not that the others ever noticed, and he never removed his armor.

"I did not lie to you, brother," Sarevok replied. "And I have no desire to betray the one who has given me another chance at life."

"Then why did you bring us to this doomed town?" Jaheira demanded.

"I did not know Saradush was under siege. If you are afraid of a trap, you need not enter the city." After a brief pause, the armored warrior added, "But then you will never learn the secrets Melissan holds, Abdel. The secrets of our father. Melissan has the answers, Abdel."

"Even if you speak the truth, there is no way into the town!" Jaheira said.

"That is not true, half-elf. My brother could walk through the front gates uninjured, if he chose. He could slaughter the entire army and save the town, if that was his wish."

"No," Jaheira spat. "More lies! We do not know the limits of Abdel's healing powers, and he will not risk his life against an entire army to test them."

"Besides, he isn't invulnerable. That lady with the arrows hurt him," Imoen said.

Abdel didn't say anything at first. He knew both Jaheira and Imoen had valid points, he knew what they said was true. But he also knew, deep down, that Sarevok was right. If he unleashed his full fury on the army gathered on the plains below, no one could stop him from entering the city gates. Any who tried would surely end up dead.

If the defenders inside the walls tried to keep him from entering, they would end up dead too, and if this Melissan refused to help him he would probably slay her, as well. He was the son of a god, a Child of Bhaal. If he wanted to, he could get inside the town. All he had to do was set the essence of his father loose and immerse himself in an orgy of bloody slaughter. But if he did that, Abdel knew, he would be lost. The part of him that was Abdel Adrian would be gone forever, swallowed by the ravaging beast that was the Lord of Murder reborn.

"If massacring an entire army is the only way in," the big sellsword said, "then I will have to learn to live without my answers."

The familiar shriek of Sarevok's armor as he shrugged set Abdel's teeth on edge, as it always did.

"I did not say that was the only way in," Sarevok answered. "I merely told you the solution that came most readily to my mind." There was a tinge of regret in his otherwise monotonal voice when he continued, "Perhaps such thoughts are why I was lost to the spirit of our unholy father while you have so far been able to resist his call, Abdel."

Imoen broke into the conversation, her high voice sounding surprisingly determined. "I think I can get us inside."

"How?" Abdel asked.

"I managed to come and go as I pleased when we were growing up at Candlekeep," she answered, laughing at the horrified disbelief registering on her half brother's face. "Every house, every castle, every keep, every walled town has a back way in, Abdel. A way in that nobody uses, a way most people don't even know about. It's just a matter of finding that back door."

"Forget it. It's too dangerous."

"If this Melissan has answers for you, Abdel, maybe she has some answers for me, too."

Abdel was momentarily taken aback by the anger in the young woman's words.

"You aren't the only one whose life has been ruined because of this damn Bhaal blood, you know. You aren't the only one struggling with this, looking for a way to deal with being the child of a god. I want to meet this woman, Abdel. And I'm willing to take more than a few risks along the way."

Abdel started to respond, but Jaheira held up her hand to silence him. "The girl is right, my love." The half-elf rested a slender hand on Abdel's muscular forearm and looked directly into his eyes. "The legacy of Bhaal is not my curse to bear, Abdel. Yet it is not yours alone, either. I have no right to challenge Imoen's decision, but neither do you. And she may succeed. Stealth is often a solution when force is not an option."

Before replying, Abdel let his eyes linger on the faces of his female companions. Jaheira's showed a familiar helpless frustration. The druid's desire to cleanse away the taint of her lover's tortured soul and her inability to do so were both evident in her beautiful features. In Imoen, Abdel saw something much different. Her face was young, but it was creased and worn by the burden of being the offspring of the Lord of Murder. Imoen's eyes reflected his own desire to be free of this cursed legacy, or at least to come to grips with it. Beneath it all Abdel recognized the same desperate hope he had felt when he agreed to bring Sarevok back to life in exchange for the promise of some answers.

"Fine," Abdel consented at last. "You can try and get us in. But at least wait until it gets dark."

* * * * *

"So the halfling says, 'That's not my sword!' Get it? 'That's not my sword!' Ha ha hah!"

Imoen could tell the soldier with the gruff voice was drunk—he spoke far too loudly for a man who was supposed to be on guard duty. Judging by the obnoxious braying laugh his companions gave in response to the vulgar joke, Imoen guessed the whole patrol was drunk. Typical.

It seemed as if the entire army was inebriated. Not that Imoen was complaining—it made her job that much easier. Under cover of darkness the young woman had slipped through the enemy lines without any difficulty at all, often passing close enough to the supposed lookouts to smell the reek of alcohol and hear their earthy banter.

The off-color jokes and the crude comments she heard as she picked her way cautiously between the fires of the night camp of the army besieging Saradush only confirmed her already low opinion of males. The stench from their unwashed bodies, the discolored stains on their garments, and the piles of filth they let accumulate with casual disregard only reinforced what Imoen already knew. Men were pigs. All of them.

They repulsed her, with their hairy, sweaty bodies and their loutish behavior. Abdel seemed different, of course, but she had grown up with him. He was her brother, and not just in blood. He didn't look at her with leering eyes or "accidentally" paw at her body when they passed in a crowd. Abdel was different. In his half sister's eyes he transcended the brutishness of his own manhood—despite his muscles and the lustful dalliances Imoen knew he had spent with many women over his life.

Imoen froze as a pair of lumbering oafs stumbled across her path less than a dozen feet away, leaning on each other for support. They paused, and Imoen felt a wave of fear swept over her. Could they see her?

Slowly, she dropped her hand to her belt. Tucked inside was a scroll she had been given as a gift from the monks at Candlekeep. At least, that was the story she would tell if anyone ever asked. In truth, she had borrowed the enchanted parchment from the massive Candlekeep library, certain no would miss this one insignificant scroll.

Imoen had displayed a certain aptitude for the arcane arts while at Candlekeep. Her quick and agile mind easily mastered the few minor cantrips she had been taught, but she lacked the disciplined and studious nature to truly develop her magical talents. Still, she had learned enough to be able to use this particular scroll if the situation should arise.

The incantation was a simple one, but useful. It would render her—and anyone standing within a few yards of her—invisible. Imoen could have read the parchment before venturing into the soldier's camp and walked right through the light of the brightest fire without fear, but she was loathe to waste the precious scroll. Once used, it was gone forever, and with the cover of darkness she had felt confident her natural abilities could keep her from being discovered.

Now, she realized, it was too late. Even if she did try to use the scroll, the men were close enough to grab her before she finished the incantation. Her hand silently slid from the scroll stashed in her belt to the dagger tucked in beside it.

But the shadowy figures made no move toward her. She heard one of them mumble something incoherent before doubling over and disgorging the contents of his stomach on the ground at his feet. The other laughed and slapped his friend on the back then they continued on, walking heedlessly through the steaming vomit in their path.

The young woman let her breath out in a long, silent sigh of relief. She hadn't even been aware she was holding it, but she knew the terrible consequences of being discovered. She was young, but not so naive that she wasn't aware of what would happen to an attractive female spy captured by an army of drunken soldiers at night.

Abdel would never do such a thing, Imoen was certain—not to her, not to any woman. Maybe it had something to do with the blood running through his veins. The more she thought about it, the more plausible that explanation seemed. Maybe it was Bhaal's blood that set him apart from other men.

Sarevok was also a Child of Bhaal, and Imoen sensed he was also different from most men. When the armored warrior spoke to her or turned his visor in her direction Imoen knew he was not ogling her with lust in his eyes. The offensive animal heat most men gave off in her presence was absent. Sarevok was cold as death itself.

In fact, Sarevok had displayed none of the worldly appetites since joining their little group. Imoen suspected he wasn't even truly alive—not in any real sense of the word. Maybe that was why he stayed with them. As Imoen understood it, Abdel had brought Sarevok back to the mortal world by sharing a minute part of his Bhaal essence with his half brother. Maybe the dark warrior was hoping he could eventually convince Abdel to share enough to restore him fully to life.

Imoen shook her head, trying to clear her mind. She needed to focus on the task at hand. A few minutes later she was silently approaching the walls of Saradush, the pathetic drunken lookouts of the army now far behind her, lost in the shadows of the night. She knew the Saradush guards atop the battlements would be more alert, watching for a clandestine invasion by the enemy beyond the gates. But Imoen was confident the night's gloom would conceal a single slim figure clad in black garments as she glided along the base of the stone wall.

She let her eyes wander. Now that she was clear of the fires her eyesight was beginning to adjust to the darkness. The walls were well built and showed little evidence of crumbling decay. The walls of Candlekeep had been just as solid, and Imoen knew of at least half a dozen ways to get past them.

Perhaps, she mused, that was her gift from her immortal father. Abdel and Sarevok were violent warriors, harbingers of death and destruction as Bhaal himself had been. But wasn't Bhaal also a god of secrets, cunning, deception, and stealth? Maybe what she lacked in brawn she made up for with her ability to become one with the darkness, to move without a sound, to slip unseen into private chambers and locked rooms.

Glancing up at the stars to get her bearings, Imoen realized she was on the south face of the walled town. She slowly made her way clockwise around the perimeter, her hand running along the stone surface feeling for changes in temperature or texture that might indicate a hidden entrance built into the rock.

Once she made her way around to the west wall it was her eyes, not her hands, that located the entrance she had been seeking. A few feet ahead of where she stood the uneven ground had been dug into a winding trench running parallel to the wall. The ditch was several feet deep and maybe a yard across.

Cautiously Imoen stepped down into the culvert and felt the damp earth sink beneath her slight weight. She crouched down, and the thick stench of human waste flooded her nostrils.

She stood up, barely able to suppress a choking cough that might have given her position away. Stepping out of the muck she did her best to clean her boots off, then followed the path of the ditch back to its source. A large stone pipe extended several feet out from the stone wall, dripping its foul muck into the drainage ditch. The mouth of the pipe was several feet across, and from the stench emanating from the access point Imoen had no doubt it would lead into the main sewer system below the city streets.

She had used the sewage drain at Candlekeep on only one occasion. The monks there held themselves in great esteem, but after slogging through the filthy muck that night Imoen could have told them with confidence that their feces did, in fact, stink. She had vowed that night that she would never crawl on her hands and knees through excrement again.

But the first hours of night had already passed. If Imoen and her companions hoped to get inside Saradush before daybreak, she couldn't afford to waste time seeking out a less distasteful route. Knowing she had no other choice, she turned and made her way back toward the distant fires of the army camped outside the walls of Saradush.

*   *   *   *   *

"I am not crawling through that filth." Jaheira kept her voice to that of a whisper, but Abdel still recoiled from the adamant tone of her words.

"We don't have time to find another way in," Imoen whispered back. "I'll go first."

As the young woman's body disappeared into the foul-smelling stone pipe at the base of the wall, Jaheira turned away in revulsion. Abdel said nothing. Jaheira had already sacrificed so much for him, he couldn't bring himself to ask her this favor. Fortunately, he didn't have to.

The half-elf gave a weary sigh. "I suppose excrement is as much a part of nature as lilacs or roses." She dropped to her knees and crawled into the sewage drain.

The stone pipe had been large enough for Imoen to fit through without any difficulty, and Jaheira was also able to slip her muscular but slender body through the small opening.

"The main tunnels of the sewer system are just up ahead." Imoen's voice sounded deep and hollow, emanating from the mouth of the stone tube. "I'm only a few yards beyond the wall and I already have enough room to stand up."

Abdel tilted his head at Sarevok, and his half brother lowered himself to his hands and knees and crawled into the pipe without protest. There were two reasons Abdel wanted his half brother to go before him. Clad in his heavy plate armor, Sarevok's body was larger and bulkier than even Abdel's enormous frame. If Sarevok could fit, Abdel had no need to worry about becoming stuck himself.

And he still didn't trust Sarevok enough to expose his back to him.

The fit was tight for the armored man. He had to drop flat onto his stomach and pull himself forward with his mighty gauntlets. Even so, the razor edges protruding from Sarevok's shoulders and back grated harshly against the stone of the pipe as he inched his way along. Abdel cast a quick glance to see if there was any reaction to the sound, but he heard no cries of alarm, and no one materialized from the darkness.

"I am through, brother." The acoustics of the pipe made Sarevok's voice even more unnerving than usual.

Abdel removed his blade from the scabbard on his back and clenched it in his right fist as he clambered down into the pipe. The cold, oozing muck squeezed between his fingers and the knuckles of his fist as he crawled along. Like Sarevok, he had to lie almost flat, supporting his weight with his hands and knees so that his chest and face were mere inches above the foul sludge seeping slowly down the length of the drain.

The stench was all but unbearable, but Abdel steeled his stomach and forced himself to go forward. Within the pipe all was black, but ahead he could see a faint, familiar glow. Jaheira must have cast another spell of illumination.

Mercifully, the length of the pipe was less than a dozen feet, and soon Abdel found himself standing with the others in the main tunnels of the sewers beneath Saradush. The tip of Jaheira's staff shone with a magical light, and in the soft brightness Abdel could clearly see the disgusting damp stains that had soaked into both Imoen's and Jaheira's clothes. The entire front of Sarevok's body was covered in the brownish green slime from the pipe. It dripped from his armor with a steady *plop, plop, plop*. Abdel's own arms and legs were similarly foul, but there was little he could do about it here.

Mercifully, the urge to retch was slowly fading as Abdel's nose became accustomed to the stench of the sewers. There was now room to stand up—at least, room for Imoen and Jaheira to stand. Sarevok and Abdel had to hunch over to keep their heads from banging against the ceilings above them.

"Well done, young one," Jaheira said to Imoen. "Though I cannot say I would readily venture on such a journey again in the near future."

Imoen took the compliment in stride. "Well, I got us in. Now where?"

The tunnel ran both north and south from where they had entered. Abdel had no doubt they would find it branching off in countless directions no matter which way they went. Without a map, any choice they made in this labyrinth would be nothing but a guess.

"North," he finally said, hoping his voice sounded more confident than he felt. Fortunately, nobody questioned him on his choice.

There was enough room for them to walk two abreast in the tunnels, so Abdel and Sarevok took the lead, splashing through the ankle-deep sludge that covered the stone floor. Rats scattered at the sound of their approach, and the beetles and roaches that covered the walls and ceilings scrambled away in terror as the light from Jaheira's glowing quarterstaff fell upon them. Occasionally Abdel felt something brush against his foot, a creature hidden beneath the slime they waded through. Fortunately none of the denizens of the Saradush sewers were curious enough, or hungry enough, to attack the strange invaders of their foul world.

They wandered for hours beneath the city, Abdel randomly choosing their path each time they came to a junction or fork in the path. They avoided the smaller side passages, sticking to the main sewer tunnel. Eventually, Abdel reasoned, it would have to lead them out.

Jaheira's spell had worn off and been re-cast several times, and Abdel was beginning to doubt his leadership ability. His back and neck ached from the perpetual hunch the low roof forced on him, and he could feel himself becoming ill from prolonged exposure to the diseased waste they were trudging through. Did that pile of dung in the corner look familiar? Had they passed this way once already?

He was just about to admit defeat when Imoen piped, "There, up ahead . . . there's a gate!"

Rushing forward, Abdel discovered Imoen had not been entirely correct. It was not a gate her sharp eyes had seen but a grate—an iron grate blocking their path, each of its round bars as thick as the sellsword's massive wrist. The bars showed no evidence of corrosion or rust. Just beyond the grate was a set of stairs leading up toward the city surface.

Abdel pulled on the bars, but the grate didn't budge.

"Can you call upon the powers of Mielikki to get us past this?" he asked his half-elf lover.

The druid shook her head. "Here in the city my magic is weak," Jaheira explained, "I can barely feel the touch of nature. She recoils from these man-made cities."

"If there was a lock of some kind I could pick it," Imoen offered, "but I don't see anything like that."

The big man sighed. "All right, we do this the hard way."

Without being asked, Sarevok stepped up beside his half brother and seized hold of the bars with his mailed fists. Abdel secured his own grip.

"On three. One . . . two . . . three."

The two giants heaved on the heavy grate with the strength of their half-immortal blood. Abdel's jaw clenched, the muscles in his back knotted up, his arms quivered and shook with the strain. His massive shoulders bulged as he tried to wrench the iron bars loose from their very settings. From the corner of his eye Abdel could see Sarevok's armor quaking from the force of the mailed warrior's own exertions.

The grate moved. Barely, but it moved. Abdel collapsed against the iron bars, gasping for breath. Sarevok slouched against the sewer wall. Though the armored warrior made no sound, his breastplate heaved in and out as if he was panting.

While the two men recovered, Jaheira came over to inspect the results of their work. "There are faint cracks in the stone," she informed them. "A few more hard tugs, and the settings will crumble away like dust."

In fact it took nearly a dozen more long, exhausting pulls from the two men before the grate was dislodged. Had it not been for Abdel's godlike recuperative powers—powers Sarevok seemed to share—the two men would have collapsed trembling from their efforts long before achieving their goal.

As it was, however, the grate wrenched free so suddenly that both Sarevok and Abdel were thrown off balance, stumbling back to land unceremoniously on their rumps in the foul liquid covering the sewer floor.

To their credit, neither Jaheira nor Imoen laughed.

The half-elf stepped over to help Abdel to his feet. Imoen hesitated to do the same for Sarevok, the blades jutting out from his armor keeping her momentarily at bay. Before she could steel herself to approach, the armored man was back on his feet.

"Shall we, my big strong hero?" Jaheira asked Abdel, her hand giving a graceful flourish in the direction of the now-accessible stairs leading up to the streets above.

Chapter Seven

The guards surrounded them less than a minute after they had emerged from the sewers. Abdel wasn't surprised. It was early morning now. They had wasted the cover of darkness wandering the labyrinth of the sewers.

In the daylight warriors as big as he and Sarevok were hard to ignore, and the drying waste on all of their clothes left little doubt as to how they had entered the town. Given the ongoing siege, it was only natural that nervous citizens would rush to alert the local militia to their presence.

"Throw down your weapons or our archers will open fire!"

A dozen men in chain shirts armed with long spears had formed a large circle around them. Beyond this circle a half dozen archers stood with bows drawn and ready. Abdel slowly drew his blade from his back, resisting the urge to unleash his fury against the men threatening him. Instead, he tossed his sword to the ground. His companions did the same with their own weapons.

"You there," the captain of the guards shouted out, "you in the armor. Remove it. I don't want you slicing up any of my men."

Sarevok made no move to comply with the order. "I cannot do that."

"I'm not giving you a choice," the captain answered. "Take it off or my men will open fire."

"We mean you no harm," Jaheira interjected, trying to change the topic. "We have come seeking a woman named Melissan."

Several of the guards turned to spit on the ground at the mention of Melissan's name, but the captain only scowled.

"That name won't win you any points with us. Now tell your friend to remove his armor."

"He is no friend of ours," Jaheira replied.

The captain shrugged and said a single word. "Fire."

Abdel leaped in front of Jaheira, determined to catch the deadly projectiles hurtling toward her chest with his own body. As he did so, the realization that he couldn't protect both her and Imoen flashed across his mind.

His concerns, however, were unjustified. The disciplined archers had launched their attacks only at Sarevok. A half dozen missiles split the early morning air and struck the armored warrior. Several bounced harmlessly off his heavy iron plates, but one pierced the vulnerable joint between the shoulder and the neck, burying itself several inches deep.

Sarevok reached up disdainfully and snapped the arrow off at the shaft, leaving a half inch of jagged wood protruding from the joint. The remainder he tossed to the floor.

There was stunned silence from the archers, and a look of understanding passed across the captain's face.

"Bloody Bhaalspawn," he whispered.

One of the pikemen encircling them snapped his head around at the captain's whispered accusation, then turned back to Sarevok.

"Damn you!" he shouted, lowering his spear and charging forward to impale Sarevok on the point.

Sarevok swung his heavy gauntlet down, his fist a blur as he slapped the weapon from the young man's grip with such force that it splintered the thick wooden shaft.

The momentum of the onrushing soldier carried him forward, bringing the now weaponless man within range of Sarevok's other fist, already arcing toward his opponent's unprotected head. Abdel had visions of Sarevok twisting his arm so that the blade jutting from the forearm of his armor would decapitate his unfortunate attacker.

Instead, Sarevok struck his opponent on the temple with the flat of his palm. The man crumpled beneath the vicious blow, and a shower of teeth flew from his mouth to skitter across the cobblestones of the street. His body twitched once then lay still, a pool of red gushing forth from his mangled mouth and a smaller trickle of blood dribbling from his nose and ear.

Abdel scooped his own sword up from the ground, intending only to defend himself. In response to his sudden movement, one of the archers embedded an arrow in Abdel's chest. The big man screamed as he tore the arrowhead free from his flesh. His wound healed almost instantly, but the memory of the pain lingered. From deep within he felt the angry flames of his father's blood sparking to life.

Dying enemies, slaughtered soldiers, butchered townsfolk—a fiery avalanche of violent images buried all reason and conscious thought. He would extract a horrendous toll on the town of Saradush for daring to attack the son of a god!

He took a half step toward the pikemen, still foolishly holding their positions as ordered by their captain. Jaheira placed a hand on his shoulder, and Abdel spun to face her with hate in his eyes.

The sight of Jaheira's troubled face instantly cooled his passion. Beneath the reassuring touch of his lover the Bhaal fire burning in Abdel's belly was quenched.

Glancing to the side he was surprised to see that Sarevok had also managed to rein in his Bhaalspawn temper and stood implacably over the unconscious soldier at his feet.

"Stop this!" Imoen screamed as the archers took aim for another volley. Amazingly, they listened to her plea and held their fire.

The captain glared at Sarevok and Abdel, his eyes smoldering orbs of resentment. He raised his hand, and the archers drew back their bows but did not fire, waiting on their captain's signal.

"They'll kill us all," Imoen warned, nodding in the direction of Sarevok and then Abdel. The captain's brow furrowed, and he lowered his hand. In unison, the archers lowered their arrows.

From around the nearest corner a small platoon of soldiers charged into view, their broadswords already drawn. The reinforcements were wearing the uniforms of the Calimshan military. Abdel found this particularly strange, since Saradush was a Tethyrian city.

The captain of the Saradush platoon shook his head in resignation when he noticed the new arrivals.

"Captain," the leader of the swordsmen called out as the troop took their positions behind the pikemen, "I demand to know what is going on here!"

"Invaders, Garrol. They're Bhaalspawn."

Garrol arched an eyebrow. "All of them?"

"Well, no... I don't think so."

Jaheira interrupted the conversation. "Some of us are indeed Children of Bhaal, but we mean no harm to you. We are here seeking a woman named Melissan."

Garrol ignored the druid's words, and continued to speak directly to the Saradush captain. "This is a matter for General Gromnir. Take your men, and return to your posts on the walls."

The captain made no reply, but at his signal two of the pikemen dropped their weapons and cautiously approached the body of their fallen comrade. Sarevok stepped back, allowing them to pick up their friend's unconscious form without having to come within range of his fierce fists.

"Uh... what about that missing grate?" Imoen asked. "And the sewer pipe?"

Garrol finally turned his attention to the four strangers. "What are you talking about?"

"The sewer drain on the west wall," Imoen explained. "That's how we got in. It's large enough for a man in full field plate to crawl through. If you want to keep your enemies on the outside of your gates, I'd suggest putting some guards down there."

"The enemies are already inside," the captain mumbled, but Garrol pretended not to hear him.

"Captain, I suggest you take this young lady's words to heart and see to this breach in the defenses immediately. I will appraise General Gromnir of the situation when I bring these Bhaalspawn before him for judgment."

"Judgment?" Jaheira exclaimed indignantly. "For what are we being judged, exactly?"

Nobody answered her. The captain and his Saradush troops were already on the move, and the Tethyrian company of Garrol had taken up positions surrounding the four companions.

"For your own safety, and that of the town, I urge you to accompany me without further incident." Garrol's voice was gruff, but polite. He spoke as a man simply doing his job.

Before Jaheira or Imoen could object, Abdel voiced his consent. "We want no trouble. Take us where you will."

The memory of how close he had just come to loosing his father's ruthless violence on the Saradush troops was still fresh in his mind. His mind recoiled as he imagined the unholy carnage the Ravager would wreak if unleashed within the walls of a besieged town. The big sellsword was willing to do just about anything to avoid another confrontation and risk a repeat episode of the all-consuming bloodlust he had succumbed to in the forest clearing when he had killed the Huntress with his bare hands. Abdel could only hope his companions, especially Sarevok, would defer to his lead.

Nobody said anything to challenge his will.

Garrol nodded curtly. "Very good. General Gromnir will be most eager to speak to you."

* * * * *

As the strangely-out-of-place Calimshan soldiers escorted Abdel, Imoen, Sarevok, and Jaheira through the town of Saradush, the half-elf was reminded why she disliked cities.

It wasn't just the paved stones beneath her feet, severing her contact with the living land. It wasn't the lack of growing grass or trees. It wasn't even the cold, hard buildings on every corner that blocked off the sky at every turn, confining and closing in on them.

The city had a scent to it, the inevitable smells that clung to people whenever they gathered in large numbers. The stale, acrid reek of sweat, the sickly odor of food carted in from the outlying farms, just slightly past fresh, horses, chamber pots, the faint whiffs of the now all-too-familiar sewers as they passed each grate. Over top of it all, the cloying perfumes and soaps the "civilized" masses used to try and mask their own foul stench. The smell of civilization.

Jaheira wrinkled her nose in disgust. The smell was the worst, but at least she had come to expect it whenever she ventured into a village, town, or city. There were other things she disliked about Saradush—things that set it apart from most of the urban centers she had seen. The streets were deserted, barren of the typical teeming life of the city. People were few and far between, and those few the druid noticed glared back at her with unmistakable resentment and even hate in their eyes. Even more remarkable, there were no animals running through the streets. No dogs or cats, not even any rats.

"Where are the animals?" Jaheira asked, eager to break the oppressive silence of their journey. "Do they not keep pets here in Saradush?"

Garrol, from his position at the front of the escort, didn't even turn his head when he answered. "They used to. But after a month-long siege supplies are scarce, and good food is hard to come by." Though he attempted to maintain the decorum of duty, Jaheira detected the faintest hint of revulsion in his voice.

"Ewww!" Imoen's unguarded reaction was evidence she had overheard their remarks. "That's disgusting."

As a druid, Jaheira understood the natural order. Many animals served as food so that other animals could survive. It was natural. But eating a pet—a faithful, loving companion—was abhorrent. The half-elf now had another reason to hate cities.

"A month?" It was Abdel who spoke now. "Where are the reinforcements? Why haven't the king and queen of Tethyr come to Saradush's aid?"

Garrol shifted uncomfortably. He was an officer in a foreign army occupying a city besieged by yet another force. Jaheira could understand his discomfort.

"Before the siege began there were widespread reports of bands of mercenaries looting and pillaging throughout the western reaches of Tethyr. The royals are too busy cleaning up the mess of raiders and bandits around Myratma and along the trade routes to bother sending their armies to the east to save our sorry hides."

"Surely if they knew how bad things have become—" Imoen began.

"They don't know," Garrol replied. "We haven't been able to get a single messenger safely past the army surrounding the walls. And even if we did, it might be another month before any help arrived. We're a long, long way from the seats of power."

"Well, you'd think the town would be a little more welcoming to us, considering the circumstance it's in. I mean, we might be the only help they're going to get, but those Saradush soldiers glared at us like they wished we were dead." Imoen said.

"The last thing the townsfolk here want is more help from outsiders," Garrol replied. "They don't like your kind here. They blame you for this siege."

"Our kind?" Jaheira asked for clarification. "You mean Bhaalspawn?"

"The citizens of Saradush offered this city as a refuge," Garrol explained. "They wanted to help protect those who were being persecuted. At Melissan's urging, they offered sanctuary to the children of Bhaal. Look what they get for their troubles. Gromnir was the last straw."

There was a pointed cough from one of the escorting soldiers, and Garrol suddenly shut his mouth, biting down hard enough to make his teeth clack. His face burned with embarrassment, and Jaheira realized he must have overstepped his authority in revealing so much information.

The rest of their walk passed in silence. Even with her sense of direction distorted by the surrounding architecture, Jaheira could tell Garrol was leading them toward the hub of the town. As they neared the city center, a large stone castle came into view. Garrol led them straight up to the gates. They opened at their approach and slammed shut behind them.

They moved quickly through the courtyard and into the main structure of what once must have been the castle of the local nobility. Inside, the halls of the keep were lined with countless more soldiers standing at attention, all of them clad in the colors of Calimshan. They saluted as Garrol passed, but he did not bother to return the gesture.

Garrol marched quickly through the castle corridors— Jaheira's long legs were barely able to keep up, and Imoen was forced to actually break into a run several times to avoid being trampled by the escort of soldiers marching behind them.

With their rapid pace it didn't take long until they reached the main audience chamber. A number of armed Calimshan soldiers were positioned strategically around the large open room, as well as nearly a dozen people dressed in civilian clothes. Seated on the throne at the far

Drew Karpyshyn

end of the room was the grubbiest, grimiest, hairiest man Jaheira had ever seen. His face was hidden beneath a heavy, unkempt black beard and long strands of tangled hair hung down from his bangs to half cover his eyes. His clothes were so filthy and stained it took the half-elf a second to realize the man was clad in the same uniform as Garrol and the rest of the Calimshan soldiers.

"General Gromnir," Garrol addressed the wild looking figure, "these people are here to see Melissan."

"Hah!" the general barked in reply, tilting his head to the side and fixing his cock-eyed stare on Sarevok. "Gromnir knows only Bhaalspawn seek Melissan! Hah-Hah! More Bhaalspawn gathered to die! Great fun! Hah!"

"Mielikki preserve us," Jaheira whispered, hoping only Abdel could hear her. "He's mad."

* * * * *

Abdel agreed with his lover's whispered assessment of their host. There was definitely something unbalanced in the way Gromnir spoke and something unnerving about the gleam in his eye peering out from behind the long, greasy strands of hair that hung down over his forehead. But Abdel was determined not to overreact. He had no intention of accidentally unleashing the ravaging spirit of the Lord of Murder again.

"General Gromnir," he said, hoping his voice sounded calm and reassuring, "I am in fact a Child of Bhaal. But I am not here to bring harm."

"Hah! Bhaalspawn bring harm wherever they go. Blood and violence follow Bhaalspawn everywhere! Gromnir knows! Hah-Hah!"

"I just want to speak to Melissan," Abdel continued, trying not to let his discomfort at the wild general's behavior show. "I am seeking—"

"Sanctuary!" Gromnir interrupted. "Bhaalspawn come to Saradush for sanctuary! Gromnir knows. Hah! Melissan

84

promises safety, but Bhaalspawn find only death! Hah-Hah! Good fun, yes?"

Shaking his head, Abdel tried again. "No, we don't want sanctuary. We just want—"

"No sanctuary? Then what do you seek? Hah! Gromnir's death, maybe?"

Sarevok spoke before Abdel could come up with a response that wouldn't agitate their already disturbed host. "I did not come to kill you, Gromnir. I could have done that long ago."

The wild general's head snapped back with the shock of recognition, his tangled locks flipping up from his eyes that were wide with surprise.

"Gromnir knows you! Hah! Gromnir heard Sarevok was dead! Hah-Hah!"

Jaheira made no attempt to hide the implied accusation in her voice. "Sarevok, you know this madman?"

"Sarevok knows Gromnir," the general replied, "and Gromnir knows Sarevok. Take them to the prisons!"

From the corner of his eye Abdel saw his companions preparing for battle. Imoen's hand was slipping down to the dagger she kept in her belt, Jaheira's seemingly casual hold on her staff tightened to a fighting grip, and even Sarevok's armored form seemed to coil in anticipation, but a quick shake of Abdel's head caused them all to relax their stances.

The guards approached cautiously and disarmed them. Abdel tried to give a reassuring look in response to the questioning glares from his female companions. He had escaped many prisons in his time, and he was willing to bet that they would find some way to escape this one as well. Abdel would rather take his chances with bars and a cell than have to endure another battle within himself against the Bhaal fire that could possess his soul and transform him into the demonic, four-armed Ravager.

Chapter Eight

There were at least a dozen cells in the dungeon, all empty except for the four now occupied by Abdel and his companions. Even the guards left them once they were secure.

"I am assuming you have a plan, Abdel," Jaheira said once the guards were gone.

"Yeah, big brother," Imoen chimed in. "What's going on? I've never known you to shy away from a fight."

Abdel hesitated before answering. He didn't want to explain the motives behind his actions to the only two people he cared about in the world. He didn't want to tell them that if he drew his sword in anger he might not sheath it again until they were both reduced to savaged, bloody corpses. He didn't want them to know he was afraid of the monster inside himself.

But Imoen and Jaheira had trusted him. He couldn't just refuse to answer them. As much as he hated to do it, Abdel was afraid he would have to lie to his sister and his lover. Abdel wasn't a very good liar, even at the best of times.

Fortunately, he never got the chance to speak.

"Perhaps your large friend merely has learned that there are other solutions besides resorting to violence," a female voice said as a tall, slender figure descended the stairs to the dungeon and emerged from the shadows.

The woman who spoke was wearing a mesh shirt of fine steel links, and a spiked mace hung from her belt.

She wore silver gauntlets and knee-high silver boots. Her cloth sleeves and leggings were black. A high, soft collar extended from beneath her armor right up the line of her jaw. Every inch of her skin was covered by either armor or the dark, form fitting cloth except for her face. There her skin was the white of gleaming marble, a striking contrast to her coal black eyes, her deep red lips and the long raven tresses that hung down well past her shoulders.

"Melissan," Sarevok said by way of greeting.

The woman nodded in the armored man's direction. "Sarevok. I thought you were dead."

"I was," Sarevok replied simply. "I should have heeded your warnings. I have been given a second chance."

Melissan turned her intense gaze in Abdel's direction. "And you can be none other than Abdel Adrian, Gorion's ward."

"How do you know Abdel?" Jaheira demanded, "how do you know Sarevok?"

"I knew Sarevok long ago," Melissan answered, though she did not pull her eyes away from Abdel, "before his mad efforts to start a war between Nashkel and Baldur's Gate.

"As for Abdel," she continued, "his name is well known to any who have taken an interest in the Lord of Murder's children, as is his description. You cannot easily hide yourself in the crowd, Abdel."

"No," Abdel replied sheepishly. "I stick out like a sore thumb."

Abdel had doubted Sarevok's promises. He was reluctant to believe his half brother could really bring him to someone who could help him escape the taint of his immortal father. But Melissan's confident, steady gaze both unnerved and excited him. Her black eyes pierced his very soul, and he was certain she could see the evil power that dwelt within him. However, she did not recoil as most others would if they glimpsed the unholy taint of Bhaal he kept caged. Instead, Melissan seemed to

Drew Karpyshyn

acknowledge and accept his monstrous nature—as if she had known it would be there all along.

"I have been told you can help me," Abdel said, enraptured by Melissan's unflinching eyes. "Sarevok says you can help me to rid myself of Bhaal's unholy taint."

"Before we delve into my lover's heritage," the druid said pointedly, "shouldn't we think of a way to escape these cells?"

Jaheira's voice snapped Abdel out of his bewitched state, causing him to blush in embarrassment and cast an apologetic look in Jaheira's direction.

Melissan nodded. "Of course. I will go fetch the keys from Gromnir."

"But he's the madman who put us in here in the first place!" Imoen objected.

"Gromnir is not as mad as he seems," Melissan assured her. "His behavior is bizarre, but he is not insane. Just very, very careful."

"Paranoid you mean," Imoen snorted, still not convinced.

"His caution is based on many previous attempts on his life," Melissan explained, "and very rational, given his present circumstances. A Calimshite general ruling over a Tethyrian town has good reason to be cautious."

"Why is this mad General Gromnir in charge here, anyway?" Jaheira asked, making no attempt to hide the accusatory tone of her voice.

Melissan sighed, her flawless features taking on a regretful, somber expression. "I thought the general and his troops could help protect Saradush and all the children of Bhaal who had come to this town seeking sanctuary. Gromnir and his men came here at my request."

Abdel nodded, remembering the way the Saradush soldiers had spat on the ground when he had first mentioned Melissan's name. Suddenly their resentment made perfect sense.

"At first Gromnir and his men were welcomed here by Count Santele, the ruler of Saradush," Melissan continued.

"But when word of an approaching army reached the count's ears, he ordered Gromnir's troops and all the Bhaal-spawn seeking refuge within the walls of Saradush to leave the city. He thought that if he banished the children of Bhaal he could spare the town."

"Let me guess," Jaheira chimed in. "Gromnir refused to go, and he and his men took over the town."

Melissan nodded. "Count Santele was forced to flee for his life. The Saradush militia was unprepared for Gromnir's sudden coup, and before they could organize themselves against the Calimshite forces, the siege had begun.

"The captains and soldiers of the Saradush militia have had little choice but to accept the rule of Gromnir for the time being. Only by working together can the two armies put up an effective defense against the invaders laying siege to the town.

"What about reinforcements?" Imoen asked. "Why haven't the king and queen of Tethyr brought troops in to end this siege and get rid of Gromnir in one shot?"

"Myratma, the capital of Tethyr, is hundreds of miles away," Melissan explained, "and there are hostile forces moving throughout the region. Surely you have heard the rumors of armies devastating towns throughout the Southlands.

"This war is being fought not only in Saradush. The king and queen must look to the security of their own backyard before they can turn their attention to Saradush."

"No wonder Gromnir's paranoid," Abdel noted. "I bet people on both sides of this siege would be happy to see him dead."

"What you say is, to some degree, true," Melissan conceded. "However, most of the citizens of this town have accepted the fact that their only hope to survive this siege is to support Gromnir's dictatorship . . . for now."

The tall woman shook her head in weary disappointment before adding, "I fear that the current situation is not the only reason for Gromnir's behavior. I suspect the curse of being one of Bhaal's offspring has recently taken its toll on the general."

"That horrible, hairy thing is a Bhaalspawn?" Imoen exclaimed in disbelief.

"The Lord of Murder's children come in many forms." Melissan arched her eyebrows and gave Imoen the same piercing stare she had earlier fixed on Abdel. "As I am sure you well know, my young lady.

"It is only because of his immortal blood that Gromnir is here, under siege in Saradush. I would never have brought him and his loyal Calimshan troops to Tethyr if I did not feel he had something personal invested in the fate of the Bhaalspawn."

Melissan probably would have said more, but the sound of Jaheira clearing her throat cut her words short. Abdel couldn't help but smile at the druid's none-too-subtle reminder.

"Of course this can wait until you are out of your cages," the tall woman in black assured them. "I am certain General Gromnir will release you all, once I have spoken to him."

* * * * *

Jaheira disliked the woman. There was something in the way she looked at Abdel, a hunger in her gaze. Jaheira didn't like any woman looking at Abdel like that—no one but herself. She also didn't like the way Abdel seemed to hang on her every word, the way a young child with a crush would focus too intently on a beautiful teacher.

Much to Jaheira's surprise, Melissan was as good as her word and returned less than five minutes later with a ring of keys.

"I'm sure there is much more you would like to ask me, Abdel. We can resume our conversation as soon as I have released you." Almost as an afterthought, Melissan added, "And your companions, of course."

The druid bit her lip to keep from speaking harshly. She knew she was being foolish, feeling threatened by this woman. Abdel loved her. He would even give his life for her.

But Melissan was undeniably beautiful. She could reveal secrets about Abdel's Bhaal blood that Jaheira could not. The half-elf knew Abdel had fallen for just such a woman before, the vampire Bodhi. Jaheira had forgiven her lover for his transgression. She knew well enough the enchanting magics vampires could wield over the living, and she couldn't believe Abdel would willingly betray her under normal circumstances. Yet she couldn't quell the whispers of doubt, the ones that said Abdel was consumed with the taint of Bhaal and would do anything to rid himself of his father's legacy. Anything.

Melissan opened Abdel's cell first, then Sarevok's. She had just unlocked the door of Jaheira's cell when the sound of three sharp blasts of a horn echoed off the walls of the dungeon.

"A breach in the wall!" Melissan exclaimed. "The invaders have broken through. Three blasts means the south wall."

The woman spun on her heel and ran for the stairs, her long hair fanning out behind her as she raced back toward the dungeon exit. In her rush, she left the key hanging in the still unopened lock of Jaheira's cell.

"We have to reinforce the men on the wall and seal the breach or Saradush will be overrun!" Melissan called over her shoulder as she leaped up the stairs two steps at a time.

Jaheira had to admit, reluctantly, that the tall woman moved with amazing speed and grace.

Sarevok rushed to follow her, and Abdel took a half step before turning to face Jaheira and Imoen.

"Go," Jaheira urged, moving toward the key dangling from the lock of her cell. "I will open our cells, and Imoen and I will come join the battle in mere moments."

Abdel must not have heard her, because he raced over to her cell.

"Go, my love," she said again, "we will be right behind you!" To prove to Abdel he had no need to worry about her safety, Jaheira reached through the bars and put her hand on the key even as Abdel arrived at her cell.

The big man reached his own hand through the bars and placed his open palm squarely on the center of her chest and shoved. Jaheira stumbled back several steps before tumbling to the ground.

"Abdel!" she cried out, more shocked than hurt.

The big man didn't respond, but he grabbed the key in his massive fist. The muscles of his forearm flexed and he snapped the metal key off in the lock, trapping Jaheira in the cage.

The druid scrambled to her feet and rushed toward him, reaching out with a free hand through the bars as Abdel hopped back just out of her range.

"Abdel, what are you doing?" she demanded, even as Imoen screamed the same question from the adjacent cage.

He turned away before she could read the expression in his eyes. "I'm sorry," was all he said before he vanished up the stairs, leaving both Jaheira and Imoen trapped in their respective cells.

* * * * *

The horror and betrayal he had seen in Jaheira's eyes twisted like a blade in Abdel's heart. If there had been time he would have explained his actions to her and Imoen. Abdel had been involved in many sieges in his days as a mercenary. He knew all too well the bloody battle that was even now raging atop the battlements of Saradush as the defenders strove to hurl the invaders from their foothold. Abdel knew the only way Jaheira and Imoen would be safe should he lose control of his own murderous fury was if they were nowhere near the violence.

It took less than a minute for Abdel to find his way from the top of the dungeon stairs to the main gates of the castle. Sarevok and Melissan had already disappeared down the streets of Saradush, rushing to aid the soldiers on the wall. Abdel had no trouble following the shouts and cries of those rushing to join the battle.

He came around a corner and found himself directly beneath the melee. Glancing up, he saw that dozens of invaders had managed to scale the wall, overwhelming the Saradush and Calimshan troops positioned atop the battlements. With each passing second, more invaders climbed up the ladders to join their fellows and drive the desperate defenders even farther back. Abdel knew reinforcements for his side would be unlikely, as the men along the other walls would be desperately defending their own positions against a similar rush of ladder carrying attackers.

There had been no more alarms raised, so it seemed as if the only breach was on the south wall. If the Saradush forces could reclaim the battlement, the advance could be halted—for now.

Abdel rushed along the base of the wall, heading for the open door at the foot of the nearest tower, one of many lining the fortifications of the town. He raced up the circular staircase and burst onto the battlement.

Melissan and Sarevok were already there, joining the half dozen defenders still standing against the score of enemy soldiers. The tall woman swung her mace from side to side with both hands, smashing aside the sword of her foe with one swipe, then quickly reversing the direction of her weapon to bring its spiked head crashing down on her opponent's skull, piercing the iron helm. By the time the dying man had collapsed into the pool of blood gushing from his mangled temple, Melissan had already moved on.

It was then Abdel realized he was charging headlong into the battle unarmed. He had let Gromnir's soldiers take his sword away when they escorted him to the prison. Without breaking stride Abdel dropped to the ground, letting his momentum carry him into a tumbling summersault. He scooped up a sword from one of the many fallen Saradush defenders as he rolled by and popped up to his feet just in time to block the incoming blade of a heavy battle axe.

Abdel never slowed, but let his charge carry him crashing into the much smaller soldier attacking him. The man was driven back by Abdel's massive body, dropping his axe and pinwheeling his arms to keep his balance as he stumbled toward the edge of the wall. Abdel took a step back and brought a boot up into his foe's chest, then thrust with his leg. The screaming man tumbled backward over the parapet to the ground below.

Beside him Abdel saw Sarevok shredding a path of destruction through their enemies. Like Abdel, the armored man had entered the battle without a sword, but unlike his half brother, Sarevok hadn't bothered to pick up a weapon.

Sarevok's mailed fists crushed the skulls and smashed the faces of his enemies into pulp. The blows of his attackers rained down harmlessly on the reinforced iron plates of his mailed suit. Sarevok struck back with the spikes protruding from his elbows or slashed out with the razor-sharp blades forged on the forearms of his black armor, carving through metal, flesh, and bone indiscriminately. Soldiers fortunate enough to avoid Sarevok's deadly arms were left crippled and dying on the ground, their lower extremities savaged as Sarevok lashed out with a bladed shin to hack open an enemy's leg.

The sight of Sarevok carving a swath of gruesome, visceral death through the battle evoked an instant response in Abdel's own soul. The fury of Bhaal answered Sarevok's wordless invitation, and Abdel began to hack down his opponents like wheat at the threshing.

Even a division of elite mercenaries could not have stood before Abdel's ruthless assault, but these men were fodder—the expendable first wave of the attack. Their equipment was substandard, their technique and training nonexistent. Abdel disdainfully slapped away their feeble attempts to parry his lethal stabs, easily sidestepped the clumsy thrusts and wildly off-balance swings of his foes. Those foolish enough to stand in his way were disemboweled, their guts ripped from their torsos by Abdel's flashing blade. Those wise enough to turn and run were chopped down from behind and left dying in the ravaging sellsword's wake.

Through the slaughter Abdel felt the hungry flames inside himself escalating, fuelled by the steady spray of hot blood that coated his hands and face. The world was tinged in crimson, his vision colored by Bhaal's mounting wrath. The fire became an inferno, until Abdel was certain his victims could feel its heat emanating from his skin even as they felt the cold steel of his blade.

But this time it didn't consume Abdel. Even in the midst of the carnage, the sellsword never lost control. He never lost *himself*. Through sheer force of will he was able to subdue the demon within and keep the Ravager at bay.

His assault had cleared a path to the nearest of the ladders the invaders had used to scale the wall, and Abdel still had sense enough to kick it down, so that it tumbled back and away from the wall. Three quick slashes of his sword and three corpses later he was at the second ladder. It, too, toppled back to the ground, taking several raiders with it.

The other two ladders had already been knocked down, one by Sarevok and one by Melissan. Abdel spun back to face the melee and saw the only men still standing were all wearing either the colors of Saradush or Calimshan. The searing bloodlust in his soul flared, urging him to unleash his fury on his allies. He felt his skin tingle and itch, the first signs of the hideous transformation he had struggled to avoid at all costs.

Abdel smothered the internal blaze and let his sword clatter to the ground, snuffing out the dark desires of his father's tainted blood as easily as he would crush a bug beneath his boot. The transformation ended before it even began. There wasn't time for the big sellsword to revel in his victory or even to wonder why the bloodlust of Bhaal's fury had been so easily quelled this time.

One of the surviving members of the Saradush troops scooped up a large brass horn from a fallen comrade, while the others began to pick through the heap of bodies searching for survivors. The man with the horn blew three long, wavering blasts to alert the other defenders that the south wall was again secure.

A series of answering blasts echoed over the besieged town.

Melissan was now standing beside Abdel, though the big man hadn't noticed her approach.

"The breach is sealed," she said, panting slightly from the exertion of the battle as she explained the meaning of the signals that had rung out over the rooftops of Saradush. "The other walls are secure, and the attackers have retreated. For now."

There were many questions Abdel wanted to ask of this woman, many answers he needed. But when he opened his mouth, only a single word came out. "Jaheira!"

He turned and ran back toward the dungeon.

Chapter Nine

"I just didn't want you to get hurt," Abdel explained, hoping Jaheira would forgive him for leaving her and Imoen trapped in the dungeon.

He wasn't being completely honest with them—he still couldn't bring himself to recount his experience in the clearing with Illasera. He couldn't admit he had been mere seconds away from transforming into an uncontrollable monster that would have ripped his lover and his sister apart with its four taloned hands. But he had to tell the half-elf something.

The locksmith working to free the end of the key jammed into the lock of the half-elf's cell nodded in agreement. "It was pretty messy up there, Miss," he said, offering Abdel some unsolicited support. "No place for a couple of ladies."

Jaheira gave Abdel an angry look and snorted contemptuously, making no effort to hide her disbelief. "You didn't seem to mind Melissan being up there."

Imoen, already released from her cell by a spare key, chimed in on Jaheira's side of the argument. "And we can handle ourselves in a fight, Abdel. You know that."

Abdel sighed, staring down at the floor. "I know," he admitted, groping for some explanation and finding nothing.

"You're free, Miss," the locksmith announced, standing up and opening the door to Jaheira's cell.

"I will go tell Melissan," Sarevok announced from his position at the top of the stairs.

Abdel's half brother had not attempted to descend the steep steps down to the dungeon. Although the only blood on his armor was that of his victims, the dark warrior claimed to have been injured during the recent skirmish. Obviously, Sarevok did not share his half brother's remarkable powers of regeneration.

Imoen watched him limp slowly away, a strange look on her face.

"I get it!" she whispered excitedly as soon as the armored man had hobbled out of sight. "It was Sarevok, wasn't it?"

Uncertain exactly what she was getting at, but desperate for any possible explanation other than the truth, Abdel nodded in agreement.

"Sarevok?" Jaheira asked, then answered her own question. "Of course . . . you still do not trust him."

Abdel's wasn't the quickest mind in the Sword Coast—he liked to keep things simple and to the point—but he was sharp enough to seize the opportunity that had just dropped into his lap.

"That's right. I was afraid Sarevok would use the confusion of the battle and try to harm you two. I couldn't take that chance."

Jaheira wrapped her long arms around her lover's massive back, squeezing him with surprising strength. "Oh, Abdel, I am so sorry. I thought Melissan . . ." She didn't finish, just buried her face against his chest and hugged him even tighter.

Imoen gave him a friendly punch in the shoulder before heading up the stairs. "You're always looking out for us."

The locksmith followed the young woman out, but not before giving Abdel an admiring smile and a knowing wink.

* * * * * *

"I want some answers, Melissan," Abdel demanded, "and I want them now!"

"Of course," she replied. "What do you wish to know?"

Abdel hesitated, uncertain what to even ask now that the time had come. Luckily Jaheira stepped in to help him out.

"Everything," she said confidently, glaring at the taller woman with a look of obvious mistrust. "Why don't you just tell us everything?"

The picture Melissan painted was not a pretty one. The persecution of the Bhaalspawn was far more widespread than any of them had imagined, extending the entire stretch of the Sword Coast and well into the southern lands of Amn, Tethyr and even Calimshan. The Children of Bhaal were being driven from their homes or thrown into prisons by pursuing armies, and in many cases they were simply executed by vigilante mobs.

Many of the unfortunate victims were not even aware of their own tainted heritage. They were as ignorant of their own immortal blood as Imoen and Abdel had once been. Farmers, merchants, storekeeps—to all appearances they had been ordinary people leading ordinary lives. Until the purge had begun.

"But why now?" Imoen asked, searching for some explanation for the madness. "Why, after all these years, is there this sudden hatred and hunting of Bhaal's children?"

"The prophecies of Alaundo," Jaheira offered. "They predict the Children of Bhaal will bring a storm of death to Faerûn . . . maybe even the return of Bhaal himself."

"The half-elf speaks the truth," Melissan admitted, "but she knows only part of the story, like the masses who so ignorantly carry out this program of genocide."

Jaheira winced at the insult.

"There is a powerful group that has spearheaded the sudden rise in the hatred of the Bhaalspawn. Through a campaign of fear and misinformation they have spread this madness, until there is nowhere a Child of Bhaal may walk without being hunted. The ones responsible for the atrocities committed against you and your kind, Abdel, call themselves the Five."

"The Five?" Abdel replied. "I've never heard of them before."

Melissan laughed lightly, though her voice was serious. "I am not surprised, Abdel. Even I have known of their existence for only these past few years, and I have dedicated my life to finding just such a group among those who share your blood. For many years I have sought out you and your kin, Abdel, while always knowing that, as I did so, I was not the only one seeking out the Lord of Murder's offspring."

Imoen shook her head. "Hold on, I'm confused. Are you saying these Five are also Bhaalspawn?"

A curt nod of Melissan's head confirmed Imoen's assumption. "The Five are indeed offspring of the Lord of Murder, and I suspect they are among the most powerful of Bhaal's children who yet live. Although, truth be told, I know precious little about the members of the Five. I do not even truly know how many of them there are. Five is a cursed, unlucky number in the culture of Calimshan and Tethyr. It is possible the Five chose this name because of the fear it would inspire in the superstitious masses.

"What I do know," Melissan continued, "is that the Five wield great political influence within Faerûn, though they always do so behind the scenes. They keep themselves hidden in the shadows, working toward a single purpose. They manipulate others into following them and serving them through lies and deceit. Entire armies have now fallen under control of the Five, though most of the troops and generals do not even realize who they are really working for."

"And what do these Five hope to accomplish?" Abdel asked.

"The Five are a secret society fanatically devoted to

bringing their dead father back to life by slaughtering their siblings."

Abdel hesitated before asking his next question. Everyone else seemed to understand what Melissan was saying, and the big sellsword was reluctant to expose his own ignorance, but he needed to understand. More than anything he had been told before, this was something he had to comprehend in every detail.

"How will killing Bhaal's other children bring him back?"

"Within each offspring of the Lord of Murder there exists a divine essence," Melissan explained patiently, "a small piece of Bhaal's own essence. In some of his progeny there exists but a faint flicker. In others it burns like an unholy blaze.

"Whenever one of Bhaal's children perishes," Melissan continued, "that bit of his father's divine, yet tainted, spirit is released. The Five seek to collect the scattered essence of their father's soul bit by bit, drawing the tiny embers together until they have built a burning pyre from which Bhaal himself will be reborn."

Sarevok, who had been standing silently off to the side, added his own emotionless voice to the conversation. "You know what Melissan says is possible, Abdel. To a lesser degree, you have already experienced it. When you ended my first life in the caverns beneath Baldur's Gate you unconsciously absorbed my essence—and you moved a small step beyond a mere mortal existence. When we met again, you willingly sacrificed a small part of that divine spirit to bring me back to life and give me a second chance."

It all made sense. Abdel had not always had his remarkable healing powers. The more he thought about it, the more Abdel realized they had manifested themselves only after Sarevok's death by his hands. He couldn't help but wonder if he had unknowingly taken some of Imoen's immortal essence. When she had been transformed into the avatar of Bhaal by the wizard Jon

Irenicus, Abdel had fought and defeated Imoen's hideous demon form. In doing so he might have absorbed much of the young woman's tainted essence. That would explain why he had become so powerful, while Imoen still seemed . . . normal.

While Abdel was wrestling with the implications of what he had been told, Jaheira continued to question Melissan.

"You seem to know an awful lot about this," she said, her voice more than slightly accusatory in tone. "How are you involved, Melissan?"

"I, too, have heard the prophecies," the tall woman in black explained, "Like the Five, I know Alaundo's words and what they foretell. I have dedicated my life to preventing Bhaal's return to this world—as any sane person would.

"For many years I fought an invisible enemy. I suspected a group of Bhaal's offspring would unite their powers to bring about his rebirth, but I could find no evidence such a cult existed. Only in the past few years have I been able to confirm the rumors and my suspicions. And now I will do everything in my power to thwart them in their mad quest."

Jaheira said nothing. It appeared to Abdel she was mulling over Melissan's words, trying to find some fault or lie in them. Eventually the half-elf gave up and turned her attention to Sarevok.

"You don't seem surprised to hear all this."

How his half-elf lover was able to judge anything about the reactions of the stoic Sarevok was a mystery to Abdel, though his half brother's response did seem to indicate Jaheira's instincts had been correct.

"I have heard this tale before, druid. Several years ago, from Melissan herself."

"It is true," Melissan admitted, cutting off Jaheira before she could comment. "When I first learned the Five were more than just a dark shadow in my own imagination, I sought out allies to my cause—those who had a vested interest in stopping the Bhaalspawn before they became powerful enough to orchestrate this campaign of murder that has now swept the land."

"You went looking for other Bhaalspawn to fight against the Five," Imoen interjected.

"Precisely, my child. Who better to aid me against the Lord of Murder's children than one of Bhaal's own progeny? At the time, of course, you and Abdel were still unknown to me. The scribes of Candlekeep had done well in burying your history and wiping your very existence from all records.

"But I knew of another who was quickly gaining power and fame, whose name was whispered with fear and awe by the darkest, most vile criminals of the Sword Coast. A young man named Sarevok."

"Melissan approached me," Sarevok said, picking up the story in his deep monotone. "She told me of my heritage, and all its implications. She hoped to persuade me to work with her for my own self-preservation, if for no other reason. But I was already consumed by the dark taint within my own soul. Instead of joining her against the Five, I vowed I would be the one to bring Bhaal back to the mortal realm myself.

"And so I plotted a war between Nashkel and Baldur's Gate, and when I learned of Abdel's existence, I was determined to kill my half brother and take his essence to augment my own power."

There was a long pause once Sarevok finished. Melissan resumed speaking to fill the almost accusatory silence. "That is the danger of having allies who are born of evil itself. They will often betray you. I have had to relearn this lesson many, many times."

Jaheira spoke up in an angry voice. "So you knew all this!" she declared, pointing a finger at Sarevok. "You could have just told us this, without bringing us into this besieged town!"

"I could have told you this tale," Sarevok answered slowly, "but would any of you have believed me?"

The silence of Abdel and his companions was answer enough.

"Whatever the circumstances of your arrival, I am glad you are here now," Melissan said solemnly. "From what Sarevok has told me, you may be the only one who can save us from the army outside. They are led by a warrior named Yaga Shura."

"Yaga Shura?" For some reason, Abdel felt the name signified more than the leader of an army. The name had power within it.

"Yaga Shura is one of the Five," Melissan explained. "Like you, he is a child of Bhaal. Like you, he burns with the essence of your immortal father.

"Abdel," Melissan whispered, "you can save us from Yaga Shura."

* * * * *

Abdel honestly didn't know what he was going to do. He was drowning in the flood of information Melissan had poured forth. Her tale ran through his head in bits and pieces as he tried to bring some order to the chaos within his own mind.

"This is madness," Jaheira insisted. "This cannot be the way to free yourself from Bhaal's taint! More bloodshed is not the answer."

Dozens of Bhaalspawn had been slaughtered by the armies who secretly and unknowingly served the Five, and countless more had been killed in the riots and panic the Five had sown across Faerûn. The children of Bhaal had fled in terror, seeking a savior, seeking sanctuary. They found Melissan.

Or rather, Melissan found them, and she led them all to Saradush.

"We can avoid this battle, Abdel," Imoen said, adding her support to Jaheira's sentiment. "I found a way to sneak us into this town, big brother, and I can find a way to sneak us out."

Many of the Bhaalspawn who followed Melissan were lowly commoners, everyday folk swept up in a storm they could never have imagined. If these were the only ones who had sought sanctuary in Saradush, perhaps Melissan could have succeeded in hiding them. Perhaps she could have kept them safe.

But others had come: powerful, influential figures, political and military leaders—even a high-ranking general in the army of Calimshan. When Gromnir and a company of his loyal troops marched to Saradush and demanded sanctuary, the predatory eyes of the Five were drawn with them.

"If you do not stand and fight now, the Five will hunt you across the entire face of Faerûn, Abdel," Melissan cautioned him, her words much more calm and rational than the impassioned pleas of Jaheira and Imoen.

The town officials had ordered Gromnir and his troops to move on. They would not allow a foreign army to take up residence within their walls. Melissan had changed their minds, and they opened the gates and offered Gromnir the same sanctuary they had granted to all his less famous kin.

"They are drawn to your tainted blood, Abdel," Melissan continued. "Eventually they will find you—eventually you will have to fight. All you can do is choose the time and place of your battle. Why not choose here and now?"

Gromnir and his men had seized control of the town, ousting the civilian rulers under pretense of being better able to prepare Saradush for the hostile army that was only a few days march away, the army led by Yaga Shura, the army led by one of the Five.

The Saradush militia might have resisted the coup and the people could have taken up arms against the invading Calimshan general and his small band of troops. But the townsfolk were more afraid of the approaching soldiers of

Yaga Shura and their savage efforts to wipe out the children of Bhaal.

Yaga Shura's army was a juggernaut, crushing everything in its path, leaving a wake of ravaged cities and burning corpses. So the people of Saradush endured the presence of Gromnir and his men, because it gave them the best chance to survive the coming onslaught and the inevitable siege that was to come.

"I have yet to meet an opponent who can best me in single combat," Abdel said, attempting to reassure his half-elf lover. "You have seen it: My wounds regenerate instantly."

"If you undertake this task you must not be overconfident," Melissan warned him. "No one knows the limits of your healing powers, but the limits are there. You are not a god, Abdel."

"This is a battle you cannot win!" Jaheira shouted in frustration. "If Melissan speaks the truth, Yaga Shura is no ordinary Child of Bhaal, he is one of the Five. If we believe what Melissan has told us, how can you hope to defeat this group?"

His lover's argument held no substance. Not anymore. Not after what Melissan had told them about the huntress who had stalked them in the forest.

"Illasera was one of the Five," Abdel said calmly. "I already killed her."

"You nearly died in the process," Imoen reminded him, anxiously offering her support to Jaheira's case. "You're putting a lot of faith in your ability to heal, Abdel . . . but I seem to remember the wounds from those arrows didn't just vanish."

"I already killed one of the Five," Abdel maintained, "I can kill Yaga Shura, too."

"And then what, Abdel?" Jaheira asked, her voice on the edge of tears. "How many more of these Five are there? Even if you kill them all, what will that solve? Hasn't there been enough deaths? Enough bloodshed? Enough . . ." The half-elf's pleas degenerated into choking sobs.

Melissan's own voice was soft and soothing as she filled the void left by Jaheira's inability to continue. "The druid speaks the truth, Abdel. I cannot say how many the Five number, or who or where they may be. I only know of Illasera and Yaga Shura because they chose to reveal themselves. The time had come for them to act in the open. The others still remain shrouded in the shadows, their machinations hidden."

Abdel was confident he could win this battle. Since the fight on the battlements, he was confident he could control the Bhaal fire within him. Now that he was aware the Ravager lived within him, he was able to fight against it. He could keep the beast caged. Or so he believed.

When Abdel spoke, his voice was quiet and sure. Without even realizing it, he had adopted Melissan's own tone. "Then whenever one of the Five dares to come out from the darkness, I will kill them as well."

He placed a comforting hand on the shoulder of Jaheira, but she flinched away from his touch and continued to sob quietly into her hands.

Imoen forced a laugh, trying to ease the tension. "This is all pointless anyway," she scoffed. "This so-called plan you've concocted will never work. What makes you think this Yaga Shura will even accept this challenge? He has an army at his beck and call—why would he agree to meet Abdel in single combat?"

"This is no laughing matter," Melissan admonished. "Yaga Shura will accept. He will want to prove himself against Abdel, prove himself worthy of being one of the Five. Yaga Shura is the Lord of Murder's son, the son of a god. He thinks he is invincible. He thinks he is a god himself."

Imoen shook her head in denial. "Impossible. Yaga Shura cannot be that stupid. I'm one of Bhaal's children, and I would never accept this type of challenge just to prove myself."

Abdel looked his half sister directly in the eye. "I would."

Chapter Ten

The gates to Saradush were opened, and Abdel stepped out alone to meet his foe. The army of Yaga Shura had retreated several hundred yards from the walls of Saradush in preparation for the coming duel, leaving a large patch of empty, well-trampled ground.

Abdel walked to the center of the vast expanse and waited. Inside the fortress behind him Calimshan soldiers and Saradush militia stood side by side, armed and ready. If Abdel managed to kill Yaga Shura the defenders of the town would charge forth, looking to catch their opponents by surprise. After witnessing the loss of their "invincible" leader, the troops of Yaga Shura would be disorganized and demoralized. A sustained charge could break their spirit, and the town would be saved.

At least, that was Melissan's plan. If Abdel survived the duel. If Abdel fell, the defenders would go back to their posts, and the siege would continue until starvation and disease weakened Saradush enough for the army outside to successfully breach the walls and raze the town.

Somewhere in the distance a trumpet sounded, a fanfare to announce the coming of Yaga Shura.

Abdel braced himself for what he knew was coming.

"Yaga Shura is no ordinary Bhaalspawn," Melissan had warned Abdel while he had been selecting his weapon in preparation for battle. "His mother was a giant from the tribes who live among the volcanoes of the Marching Mountains."

"That's disgusting!" Imoen had gasped.

"Don't be naive, child!" Jaheira had snapped, taking her anger at Abdel out on the young woman. "Bhaal was no mortal man. He could assume any form he desired. A giant is as close to a god as a human or an elf."

Imoen had shaken her head, stubbornly declaring, "It's an abomination."

"Bhaal's taint is an abomination in any form," Melissan had replied, effectively ending the conversation.

The soldiers parted, clearing a path for their champion. The sight of Yaga Shura's approach snapped Abdel's mind away from his recollections and to the present.

The shirtless giant towered over his men by several feet as he made his way through the crowd. His broad shoulders, muscular chest, and massive arms were clearly visible above their helms and even the points of the spears they raised in salute. His skin was the color of ash and soot, his beard the same flaming red hue as the long hair that hung down in a single braid past his shoulders. The double-edged head of the enormous axe strapped to Yaga Shura's back seemed to devour any light that struck its obsidian surface.

Abdel tightened his grip on the broadsword he had chosen to bring into battle and shifted his weight rapidly from one foot to the other to try and work out any lingering stiffness before the duel began. He wore no armor—he wanted to use his quickness and agility against his much larger opponent. Abdel had surprised men half his size with his inhuman speed. He was certain he could do the same to a foe the size of a lumbering giant.

Yaga Shura's long, heavy strides quickly brought him free of the crowd and closed the distance between the two combatants. The giant stopped less than twenty feet away and slowly reached back to draw his own weapon from its harness, the muscles of his bare torso flexing as he did so. Abdel was now close enough to see the head of the weapon was not solid black, as he had first imagined. The weapon's edges were inscribed with blood red glyphs and symbols.

The implications of those markings were not lost on Abdel. Instinctively, he knew these sigils were the same as those that had marked the arrows of Illasera, the archer in the clearing. Like Illasera's arrows, Abdel knew any wounds he received from Yaga Shura's axe would not disappear.

He spread his feet wide, lowering his stance. The knowledge that his enemy could harm him, perhaps even kill him, didn't scare Abdel. It just changed his battle plan to a more defensive strategy.

The two men slowly circled each other, Abdel in the unfamiliar position of looking up into the eyes of his opponent. The sellsword hesitated, uncertain if a signal would be given to begin. An impatient roar of anticipation went up from the assembled host, and Yaga Shura lunged forward.

As Abdel had hoped, Yaga Shura's own bulk worked against him, slowing the giant down. He bull-rushed Abdel, his great axe held high above his head. Abdel waited until the last second then ducked to the side and rolled clear of the clumsy chop of his opponent. As he did so, he slashed his own blade across the rippling muscles of Yaga Shura's unprotected stomach, slicing him open.

Abdel spun around to deliver the coup de grace to his dying opponent's exposed back, only to find the giant had also spun around to face him. Already the gaping gash Abdel had inflicted had become nothing but a faint scar of blazing white against Yaga Shura's soot-colored skin. A second later that too was gone, leaving no evidence of Abdel's attack.

The shocking realization that Yaga Shura shared— maybe even surpassed—his own remarkable invulnerability to injury momentarily confused Abdel. He had expected to finish off a dying opponent writhing on the ground. He wasn't prepared to pierce the defenses of a ready adversary.

The giant was already swinging at him again. Abdel easily redirected the path of the giant's awkward attack and carved out the eye of his foe in a series of fluid sword strokes learned through years of practice and training. Yaga Shura screamed in pain and stumbled back, bringing one massive hand up to clutch at the blinded, mangled orb in his head.

As one, his troops cried out in surprise and dismay. But when Yaga Shura dropped his hand, now covered in blood and ocular fluid, Abdel was only mildly surprised to see the eye had been fully restored. In the pit of his stomach, Abdel felt a heavy, sinking feeling. He realized this must be the same hopelessness many of his past enemies had felt when they understood the ineffectiveness of their weapons against Abdel himself.

The giant's amused laugh was drowned out by the cheers of his followers, and he engaged Abdel once more.

The battle quickly fell into the pattern established in the first two exchanges. Yaga Shura attacked without technique or style, as he knew only brute force and sheer strength. Abdel, with the expertise of a trained swordsman, was easily able to evade or parry every blow and deliver a savage counterstrike each time. Abdel didn't know the scope of his own regenerative abilities, but he was determined to push Yaga Shura's healing powers to the absolute limits.

He carved the giant's throat, he impaled vital organs on the point of his sword, he inflicted dozens of wounds, each one fatal. Again and again he mutilated the unskilled foe opposing him, but the injuries he inflicted were transitory, the damage temporary and ultimately ineffectual.

The battle had raged for only ten minutes, a brief time for the cheering spectators but an eternity for the combatants. Abdel's breath came in gasps, his massive chest heaving like a bellows to try and bring fuel in to his oxygen-starved limbs. The muscles in his legs screamed each time he crouched to duck under one of Yaga Shura's swings, and they threatened to cramp up every time he leaped clear of a descending chop. His shoulders burned with fatigue, his hands and fingers were numb from the ceaseless vibrations as Abdel parried blow after blow from the mighty giant's great axe.

Only then, as his body threatened to collapse in a trembling exhausted heap, did it dawn on Abdel. Yaga Shura had never learned technique or style because the giant had never needed them. Abdel could strike his enemy virtually at will, but no matter how over-matched Yaga Shura was in skill and ability the giant's physical invulnerability gave him an insurmountable advantage.

With each swing of his axe, Yaga Shura's advantage grew. Each time Abdel spun, or ducked, or dodged he felt the deadly blade miss by a smaller fraction. The big man was wearing down; his quickness and mobility ebbed as his stamina faded. Still the giant pressed him, relentless and irresistible as a force of nature.

Abdel tried to summon the rage of his immortal father. He reached down into the depths of his soul and stoked the flames of Bhaal's fury to give him strength, but there was nothing there. The knowledge that all the bloodshed and violence he was inflicting was meaningless against this foe had cooled the Lord of Murder's savage heat.

Abdel Adrian, drained and weapon-weary, knew he was going to die.

His feet betrayed him first, now far too heavy to perform the rapid backpedaling Abdel demanded in his latest effort to avoid the giant's latest brutally simple assault. The axe whistled through the air, its keen edge slicing a long, superficial wound across Abdel's chest as the big man fell backward, tripping over his own heel.

The sword fell from Abdel's grasp as he threw his hands back to cushion his fall. Even so, he struck the ground hard enough to momentarily see stars. When his vision cleared he saw Yaga Shura straddling him, his rune covered axe already arcing down to end Abdel's life.

Abdel wanted to surrender. His exhausted body begged to lie back and welcome the grisly end, but his warrior's instincts took over, and Abdel kicked out with his heavy boot. His heel struck the axe's handle half way down its ten-foot length, cracking the thick wood completely through. The lower half of the rune-inscribed shaft burst apart, disintegrating into several chunks of splintered wood, each over a foot long.

Yaga Shura toppled forward, his balance thrown off by the force of the unexpected kick and the suddenly unbalanced weapon he wielded. The bits and pieces of the lower end of his axe's shaft had fallen to the ground, but his right hand still clutched the top half of his broken weapon. The giant drew the blade back to strike at Abdel even as he fell on top of him. With his free hand, Yaga Shura reached out to brace his fall.

Abdel seized the wrist of Yaga Shura's empty, extending hand and pulled, bringing his other foot up and bracing it against the muscular chest of his foe. Abdel might have been the only man alive who had the strength to redirect the momentum of a falling giant's weight, but then, Abdel was truly more than a man. To the amazement of the onlookers and Yaga Shura alike, the giant suddenly found himself hurtling through the air, his entire body flipping heels over head as he crashed on his back.

Before his foe even hit the ground Abdel had scrambled to his own feet, scooping up the largest chunk of the axe's broken shaft as he did so. Before his fallen opponent could recover from the throw, Abdel was on him.

Along with his swordsmanship, Abdel had spent many years training himself in grappling and other unarmed forms of combat, and he knew how to gain an advantage on a prone opponent. The big man leaped onto Yaga Shura's enormous chest, pinning the giant's arms with his knees. He felt like a child wrestling with a grownup—the same way an ordinary man must have felt when wrestling with Abdel. Yaga Shura would be able to free himself quite easily simply by rolling to the side, twisting his shoulder and using his bulk to over-balance Abdel. The sellsword just hoped the giant wouldn't know how.

Yaga Shura's torso heaved and bucked as he tried to fling Abdel off through sheer strength and brute force, but Abdel could not be dislodged so easily. He simply shifted his weight in rhythm with the larger man's thrashing, maintaining his mounted position straddling the giant's chest. The giant's free hand clutched at Abdel, the other flailed with the axe in a desperate attempt to bring the weapon to bear. With Abdel's knees still firmly pinning the mighty arms of the giant to the ground, all of Yaga Shura's efforts were ineffective.

Abdel raised the broken, rune covered piece of wood with both hands above his head, and plunged the jagged, splintered point into the giant's exposed throat—impaling Yaga Shura with a piece from the shaft of his own enchanted weapon.

The writhing death throes of the doomed Bhaalspawn finally hurled Abdel from his perch, sending him rolling across the ground. The big sellsword tried to leap to his feet, but his muscles refused to respond. He had spent every last ounce of energy burying the shaft in Yaga Shura's neck.

Somehow, Abdel managed to raise his head in time to see Yaga Shura struggle to his feet, clutching at the length of wood protruding from his neck. The giant's chest was coated in a bubbling magma, the fiery lifeblood pumping from the puncture wound in his neck. He tried to yank the massive splinter from his throat, but the haft was slick with flowing fluid and the giant's hands slipped off.

The monstrous Bhaalspawn fell to his knees and grasped the shaft again. This time he managed to pull it free but only succeeded in unleashing a veritable flood as the steaming blood burst forth like a geyser from the wound with every fading beat of his massive heart.

From behind him Abdel heard the sound of a trumpet and a great crash as the gates of Saradush flew open and the army attacked. Still too weary to stand, he turned his head to see Gromnir, Melissan, and Sarevok leading the charge as the defenders suddenly took the offensive.

The gurgling gasps of his dying foe were swallowed by the deafening din as Abdel's allies surged past him to engage the panic-stricken forces of Yaga Shura. Then the world began to dissolve, melting away as it had done in the clearing when Abdel had slain Illasera.

The last thing he saw before the world vanished entirely was an enormous winged beast descending on the city of Saradush, ruby scales blinding and bright in the reflected glow of the fire belching forth from its reptilian jaws.

* * * * *

He was back in the void. Although, as he looked around, Abdel realized the name no longer fit. There was clearly ground beneath his feet now. An empty gray sky arched overhead. The mists were gone, revealing a barren, lifeless plain extending to the limits of his vision in every direction.

The void had become a sterile, dead world with nothing to break the monotony of the landscape except the free-floating doors that stood before him. Abdel noted there were only four now.

"They represent your possible destinies, Abdel Adrian," an unseen speaker answered in response to his

unasked question. "And as you continue down your path
your possible futures become fewer."

Abdel instantly recognized the infinite yet singular
voice of the being from his dream in the clearing.

"Show yourself!" he demanded.

Suddenly the figure stood before him, as physically
magnificent as before, the blinding light of perfection still
radiating out from its being. But for some reason, Abdel
now found the creature less impressive, less imposing,
less wondrous, less . . . well, just less.

"I am not less, Abdel Adrian. You have simply become
more. Much more. Your progress has been amazing, even
to one such as myself."

Abdel spat out his next question quickly, unnerved by
the being's habit of answering the thoughts in his head.
"Why have you brought me here?"

"As before, I am not responsible for your presence here,
Abdel. You are."

He remembered his last glimpse of the material world,
the terrifying vision of the dragon descending on Saradush.
"I have to get back! You have to send me back!"

"You know the way back, Abdel. You control your leaving
just as you controlled your arrival."

The doors. Abdel took a step toward them, then hesitated. Slowly he turned back to face the immortal creature,
still not even certain what he intended to say.

"I cannot do this alone, Abdel," the being explained. "I
can only answer the questions you ask."

"I did as you told me. I found those who share my
tainted blood. And the only thing I learned was that I have
to keep killing. I've known that lesson my whole life!"

The creature made no response but stood perfectly
still, waiting for Abdel to continue.

"There has to be more to my destiny than just
slaughtering my Bhaalspawn kin! But you refuse to
help me. Why? You know something. Why can't you just
tell me?"

"There are forces greater than you can yet comprehend at work. Many of them are working through you. They can save you or destroy you. I must be cautious, for your own sake as well as the sake of the future.

"If you are not yet ready to ask the question, Abdel Adrian, you are not yet ready to truly understand the answer."

Abdel laughed, uncertain if he meant the sound to be wistful or bitter. "You sound like Gorion."

"Your adopted father was a wise man."

The big sellsword glanced briefly at the doors, then turned his attention back to his strange companion. As desperate as he was to get back to the real world, he could not simply throw away a chance to learn something about what was going on. He opened his mouth to speak, and a million questions tried to come out at once. The result was only choking silence. He took a deep breath and tried again.

"The Five . . . do they really exist as Melissan claims? Are they truly attempting to resurrect Bhaal?"

"What Melissan has told you is the truth," the being admitted, then hastily added, "but there is much about the Five she has not revealed."

Abdel was momentarily caught off guard by the answer. The rushed qualification seemed vitally important, yet at the same time the being seemed almost ashamed, as if it had violated some extra-planar law or an obscure immortal code of honor by sharing too much.

"You aren't in charge here, are you?" Abdel asked, slowly beginning to understand.

The being shook its head slowly. "I am but a servant of divine will, Abdel. I cannot take an active part in your destiny. Events must unfold as they will."

"And I suppose you won't tell me my destiny," Abdel said wearily.

"Even the powers I serve cannot say."

Abdel spat in disgust. The parched ground devoured the moisture.

"You are of no more help to me than my mortal advisors," he sneered. He turned toward the doors and marched through the nearest one without looking back.

Chapter Eleven

The vast expanse of the lifeless Abyss vanished, replaced by the unmistakable sights and sounds of battle. Armored men hacked and chopped at each other. Arrows and sling stones flew through the air indiscriminately striking their targets. Foot soldiers used pikes and pole-arms to unseat their mounted rivals or were trampled beneath the churning hooves of enemy steeds. The horses reared and neighed, froth spraying from their snapping teeth, their flanks covered in sweat and blood.

The dead and dying lay underfoot, crushed, cut, stabbed, and gored. The clash of steel on steel, the panicked screams of horses and men, and the groans of the mangled, muti-lated soldiers writhing on the turf mingled in a single dull roar—the song of battle.

Abdel was surrounded by the carnage on all sides. He had materialized in the exact spot he had stood when Yaga Shura had breathed his last. The giant's corpse lay only a few feet away, now pounded into a barely recogniz-able pulpy mountain of flesh by the boots and hooves of the battling armies. The big sellsword had no idea how long he had been gone, but from the condition of Yaga Shura's corpse he knew it was long enough for the tide of battle to have swept over this one spot several times.

From his vantage point amidst the chaos Abdel couldn't gauge the ebb and flow of war. He had no idea which side was winning, and he didn't care. It was all moot anyway. The dragon that he had glimpsed before being snatched away into the Abyss would destroy Saradush—it would destroy both armies, and it would destroy Jaheira and Imoen if Abdel couldn't save them.

First he had to find them.

He glanced down at what remained of Yaga Shura's axe, then turned his attention elsewhere. He had no need of the enchanted weapon to hack his way through the wall of mortal soldiers between him and the women he loved, and Abdel was a swordsman, not a woodcutter. Fortunately, swords were in great supply at this point in the battle.

He snatched a heavy, broad blade from the hand of one of the fallen, ignoring the feeble protests from the clutching corpse too stupid to know it was already dead.

Abdel struck without thought, savagely hacking down anyone in range in his mad attempt to simply thin the throng surrounding him. He ignored the counterattacks directed at his own unarmored body. His mind blocked out the pain, and his immortal spirit absorbed the countless blows and healed his wounds. The small corner of Abdel's mind not obsessed with mowing down the hapless men between himself and his missing companions noted that his healing powers were stronger than ever—many of the wounds closed so fast Abdel didn't even to start to bleed.

Nevertheless, he was soon covered in sticky crimson fluid and warm gore from head to toe. The blood of his opponents matted his hair and soaked into his clothes. The cloying scent clung to his nostrils, and he could taste the coppery tang on his tongue. Rubbing the back of his blood-soaked hand across his eyes couldn't clear the crimson veil from his vision.

And through it all, the essence of Bhaal within Abdel stayed calm. He did not revel in the massacre of friend and foe alike, this was not death to be savored. This was slaughter with a single cold purpose: Find Jaheira and Imoen before the dragon turned its attention to the battlefield.

The impossibility of Abdel's task never entered his mind. He ignored the facts—thousands of combatants milling about over an area expansive in size—and allowed himself to believe he would somehow stumble across his lover and his sister.

Through the confusion of bodies Abdel occasionally saw distant visions of death and destruction raining down on the city of Saradush. A single flick of a great scaled tail toppled the spires of a noble's mansion. A blast of deadly fire from the sky incinerated entire city blocks. A gigantic reptilian beast descended on leatherlike wings to rend and devour a dozen unfortunate victims fleeing through the streets. The glimpses of the great wyrm ravaging Saradush merely spurred Abdel ever onward in his hopeless search.

Then he heard his name, screamed with primal, animal rage over the cacophony of the conflict.

"Abdel!"

He turned toward the desperate, crazed cry and saw a single disheveled figure on horseback bearing down on him. The man looked more beast than human, hunched over the saddle of his wild-eyed mount, his tangled, greasy mane streaming out behind him as he rode, a single hairy arm brandishing a heavy spear high above his head.

Abdel, despite his best efforts, had been unable to locate either Jaheira or Imoen. But somehow Gromnir, the mad general of the Calimshan forces, had managed to find him.

"Abdel!" Gromnir bellowed, "We meet again! Good fun. Hah!"

The horse bore down on him, but Abdel held his ground. At the last second he stepped forward, ducking under Gromnir's thrusting spear and wrapping his muscular arm around the steed's thick neck. Abdel braced himself, but was still thrown backward by the impact of the charging beast and sent hurtling through the air. The pop of Abdel's shoulder dislocating was lost beneath the thunderous crack of a dozen bones in the horse's neck snapping like dry kindling.

By the time Abdel was back on his feet, his shoulder had already slipped back into place, with no ill effects. Gromnir was not so fortunate. He might have been a Child of Bhaal but like Imoen and most of the others he lacked the superhuman regenerative powers of Abdel or Yaga Shura.

The general was crawling weakly out from beneath the convulsing body of his horse, pulling himself forward with only his hands. Abdel could see Gromnir's pelvis had been smashed in the fall. Already a dark stain was seeping up over the belt and from beneath the chainmail leggings that covered Gromnir's body below the waist.

"Abdel," the crippled, twisted man croaked. "Abdel betrayed Gromnir. Ha-ha! Gromnir fell for Abdel's trap."

He could have turned his back on the helpless man and simply resumed his search to find Jaheira and Imoen. But something within Abdel couldn't endure the unfounded allegations the Calimshite general had leveled at him.

"I am no traitor, Gromnir," he said in an even voice.

"Hah! Good fun, Abdel. Joking while Gromnir dies! Ha-ha!"

Abdel shook his head. "You're crazy."

"Crazy? Gromnir and his men rode into an ambush! Hah! A thousand cavalry troops hidden behind the hills, reinforcements to smash Gromnir's army!" The dying man's words frothed up on his lips as he spit them out. The spray was tinged pink from the blood welling up from his gut wounds.

"They knew Gromnir was coming out from behind his walls! Ha ha! And the dragon . . . it knew, too. Watching and waiting for Gromnir to take the bait! Abdel's plan worked! Ha! Saradush was left defenseless!"

"It wasn't my plan," Abdel protested, but his arguments went unheard as a spasm of choking coughs wracked Gromnir's broken body.

"The druid and the girl," Gromnir continued, his voice growing softer with every word, "they knew. They fled back to the city, they did not walk into the trap. Ha!"

Another series of coughs shook Gromnir and then his body lay still. Abdel didn't stay there to witness his death. The big sellsword was already charging through the mass of combatants again, carving his way directly toward the city—or what was still standing beneath the dragon's wrath.

As he traversed the battlefield, Abdel cursed his own stupidity. Of course Jaheira and Imoen were in the city! Gromnir had thought they fled the battle, but the general's mind was limited by his own instincts for self-preservation. Abdel knew the real explanation.

He could clearly imagine the scene. He saw the women he loved herding the civilians to safety, trying to help them find some shelter, some refuge from the terrible monster ravaging their town. Jaheira and Imoen were, as usual, risking their own lives to save the innocent and helpless.

Now that he had a goal, Abdel made quick progress. He had reached the still-open gates of Saradush and was rushing down the rubble-filled streets, ignoring the flame-engulfed buildings on either side of him. The city was choked with a thick veil of smoke, forcing Abdel to hunch his seven-foot frame nearly in half to stay beneath the acrid clouds.

He knew Jaheira and Imoen would be where the destruction was the greatest—all he had to do was find the dragon, and he would find his friends.

Finding the dragon was easy. He just ran toward the screams. He was still several blocks away when he saw the enormous beast rampaging through the street, reducing buildings to dust and slaughtering every living thing that came within reach of its claws, jaws, or tail. As with all dragons, this specimen was both awe-inspiring and terrifying. As he approached, Abdel realized this dragon was but a youth, barely even full grown. Its scales were smooth and unmarked by the scars of great battles yet to come. Its hide was still a bright, shiny red. As it aged, its coloration would darken and deepen. If the creature was as inexperienced in tactics and combat as its immaturity would suggest, Abdel might have a hope of defeating it.

At the far end of the block Abdel caught a glimpse of half a dozen figures huddling in the ground level of a burned-out hull of a building whose upper reaches had already been destroyed by dragon fire. Even at this distance, Abdel recognized the silhouetted outline of Jaheira through the haze and the smaller form of Imoen beside her. Imoen's arms moved in the intricate patterns Abdel had seen mages and wizards use when performing an enchantment, and through the darkness Abdel could clearly see a parchment scroll with glowing symbols at her feet. A second later the entire group vanished from sight.

Momentarily stunned, it took Abdel a second to realize they were still there, their presence cloaked by a spell of invisibility. However, he didn't have time to wonder at Imoen's previously unrevealed magical talents as the dragon's attention was now even more focused on the small structure in which the group had sought shelter.

Slowly, as if savoring the coming slaughter, the dragon began to march along the street toward the invisible Imoen and those she would protect. A deep mocking laugh rolled out from the monster's throat, rising above the deafening crackle of flames and the screams of the other townsfolk fleeing in terror at its approach.

Abdel never hesitated in his charge, never even slowed his stride—though part of his mind was screaming at him to turn and run. The beast could rip him apart with one swipe of its massive talons or reduce him to a pile of ash and charcoal with a blast of fire so hot it would cause great chunks of the stone walls fortifying the city to melt.

Abdel knew his own instantaneous healing couldn't save him from death in the face of such traumatic, grievous njury, though it might have appeared that way to the soldiers ineffectually hacking at him back on the field of battle. Abdel knew he wasn't immortal.

It was more than just the knowledge of his own mortality that made a section of Abdel's mind cower in terror. Despite its obvious youth, the great red wyrm dwarfed the humans and halflings scurrying before it. It spread its enormous wings to span the breadth of the entire street, casually batting the tiny figures who stumbled too close to the leathery appendages, leaving the victims in crumpled, unconscious heaps.

Though large enough to carry off a pair of owlbears in its claws, the awesome spectacle of the dragon's presence was the result of more than just sheer size. Its young scales gleamed with an inner brilliance, each as beautiful and bright as a priceless ruby. Yet they were woven together so tightly they seemed to form an impenetrable coat of armor over the beast's back. From the tips of its razor-sharp teeth to the ends of its serpentine tail thirty feet away, the creature exuded glorious power. There was a majesty about dragons, even young ones, that transcended even their own incomprehensible physical presence: a physical aura of grandeur, magnificence, and pure malevolence that made Abdel want to throw himself to the ground and tremble in fear. Dragonfear, the sages called it.

Ignoring the corner of his consciousness that begged him to hurl his puny sword to the street and flee in terror, Abdel moved within striking distance. Too lucky or too insignificant to have even been noticed by his gargantuan foe, Abdel rushed in unseen and slashed at the dragon's hind leg just above the heel. Most weapons would merely bounce harmlessly off the beast's scales, but Abdel's sword was propelled by a strength unequalled by any other mortal.

A geyser of steaming blood erupted from the wound, though Abdel's weapon was shattered by the impact. The dragon howled in pain, kicking out with its wounded leg and twisting its head around on its long, sinuous neck to snap at the unseen enemy.

Abdel leaped back, avoiding both the kicking leg and the lethal jaws even as he ducked beneath the wing that swept over his head. He didn't avoid the heavy tail whipping around to slam into him from behind. It hurled Abdel through the air into one of the few stone walls still standing on the street. The wall disintegrated when Abdel smashed face first into it, breaking his ribs, cracking the vertebrae in his neck, shattering every bone in his face, and rupturing several internal organs.

It took Abdel nearly ten seconds to recover enough from the horrendous injuries to stand on his feet again. Luckily, the inexperienced dragon hadn't bothered to finish him off. Assuming the hero had been pulverized by its lashing tail, the creature returned its attention to the building where Imoen, Jaheira, and the others had sought shelter before being cloaked with the spell of invisibility.

Raising up onto its hind legs the beast let loose with a roar that shook the ground. The reverberating echo of the battle cry drowned out all other sound. Abdel couldn't even hear his own scream as the beast slammed its entire body down on the building's roof, collapsing the entire structure in a roiling cloud of dust that quickly mingled with the heavy smoke hanging like a curtain in the air.

Nothing inside the mashed building larger than a roach could have survived the destruction.

Abdel howled to the blackened sky in grief over his lover's certain death.

"Jaheira!"

Abdel's eyes welled up as he ran his hand across the mix of blood and dirt on his face. He took in a great deep breath to give voice to his rage and sorrow once again when he abruptly stopped. Abdel noticed footsteps in the dirt and soot that covered the city streets. Footsteps leading away from the building, churning up tiny puffs of dust as they scampered away. From the number of footprints left behind

nd the amount of broiling dust in their wake, Abdel
guessed there were maybe half a dozen people on the run.
He couldn't see them. Whatever spell had caused Imoen,
Jaheira and the others to vanish from sight when Abdel had
first noticed them huddled inside the threshold of the now-
destroyed doorway was still keeping them hidden from
view. Imoen and Jaheira were alive. Abdel released his
breath, and his anguished cries became relieved laughter.

As the dragon turned back toward the big sellsword,
Abdel's laughing stopped. The wyrm tilted its head back
slightly and took a deep breath. As the beast inhaled, its
enormous chest expanded ever farther, and Abdel realized
it was gathering itself to unleash a blast of fire that would
incinerate him where he stood.

The big man spun on his heel and ran. Behind him,
Abdel heard a deep rumble and a sizzling hiss. He dived
for the cover of an open doorway, hurtling himself through
the air even as the wall of flames swept down the street,
engulfing everything in its path.

Had the full brunt of the dragon's attack struck Abdel,
he would have died instantly, his blood evaporating, his
skin melting, and his bones turning to charred ash. But
the youthful beast's own impatience saved Abdel. The
dragon had tipped its hand too soon, allowing his foe's
hasty retreat to bring him to the farthest edge of the
wyrm's fiery breath. Abdel made a desperate leap for
cover, and instead of instant, merciful annihilation he felt
an unbearable burning pain reserved solely for the living.

His clothes and hair ignited, the skin on his back,
neck and shoulders blistered instantly in the intense
heat. He clenched his eyes against the sizzling cocoon of
fire momentarily enveloping him. His nasal passages,
throat and lungs were scorched as he breathed in sul-
furous air and stinging smoke.

The agony of being burned alive momentarily sent his
body into shock causing Abdel to black out. The blaze swept
over his unconscious form. Recovering consciousness, he

found himself in the now-blackened doorway, the last flickers of the dragon's breath still burning around him. He tried to leap to his feet, only to find his limbs would not obey. He lay still for several seconds, waiting for his otherworldly regenerative abilities to kick in, but when he tried to stand he found his injuries hadn't healed.

Fire. Many times Abdel had felt the internal blaze of Bhaal's fury and bloodlust, but those were flames of the spirit and the soul. In the real world, Abdel had never been seriously burned in his life—not before he had become an avatar of a dead god, and not after. He had just assumed he could recover from horrible burns as easily as he recovered from slashes, cuts, and other physical injuries. Now, as he lay helpless beneath a sticky blanket of his own melted clothes and the oozing wounds from his cracked, blistered back Abdel understood this was not the case.

Mustering all his strength, the crippled warrior managed to crawl around to peek out from the doorway that had saved his life. He had to see why the dragon hadn't finished him yet. He had to see if Jaheira and Imoen had escaped. With great effort he lifted up his head, and the answers to both his questions were revealed.

The dragon was under attack. Two gigantic tigers threw themselves on the creature's back, ripping and tearing at its scaled hide. Leaping clear as the dragon lashed out at them with its wings and tail, the two great cats roared and pounced again as soon as another opening presented itself. From the blue nimbus surrounding their powerful feline forms, Abdel knew the beasts had been summoned by Jaheira. The druid must have called on Mielikki for aid, and in answer the forest god had sent the striped cats to protect her servant. Their coordinated assault confused the young dragon, harrying it incessantly and preventing the wyrm from concentrating its attacks effectively on either foe.

Jaheira herself stood just beyond the edge of the melee. The incantation she had used to call the striped efenders to her side had destroyed the invisibility that ad previously kept her hidden from view. She was minstering to a third tiger that lay broken and bleeding in he middle of the street. Though pain clouded his vision, Abdel could see the half-elf was weeping at the dying iger's suffering.

The dragon flailed around recklessly with its claws and napping jaws, desperately trying to unseat its two surviving foes from their perch atop its back. But the tigers vere quick and cunning, and they continued to savage the nonster's hide—though their razor claws were unable to pierce the dragon's scales.

Abdel tried again to stand and failed. He tried to drag himself forward, willing his crippled form to crawl to Jaheira's aid. The exertion forced him to draw ragged, rasping breaths with his seared and damaged lungs. The crid smoke still lingering in the air crawled down his throat, wracking his charred body with choking coughs. In he end his muscles betrayed him. The avatar of Bhaal vas as weak and helpless as a newborn child. Barely able o even raise his head, it took all his strength just to vatch the battle and pray Jaheira survived.

From far away, Abdel heard a fierce war cry he recognized from the battle atop the Saradush battlements. Melissan was coming to join them. The dragon heard her too and turned to unleash another fiery blast against this new enemy. Melissan seemed oblivious to he horrible fate that was about to engulf her and rushed headlong through the ruined city street to challenge the wyrm, the head of her mace whistling through he air in deadly circles.

The flames swallowed her, and Abdel's own wounds cried out in sympathetic protest. When the wall of fire had passed, Melissan stood unharmed, though the force of the dragon's breath had stopped her charge.

Puzzled by Melissan's unexpected survival, the young dragon allowed its attention to be distracted long enough

for Jaheira to leap into the fray. The staff she normall
carried in her hands was gone, replaced by a magicall
conjured scimitar of cold blue fire. She brought th
enchanted blade down on the unsuspecting dragon's tai
slicing deep into the wyrm's flesh. Cold steam burst fron
the wound, and the dragon bellowed in shock and anger

Still ignoring the tigers futilely clinging to its grea
back, the beast spun toward Jaheira. In her haste to duc
clear of the dragon's snapping jaws, the druid's foo
snagged on a jagged piece of debris from one of the street
many demolished buildings and the half-elf fell to th
ground. She tried to roll clear, but the dragon was to
quick, pinning her to the ground with a taloned foot.

In response to Jaheira's tormented shrieks, Abdel trie
again to stand. Through sheer force of will he managed t
get to his feet, but when he took a step toward his scream
ing lover he collapsed back to the ground, too weak t
even cry out in grief or frustration.

Somehow, he managed to lift his head again. His visio
had become a narrow tunnel of light, and darkness wa
closing in from all sides. Abdel knew he was on the verg
of blacking out again. The world was fading. He could se
Jaheira's body writhing beneath the dragon's claw, but h
could no longer hear her cries.

Melissan stepped into his rapidly shrinking field o
vision, her mace now jammed inside her belt. Her empt
hands were engulfed in a white ball of energy that sh
hurled at the dragon. The spell struck between the mon
ster's winged shoulders, and it screamed. Few beings ha
ever heard a dragon's scream, but any who survived th
siege of Saradush would remember the awful sound i
their nightmares forever.

The few buildings on the street still standing wer
toppled by the concussive force of the wyrm's keenin
cry. The tigers still atop the creature's back fell to th
ground twitching, stunned by the wave of sound. Para
lyzed by his injuries, Abdel could not bring his hands u

to shield his ears against the horrific noise. His eardrums burst, exploding in a burst of blood that trickled from his ears down the sides of his cheeks.

Yet Melissan seemed unaffected. Already, she had gathered another ball of the glowing energy and hurled it at the dragon. The beast screamed again. Deafened by the first cry, Abdel could not hear this one. Even so he felt the vibrations rippling through the ground.

Abdel struggled to hold back the curtain of darkness, refusing to succumb to the blackness while the battle still raged less than thirty feet away. Unwilling to endure another assault from Melissan, the beast flapped its wings and rose from the ruined streets of Saradush, still clutching the feebly struggling body of Jaheira in its claws. The last image Abdel saw before unconsciousness took him was his lover being carried off by the young dragon.

Chapter Twelve

Abdel drew a slow, shuddering breath as consciousness returned. Too weak to open his eyes, he was still able to sense he was indoors now. Someone had moved him from where he collapsed in the street. By the faint sting of smoke and ash he could taste on his tongue he guessed he was still somewhere in the burning city of Saradush.

He took another deep breath. A cool mist spread down into his chest, the moist cloud soothing his scarred throat and lungs. His hearing, destroyed by the dragon's battle cry, had returned enough for him to detect the monotonous droning of a religious chant echoing from far above.

Struggling against his own weariness, he opened his eyes and found himself lying naked on a cold stone floor, staring up at a high arched ceiling. The walls and roof were adorned with elaborately painted images of men and women suffering from disease, injury, and torture—though their expressions showed not torment, but relief. Common to each scene was the figure of a cowled man, his sympathetic face stained with tears. Abdel recognized the portrait of Ilmater, the crying god.

It was then that he realized he felt no pain, even though he was lying on his horribly burned back. Unsure if his natural healing abilities had finally kicked in or if there was another explanation, he forced himself to sit up. The effort blinded him, as stars momentarily filled his vision.

"Thank Ilmater you're alive!" Melissan's voice exclaimed through the glittering tapestry.

132

Abdel heard the sound of scampering feet and a second later felt the familiar embrace of Imoen as she wrapped her thin arms around Abdel's massive neck. "Abdel," she cried, pressing herself against his obviously completely healed back, "I thought I'd lost you."

As he wrapped his massive arms around his half sister and hugged her back, the stars in his vision began to vanish. Abdel found himself surrounded by not only Imoen and Melissan but by several robed figures anxiously studying his every movement. No doubt it had been these priests of Ilmater who had saved him from his injuries.

There was little time to waste on thanks. "Jaheira?" he asked hesitantly, looking directly at Melissan. The tall woman turned away.

Imoen released her grip and withdrew from Abdel, her face heavy with grief. "The dragon took her," she said softly.

Abdel gently pushed Imoen away and rose slowly to his feet. Seeing something in his eyes, the robed figures took several steps back from the warrior who now towered over them, clad only in the charred remnants of his clothes. Melissan held her ground.

"I am truly sorry, Abdel," she said.

Launching himself at her, Abdel managed to wrap his hand around her throat before anyone else had a chance to react. With his hands squeezing ever tighter he lifted her off the ground, her heels kicking feebly in the air. The priests of Ilmater reacted with horrified gasps but made no move to intercede on Melissan's behalf.

"Abdel!" Imoen screamed, leaping on his back and futilely trying to pry his hands from Melissan's neck. "Abdel, it's not her fault! There was nothing we could do."

Melissan clutched feebly at Abdel's massive arms, her eyes bulging as she gasped for air.

"She betrayed us!" Abdel roared. "She lied to us about the Five! She wants us all to die!"

133

"No!" Imoen shrieked, now pounding on her invincible half brother's back with her tiny fists. "Melissan drove off the dragon! She found you and brought you to this temple. If she wanted to kill us why did she save us?"

No longer so certain of Melissan's treachery, Abdel's grip loosened. He lowered the tall woman until her feet were on the floor and let go of her neck, giving her a disdainful shove that sent her reeling back into the surrounding priests of Ilmater, who caught her as she stumbled.

Imoen dropped from Abdel's back and rushed over to see if Melissan was all right. Assured her new friend would survive, the young woman shot a harshly disapproving glance back at Abdel.

"What were you thinking, Abdel? Have you gone mad?"

Abdel didn't answer but merely swore and spat on the hallowed floor of the church as he turned away from them.

With Imoen's help, Melissan managed to stand. Her long, delicate fingers massaged her neck beneath the high, dark collar that reached up to just beneath her chin. Her throat was bruised beneath the fabric of her collar by Abdel's savage and unwarranted assault, but when she spoke, there was no hint of Imoen's anger in Melissan's voice.

"Your brother has lost someone he loved," she said softly, her abused throat making her voice rough and rasping. "He has a right to be upset."

"Not like this," Imoen protested, a protective arm around the taller woman's shoulders as her eyes shot daggers at Abdel's back. "After everything you've done for us, he has no right to treat you this way."

The big man spun on his heel to face the two women. The ring of cowled priests slipped silently away, leaving the trio of interlopers alone to solve their disputes.

"She set us up, Imoen," Abdel declared. "She led us right into a trap."

Imoen started to protest, but Melissan raised her hand to hush the young girl.

"I will not deny Gromnir's army was ambushed," the tall woman said softly, her voice now closer to its normal tone. "But I assure you, I had nothing at all to do with the betrayal."

"Who then?" Abdel demanded.

Melissan shook her head. "Regrettably I cannot say. There were many Bhaalspawn gathered in Saradush seeking shelter from Yaga Shura's army. Perhaps one of them sought to trade his own life for the lives of all his kin."

Despite his best efforts, Abdel felt his anger fading. He had accused Melissan based on his own assumptions. They were assumptions based on the dying accusations of the mad General Gromnir. Forced to look at the facts, he couldn't find any evidence Melissan was the one responsible for the ambush. In fact, Melissan had saved Abdel's life—at least according to Imoen.

Looking into his half sister's eyes, Abdel realized she was infatuated with the powerful, beautiful woman. Abdel had seen that look in her eyes before, but in the past it had always been when she looked at him. Melissan was Imoen's savior, and apparently she had supplanted Abdel in his role as the young woman's hero.

Abdel himself wasn't so awestruck.

"You haven't been completely honest with me," he said, remembering the parting words of the mysterious being in the Abyssal plane. "You know more about the Five than you have told me."

Before Imoen could leap to her new idol's defense, Melissan spoke. "It is true, Abdel. I have not been completely honest with you. But you must understand I could not trust you until you had proved yourself by defeating Yaga Shura."

"Yet you expect me to trust you."

Melissan sighed. "Abdel, my work is difficult. I seek to save the offspring of an evil, treacherous deity from their own kin. I must constantly be on guard against betrayal from my own allies. You know many of your kin are not to be trusted."

Reluctantly, Abdel nodded. He could not deny the truth of her words, just as he could not deny his own tainted heritage.

"Many years ago I approached Sarevok and told him everything I knew about the Five and their purpose," Melissan continued. "He used that information for himself and nearly started a war in his mad efforts to supplant the Five as the one who would resurrect your dark father. I have learned from such mistakes to guard my secrets well, Abdel Adrian."

"And look at what happened with Gromnir," Imoen chimed in. "The people here in Saradush offered him sanctuary, and he took over their town. No wonder Melissan was reluctant to tell us everything. You can't blame her."

"Where is Sarevok now?" Abdel asked, suddenly aware of his half brother's absence.

With a shrug, Melissan replied, "He rode by my side when we charged from the gate, but we were separated during the chaos of battle. He has not returned. Perhaps he is one of the thousands who lie dead on the battlefield. Perhaps he was slain by the army that ravaged Saradush and only fled when they saw the dragon take to the sky."

"I doubt these soldiers would have been capable of ending my half brother's existence," Abdel muttered.

"Maybe he was the traitor," Imoen offered. "It wouldn't be the first time he's tried to destroy a city."

"Perhaps," Melissan admitted, though she did not seem convinced. "Sarevok was aware of our battle plan. He could have somehow arranged the ambush. When I first met Sarevok, he was easily capable of such treachery.

"But I sensed something different about him now," the tall woman continued. "Sarevok has changed since I first met him. Do you believe he is still capable of such evil?"

"I . . . I don't know," Imoen admitted, "I guess not. But I didn't really know him before."

She turned to her brother. "What do you think, Abdel? Did Sarevok betray us?"

Abdel considered his answer for a long time. Sarevok had murdered Gorion and Khalid. He had nearly killed Jaheira, and he had done it all without conscience. But that was long ago. Like Melissan, Abdel sensed something fundamentally altered in the Sarevok who had accompanied them to Saradush.

"It hardly matters now," Abdel finally answered, his voice weary. "If Sarevok is the traitor, I suspect he retreated with the rest of the army. I doubt we will run into him again. We have to focus on the task at hand. Tell me about the Five, Melissan."

When Melissan hesitated, Abdel pressed his case. "I proved myself by risking my own life to slay Yaga Shura. Surely you realize that I have no desire to bring Bhaal back to life. If you expect me to aid your cause, you must tell me everything you know about the Five."

Tilting her head to the side, Melissan seemed to be weighing Abdel's words, balancing the risks of revealing too much against the rewards of obtaining Abdel's help.

"Please, Melissan," Imoen implored, "I've known Abdel my whole life. He's a good man. You can trust him to do the right thing."

The tall woman gave the younger girl a warm smile. "Very well, child. I will tell you both what I know about the Five, and you will understand why I was not surprised to see the dragon joining the battle against us."

* * * * *

"Please, Abdel, come with us," Imoen begged. "Melissan will take us both to the monastery at Amkethran. She has promised that Balthazar, the leader of the monks there, will hide us. They'll protect us from the Five while we rest and regroup."

Her brother shook his head. "You go with her now. I'll catch up later after I find Jaheira."

Imoen couldn't bring herself to say the awful fact they

both knew to be true. But Melissan was not afraid to speak the words.

"Your lover is dead, Abdel Adrian. You cannot save her."

Abdel strapped the large, heavy blade he had claimed from the armory of Saradush across his back. "If I cannot save her, then I will avenge her death."

"You intend to slay a dragon by yourself?" Melissan demanded. "Perhaps several of them?"

"If I have to."

"What about Abazigal?" Imoen asked. "Their Bhaal-spawn master Melissan told us about? What if he's waiting for you, using Jaheira as bait to lure you to his lair?"

"I've already killed two of the Five. I don't see why a third should be any different. In fact, killing this one should be easier. If Melissan is right this wizard doesn't share Yaga Shura's immunity to conventional weapons."

"All the information I have gathered seems to indicate that you and Yaga Shura were the only Children of Bhaal to have such remarkable invulnerabilities," Melissan admitted. "But just because it is physically possible to run Abazigal through with an ordinary sword does not mean he will give you that chance.

"Your confidence is admirable, but foolish," Melissan warned. "Have you not been listening to what I have said? Abazigal is a master of both dragons and sorcery. Unlike Yaga Shura and Illasera, he is not merely some warrior you can hack down with your sword."

"Killing wizards is hard work," Abdel admitted as he pulled on a pair of sturdy boots that were at least two sizes too small. His own clothing had been incinerated by the dragon's fire, but Melissan had managed to find him a shirt and breeches that fit his enormous frame— barely. "But Abazigal won't be the first mage whose plans I've thwarted."

He stood up and gave Imoen a hug. Over her shoulder he could see out into the streets of Saradush. Already the survivors were beginning the task of rebuilding their city, clearing away the debris and bodies that littered their ruined streets.

"Imoen, you stay with Melissan," he instructed his sibling. "Don't do anything stupid like trying to follow me, you'll just get in the way. I'll meet up with you later. I promise."

"Abazigal is far more powerful than the wizard you defeated at the Tree of Life," Melissan cautioned as the big sellsword headed toward the door. "Irenicus lusted to be immortal, but he did not have the blood of a god coursing through his veins. Do not discount Abazigal's status as one of the Five. He is the son of Bhaal himself."

Abdel slung a large pack of provisions over his right shoulder. "And so am I."

* * * * *

Driven by urgency and fueled by his immortal blood, Abdel didn't even stop to rest the first day. Even so, he could not traverse the ground as quickly as a dragon in flight. The lost time galled him, but Abdel couldn't move any faster. In fact, as weariness set in he was forced to slow his pace. Though his stops were few and far between, even the son of a god needed to rest.

Tracking the dragon was easy. Everywhere the creature passed, it left an indelible impression on both the landscape and the minds of the people fortunate enough to witness the spectacle and survive. The creature was flying almost due south. At first, Abdel suspected it was headed for the dense woods of the Forest of Mir. There the trees grew so thick, it was said, that the light of the sun never touched the forest floor. In many places the trunks grew so close together it was impossible for either man or beast to pass—or so Abdel had heard. In fact, everything he knew about the Forest of Mir was hearsay and legend. Eyewitness accounts were exceedingly rare, as few who ever entered the dark wood ever emerged again.

Drew Karpyshyn

Abdel hoped the creature wasn't heading into the deepest recesses of those accursed woods. The sellsword wasn't afraid of whatever monsters might lurk within the trees, but he was worried that the tales of vast stretches of thick, virtually impassable growth were true. If he had to constantly hack his way through branches, roots, and thickets in his pursuit of the dragon the already slim hope of arriving in time to save Jaheira would become even fainter.

By the middle of the third day Abdel realized the dragon wasn't heading for the Mir Forest. The near edge of the wood was now a half day's march to the west, but the creature's path had not veered from its southerly course. Calling upon the long-buried memories of the maps he had been forced to study in his lessons at Candlekeep, Abdel made an educated guess as to where the beast was heading. It was probably heading toward the Alimir Mountains on the coast of the Shining Sea, a small range located a tenday's journey south of Saradush.

It was there, Abdel guessed, that the beast had made its lair. It was there he would confront the Bhaalspawn Abazigal, and it was there, Abdel hoped, he would find Jaheira.

Part of his mind knew his half-elf lover had left this world, but Abdel refused to consciously acknowledge that part of himself. Against all logic and reason, he still harbored the faint hope that somehow, someway he would find Jaheira alive. If he didn't, the small corner of his mind he refused to acknowledge vowed that he would extract a gruesome vengeance.

Abdel pressed onward, his thoughts a churning maelstrom of improbable hope and despair and violent images of retribution. His being was focused on the goal before him, and he was oblivious to the man pursuing him.

* * * * *

A half day's march behind the determined sellsword, an immense figure in dark plate mail followed Abdel's

140

path. Sarevok had picked up Abdel's trail on the plains outside the ruins of Saradush, and he had been tracking him ever since.

The relentless pace of his half brother kept Sarevok from closing the distance between them, but the armored warrior shared enough of Abdel's blood and physical prowess to keep himself from falling farther behind. Sarevok knew his brother sought revenge for the female druid's death. Sarevok also knew Abdel was heading to a confrontation with another of the Five that might very well end Abdel's existence, and Sarevok was determined to be there when the confrontation took place.

Chapter Thirteen

Even now, long after the ritual had ended, the flames in the pit at the center of the abandoned temple burned high and hot, fuelled by the essence of the countless Bhaal-spawn slaughtered in the sacking of Saradush. The orange light of the fire reflected off the walls, giving the painting of Bhaal's grinning gray skull on the wall a hideous glow and bathing the entire room in its ghastly illumination.

The three cowled figures huddled in the farthest corner of the temple. Conditioned by years of operating in hiding and secrecy, they were still loathe to let the revealing light of Bhaal's ceremonial fire touch their hooded forms.

"The blaze has never been so strong," the smallest of the figures whispered, brushing a strand of silver-white hair from her dark skin. Of the three, the light bothered the drow most of all. Extremely young by elf standards, most of her thirty years of life had been spent among the blackness of the Underdark where the only illumination was the diseased glow of pale lichens. Recruited by the Anointed One several years ago to join the Five, the drow still found bright light painfully uncomfortable.

"The blaze is strong because our triumph is near," the second figure replied. The tattoos on his face and hands seemed to pulse and shimmer in response to the ghoulish radiance of Bhaal's burning essence.

The third and largest figure flicked his long forked tongue to taste the scent of Bhaal's sacrificial glory that hung like smoke in the air. In the harsh light his pupils were mere slits of black in the yellow of his reptilian eyes. "Yet Gorion'sss ward ssstill thwartsss usss."

The drow scoffed at the fear in the voice of her larger companion. "Abazigal, surely you are not afraid of this stupid oaf?"

The half dragon hissed at the revelation of his name. "You dare betray my identity?" he growled.

The tattooed man halted the impending argument with a simple wave of his hand. "Do not be a fool, Abazigal. Your identity is already known to our enemy. The Anointed One has informed me that even now Gorion's ward tracks your pet to your mountain enclave."

"Perhaps I should accompany you back to your home, Abazigal," the drow suggested in a sinister whisper. "If you are frightened I can deal with Abdel for you."

"No!" Abazigal spit out hastily. "I ssshall deal with him alone. You will not befoul my sssacred cavrensss with your unholy presence."

The drow laughed, amused at Abazigal's righteous indignation. "Do you seek to hide secrets from us, Abazigal? Do you think we are unaware of the dragon army gathering near the foot of your mountain home?"

She shook her head in mock sympathy. "Poor little half-breed," she sighed. "You are fooling yourself if you believe the true dragons will flock to your banner. They will never demean themselves enough to follow a bastard wyrm like yourself!"

The clawed hand of Abazigal lashed out to rip the drow's windpipe from her throat but found only air. The drow ducked under the attack and slipped around behind her heavyset opponent, her knife pressed against his throat.

"Perhaps Yaga Shura will not be the only member of the Five to fall tonight," she whispered in his ear.

"Enough," the tattooed man said in a firm voice.

The drow sheathed her blade and stepped back from the chastened Abazigal. The half-dragon turned his back on his two companions and walked slowly toward the exit.

"I can ssstay no longer. I have more presssssing matterssss to attend to." Embarrassed by the drow's display, Abazigal's voice was sullen and petulant.

"Yes, hurry, half-breed," the drow taunted. "You must not keep your betters waiting!"

Beneath his cloak, Abazigal's body stiffened.

"We shall leave Abdel to you," the tattooed man promised, causing Abazigal's body to relax. "Do not underestimate him," he warned his companion. "Illasera and Yaga Shura paid for their arrogance with their lives."

Without turning to face them, Abazigal replied, "They were weak and foolish. I am not."

Without another word, the humiliated half-dragon stepped through the nearby door and into the cool night. He crouched low to the ground then launched himself high into the air. His biped form morphed, and his body grew into an enormous mountain of scaled flesh. Great wings erupted from his back, his arms became small vestigial claws, his legs changed into massive, taloned haunches. With the sound of cracking bone, his face transformed into the tooth-lined visage of a dragon, perched atop his suddenly elongated neck.

The entire transformation took less than a second. With a flap of his enormous wings and a swish of the tail that had sprouted from his hindquarters, Abazigal rose up into the blackened sky.

Not at all surprised, the other two members of the Five watched the silhouette of his massive new body as it grew smaller and smaller against the full moon that hung low in the sky. Only when it had diminished to a faint speck did they speak again.

"Abazigal is more focused on winning favor with the council of dragons than on fulfilling his duties as one of the Five," the drow noted. "He thinks with an army of wyrms under his command he will have no further use for us."

"The dragons will not follow him," her companion assured her. "And Abazigal lacks the strength and the courage to disobey Bhaal's Anointed.

"Still," the tattooed man admitted, "his attention is diverted. He does not fully appreciate the threat Gorion's ward represents."

"If Abazigal should fail, we two shall figure more prominently in our father's return," the drow whispered.

When her companion made no reply she added, "And if the Anointed One should also perish by Abdel's blade, Bhaal's favor will be split between we two alone."

"And perhaps you are plotting ways to eliminate me as well," the tattooed man answered without a hint of emotion. "Though I suggest we concentrate on destroying Abdel Adrian before we turn against each other."

The drow smiled. "Of course, my half brother. Your words are as wise as ever. Are you certain the blood of my kind does not flow beside that of our immortal father through your veins?"

"While Abazigal is engaged with Gorion's ward," the tattooed man said, ignoring the drow's compliment, "we should attend to that other Bhaalspawn from Candlekeep."

"Imoen?" the drow sniffed disdainfully. "She is hardly worth the effort."

"She is Abdel's friend, and the essence of Bhaal still dwells within her, however faintly. If Abazigal should fail, killing the girl will make Abdel's grief even greater and our plans for his death easier."

Unconsciously, the drow's lithe hand slid down to caress the hilt of her rune-covered dagger. "Then we must see to it she dies."

The tattooed man shifted uncomfortably. "Melissan is bringing her to Amkethran."

The drow laughed, a sound of malevolent evil. "Melissan, the great protector of the Bhaalspawn, is bringing Imoen to the fabled protection of Balthazar and his monastery? How deliciously ironic!"

"I do not wish to reveal myself by moving against her," her companion replied. "The time is not yet right for me to take such open action."

"Then give me the pleasure of killing this girl!" the drow insisted. "You know the protective walls of the monastery are nothing to me—I am but a shadow. Melissan herself will not even know I am there until she finds the Bhaalspawn's corpse!"

The man hesitated briefly before nodding his assent. The drow laughed again and slipped out the doors into the cover of night, shedding the heavy hooded cloak once she was beyond the glow of the temple's fire. Her dark skin and clothes were instantly invisible in the evening's gloom.

A lifetime of emotional discipline and training could not prevent the tattooed man from feeling a faint glimmer of hope as he watched the drow assassin disappear into the night. He had no doubt Sendai would succeed in her mission. The monks of Amkethran's monastery, though powerful, were incapable of keeping the drow from slaying the young woman from Candlekeep. Perhaps, if fortune smiled on him, Sendai would slay Melissan as well.

Alone in the house of his father, the tattooed man turned his attention back to the conflagration in the center of the temple. Beneath the crackle of Bhaal's flaming fury he could hear the anguished screams of the slain Bhaalspawn. He felt their torment pulling at his tainted soul, drawing out the unholy lust of his father. He resisted the urge to submerge himself in the glorious suffering.

This night had not gone as he had expected. He had hoped to feed the sacrificial fire with the souls of the drow and the half-dragon tonight. But with Abdel Adrian still alive he could not afford to betray his allies just yet. As the tattooed man had explained to the drow, the continued existence of their common enemy forced the members of the Five to forestall their natural inclinations to turn on each other.

But if his study and training had taught him anything, it was patience. He would bide his time. Eventually he would see them all dead: Abdel, Imoen, Abazigal, Sendai, Melissan—all of the Bhaalspawn, all of the Five, even Bhaal's Anointed would fall. If they killed each other off, so much the better, and in the end he would be the only one left.

Chapter Fourteen

Abazigal flew the entire night spurred on by his shame, his hatred of Sendai, and the knowledge that the arrival of Gorion's ward could ruin all his carefully laid plans. Still many miles from his destination, his keen serpent's eyes could already see the assemblage of dragons who had gathered on the top of the mountain plateau where Abazigal had built his mountain fortress. Blue and green dragons from deep within the Mir Forest, brown wyrms from the sands of the Calimir desert, black dragons from the spider swamp—a glittering kaleidoscope of hues and colors all impatiently awaiting the half-dragon's arrival.

Abazigal had sent his request for audience to every mountaintop, hidden cave, and underground cavern within a thousand miles. Over a dozen of the magnificent creatures had responded, drawn by Abazigal's promises of treasure, glory, and a return to a time when dragons ruled the lands of Faerûn. Though he was disappointed to notice the absence of the ancient reds Balagos and Charvekannathor, he was exceedingly pleased to mark the gleaming hide of Iryklagathra, the great blue dragon known to most mortals as Sharpfangs, among the assembled throng.

Arriving just as the first rays of sun knifed through the morning clouds to ignite the snow-covered peaks, Abazigal alighted in the center of the circle formed by the great wyrms. As his feet touched the hard rock he resumed his humanoid form. The others would not be fooled by his appearance. Even in dragon form they could smell he was a half-breed. Proud as he was, Abazigal knew enough to humble himself before the pure bloods. It had cost Abazigal a small fortune in gold and gems just to gain this audience, and he was not about to offend his guests by speaking to them in the form of a true dragon.

"You are nearly late," Saladrex, an ancient green wyrm, said by way of greeting, his great voice echoing throughout the surrounding hills. Smaller and less powerful than the red and blue dragons that struggled for dominance in the region, Saladrex was crafty and ambitious. Sensing an opportunity to gain a powerful ally, he had been open to Abazigal's initial queries. Saladrex was the first wyrm to agree to come and listen to Abazigal's offer. For a price, of course.

Now, apparently, Saladrex was also serving as the voice of the collected council. Abazigal suspected the green dragon had been chosen because many of the other wyrms, like the glorious Sharpfangs, felt it beneath them to bargain with a creature as insignificant as Abazigal knew he was in their eyes.

"My most sincere apologies, great Saladrex," Abazigal replied, careful to keep the snakelike hissing lisp from his speech lest it insult his guests in some way he could not even imagine. The effort made his jaws ache, but he knew it was a small price to pay if he could win the support of Saladrex and the others. "I flew all the night without rest to arrive on time. I would never dishonor this revered assemblage by making you wait for one as insignificant as me."

His fawning answer seemed to assuage the irritation his last-second arrival had caused among the collected dragons.

"We shall listen to your offer," Sablaxaahl, a large but relatively young black dragon blurted out, exposing the impetuousness of youth by speaking out of turn. "Though

149

what a man spawn such as yourself could have to interest us we could not imagine."

The other wyrms accepted the black's breach of etiquette without comment. Another sign they didn't feel Abazigal worthy of proper respect.

"Ah, there is where the potential lies," Abazigal replied. "I am not the offspring of a mere mortal. I am a child of the god Bhaal."

The assemblage rumbled with laughter. "The lineage of a human god? And a dead one at that?" There was amusement in Saladrex's voice as he spoke. "This is meant to impress us, half-breed?"

Abazigal bit his tongue to keep from speaking out of turn.

"You have yet to hear my offer, mighty Saladrex" he replied once he had quelled his anger. "Bhaal was indeed a god of the man creatures, but he was also a god of death and destruction, the Lord of Murder. When he rises again, he will be a god bent on vengeance."

"You speak as if the return of Bhaal is inevitable, but we know the future of this matter is not yet decided. Now our patience wears thin," Saladrex warned. "And we have yet to hear how this will benefit dragonkind."

"Are not dragons the most majestic of beings to grace the face of Faerûn?" Abazigal asked rhetorically. "Are dragons not the most powerful? The most intelligent?" The wyrms could not resist nodding their heads in agreement. Dragons were truly intelligent creatures, but even the wisest was not above allowing himself to be shamelessly flattered.

"Yet dragons do not rule," Abazigal continued, knowing he had captured the wyrms' attention. "The lesser creatures—humans, halflings, orcs, goblins—they breed like insects! They spread like the plague across the face of Faerûn, burning forests and turning your hunting grounds into pastures and towns. They steal from your hoards, their foolish heroes band together and track you to your lairs, plotting to end your existence so that they may seize your hard-won treasures for themselves and advance their own petty reputations with the title of dragonslayer."

There were murmurs of assent from his reptilian audience.

"Through sheer numbers these undeserving vermin have pushed dragonkind farther and farther into the wilderness as they expand their territories. How long until they seek to exterminate your kind forever?"

"Impossible!" a fiery young brown spat out. "Our species will never be destroyed by these pathetic little bipeds!"

But the other dragons did not second her hasty protest. They were old enough to have experienced the spread of the lesser creatures. They were wise enough to see Abazigal's ominous prophecy was not so far-fetched.

"And you claim you can stop this, Abazigal?" Saladrex challenged.

The half-dragon nodded. "When Bhaal returns, he will begin a campaign of bloody vengeance, a war to make Faerûn suffer for his death. He will slaughter the humans and their two-footed cousins in numbers history's most infamous tyrants could not even begin to comprehend.

"That is when we will act! With their populations ravaged by war, the lesser creatures will not have the numbers—or the will—to stand up to the united might of the dragonkind! You will loot and plunder the gold of their cities! The humans and their ilk will bow before you! Those who submit will be enslaved, those that do not will be driven into the seas and oceans by the combined might of our army of wyrms. Dragons will once again rule Faerûn!"

There was only silence in response as the dragons contemplated Abazigal's glorious vision. It was Saladrex who asked the question Abazigal feared most.

"And why exactly do we need you, half-breed?"

"I will be the liaison between the dragon army and the forces of Bhaal. I will guide my immortal father's war machine in directions that will prove the most beneficial to the goals of the Dragon Council."

"Why should Bhaal aid our efforts?" Saladrex asked. "He is a human god."

"Yet the Lord of Murder understands the glory of dragons," Abazigal assured them. "He assumed the form of a great wyrm to sire me—the heir to his immortal legacy. Surely this is proof that he understands dragons are the pinnacle of creation and humans are fit only for servitude.

"If your human slaves are forced to pay homage to Bhaal, what is that to you, Saladrex? Nothing. And Bhaal will not care if his followers are forced to serve dragonkind, so long as they are also forced to worship him."

From the sneer curling up Saladrex's great green lip, Abazigal knew the wyrm was not yet convinced.

"I assure you, mighty Saladrex, this alliance will be beneficial to both Bhaal and the dragons. As the offspring of both parties I will look after the interests of each side fairly."

Saladrex snorted. "Perhaps you speak the truth, but we few gathered here are not enough. We will need to recruit other dragons to the cause. The ancient reds will need to join us before others will agree, and they will be loath to follow you. None of my ilk will trust a mongrel half-breed."

Abazigal bowed his head respectfully, accepting the insult as the truth it was. "I shall not always be a mongrel," he said softly. "When my father is reborn, he will grant me any boon I request. And I shall ask of him to make me into a true dragon of pure blood."

There was laughter from the assembled dragons, and Abazigal kept his head bowed, unable to face the humiliation of their mockery. Saladrex was not laughing.

"If Bhaal truly understands the majesty of dragons," the green wyrm whispered beneath the roaring mirth of the others, speaking so that only Abazigal could hear, "he may indeed grant your wish. Seek me out when you have the pure blood of a true dragon, and I will join your cause. Together, we will unite the others."

His heart bursting with gratitude and relief, Abazigal raised his head—but Saladrex was already gone, his powerful wings flapping as he rose up into the morning sky. The other dragons, still laughing at the half-breed who would become one of them, also took flight.

Their beating wings stirred up great clouds of dust and dirt and created powerful whirlwinds and eddies that battered Abazigal's body. The half-dragon held his ground, determined not to show any weakness in the face of those he would call his peers. He stood in the same spot long after the dragons had vanished, the promise of Saladrex repeated over and over in his jubilant mind.

* * * * *

It was late afternoon on the fourth day when Abdel finally reached the northern tip of the Alimir Mountains. Here the trail of the young dragon that had fled with Jaheira grew cold. There were no witnesses to the beast's passing in this remote, inhospitable region, no trees or grasses flattened by the great winds that traveled in the wake of its flight to indicate the wyrm's direction.

Here in the foothills there was only hard stone, baked by the sun and carved by the winds of the centuries. The full range of the Alimir Mountains stretched far to the south, extending well beyond the limits of Abdel's vision. If the beast made its lair deep within the range, Abdel might never find it, or his lover.

Melissan had told him the creature worked for Abazigal, and Abazigal was one of the Five. He had to maintain frequent contact with the others in his covert group to help orchestrate their war to eradicate the Bhaalspawn. It would be necessary for the wizard to keep himself appraised of events in the lands beyond the edges of his mountain kingdom, and this task would be made simplest if Abazigal located his enclave in the northernmost reaches of the range. It was only logical to assume Abazigal's pet, as

Abdel believed the young red dragon that had taken Jaheira to be, would also have made its lair in the northern tip of the range.

Still, Abdel knew scaling the dozens of peaks and spires within even a single day's march would take weeks, if not months. A pointless endeavor. Fortunately, Abdel had devised a plan. He had no doubt Abazigal would employ his young flying lizard in a number of capacities—messenger, transportation, reconnaissance, martial reinforcement. All Abdel had to do was wait for the beast to appear again on one of its many missions and spy on it as it returned to its lair. Once he knew which peak the beast made its home on, Abdel could ascend to his vengeance.

He scouted until he found a small cave—somewhere he could bed down for the night and be out of sight but still be able to emerge quickly when he heard the unmistakable flapping of a dragon's wings. He also needed somewhere with clear sight lines of the numerous peaks dotting the horizon, so that he could track the flight of his quarry. Satisfied his location met all of his requirements, Abdel retreated inside and waited.

Night fell, but Abdel didn't sleep. While marching, even Abdel had needed to stop and rest for an hour or so each day, but now that he was merely keeping vigil, the physical specimen that was Bhaal's avatar had no need to sleep or rest. Alert and anxious, Abdel watched and waited, and with every passing second he knew the already miniscule chances of finding Jaheira alive were growing smaller.

Close to midnight he heard a sound, something searching the area outside his cave. It wasn't a dragon—this intruder was much smaller. Abdel crept to the entrance of his makeshift lair, his movements silent. The big sellsword had no intention of revealing himself. He didn't want to risk an encounter that could alert Abazigal or the wyrm to his presence. Abdel only wanted to see who was scuffling across the nearby rocks.

In the light of the full moon, Abdel could make out a single dark silhouette—a giant of a man in heavy armor adorned with savage spikes and lethal blades forged into the metal plates. At the sight of the half brother who had betrayed him at Saradush, all thoughts of concealment and discretion vanished, replaced by a hatred so primal Abdel could only scream a single name to express his fury.

"Sarevok!"

The armored man turned to meet the sellsword's reckless charge, batting away the thrusting sword seeking to plunge itself into a vulnerable spot between the impenetrable iron plates. Abdel's body crashed into Sarevok's, driving them both down.

They rolled on the ground, Sarevok wrapping his arms in a bear hug around Abdel's own, pinning the sellsword's limbs to his side and preventing Abdel from using his sword to hack through his half brother's protective iron shell.

Abdel twisted his body, trying to break free of Sarevok's grip and bring his weapon to bear. As they grappled, he felt the blades on his opponent's shins and forearms slicing through his flesh again and again. Each time the wounds healed instantly, but the incessant pain enraged Abdel further.

Sarevok still possessed inhuman strength, but Abdel knew that the power he had gained with Yaga Shura's death had made him physically superior to any foe—even this brother who shared Bhaal's blood. But he couldn't break Sarevok's grip. The armored man had better leverage, and he had locked his left fist around his right wrist, making his hands virtually impossible to separate.

Still, Abdel refused to give up. He bucked and thrashed, throwing his entire weight from side to side. A smaller man would have been flung around like a rag doll, but Sarevok's own great size allowed him to counter Abdel's

155

throes. Eventually though, Abdel knew, his enemy would tire. Or his grip would slip, and Abdel would be free to hack his half brother into trembling, quivering bits.

Sarevok was holding on for dear life, trying to speak, but Abdel wasn't about to listen to any more of his half brother's lies. Heedless of the pain and injury he was about to inflict on his own body, Abdel smashed his forehead against Sarevok's visor. It was a desperate move, a ploy he had used to great effect in many a bar brawl when his hands had been restricted. Abdel soon learned that head butting a foe with a full iron visor did not produce the same results.

Again and again Abdel slammed his own head against the metal faceplate, his nose breaking in a burst of blood then healing just in time to be broken once more as Abdel banged his head against Sarevok's armor over and over.

The taste of his own blood did little to cool Abdel's wrath, but Sarevok would not be shaken free. For nearly an hour the two combatants struggled against each other, locked in the unbreakable embrace. Pushing their bodies to the point of exhaustion, each warrior strained against one of the only other beings on Faerûn able to match their own immense strength. Finally, Abdel's remarkable regenerative powers came into play.

Sarevok's cramping fingers lost their hold, the locking grip of his bear hug slipped. Bringing his arms up, Abdel was able to push himself away from Sarevok and spring to his feet. His armored foe, muscles heavy and weary from the prolonged struggle, lay motionless on the rocky ground. Had Sarevok been human and not some specter given corporal form, Abdel imagined, he would have been panting and gasping for breath. Sarevok might as well have been a dead thing. He looked no more than an inanimate suit of plate mail on the ground.

Abdel slowly raised his sword, intending to take back the existence he had granted his hated half brother. The savage rage was gone, it had slipped away during the protracted,

xhausting battle to free himself from Sarevok's grip. Now
Abdel moved with the measured actions of a man bent on
inishing a long, hard task.

"I cannot defeat you, Abdel," Sarevok admitted in a
old monotone. "We have both seen that the injuries my
rmor accidentally inflicted upon you during our struggle
vere inconsequential. I am at your mercy, brother."

Almost against his own will, Abdel's hand had stayed
at the sound of Sarevok's voice. Realizing he was hesitat-
ng, he tensed his muscles to deliver the killing blow.

"At least grant me the satisfaction of knowing why you
lay me now," Sarevok asked, his voice completely devoid
of emotion.

Despite himself, Abdel answered. "You dare ask such a
question? After betraying us at Saradush?"

The armored helm, splattered and stained with the
blood from Abdel's repeatedly broken nose, moved slightly
rom side to side. "I am no traitor, Abdel. If you do not
believe me, strike now and end my return to this phys-
cal plane. But if you want to learn the truth, set aside
your sword."

Abdel raised the blade up above his head but did not
hrust it home. His mind churned and spun, too tired to deal
vith another dilemma of who to trust. Unable to decide if
his suspicions about Sarevok were justified, Abdel could not
bring himself to strike. In disgust he let the sword slip from
his grasp to clatter on the stones at his feet.

The sheen of sweat on his muscles caused him to
shiver as a chill gust of wind blew across his body. Abdel
collapsed in frustration beside his brother.

Slowly, Sarevok lifted himself to a sitting position. "So
you believe I am innocent of treachery?" he asked.

"I no longer know what to believe," Abdel replied, forc-
ng himself to his feet. He retrieved his sword, turned his
back on Sarevok, and returned to the shelter of his cave.
A second later, he heard the grinding of metal on metal as
Sarevok stood up and followed him.

"I am here to offer my aid," Sarevok assured Abdel as he took a seat beside his half brother inside the small cavern. "When you restored my life I vowed to stay by your side, brother. I shall not break that vow. That is why I followed your trail from the battlefield outside Saradush."

"Is that the reason?" Abdel asked sarcastically, "Or are you here to finish the job Abazigal's dragon could not?"

Sarevok shook his head. "Abazigal? I am not familiar with that name."

Abdel sighed, still uncertain if Sarevok was telling him the truth. "He is one of the Five. A half-dragon, if Melissan's reports are accurate. His pet sacked Saradush— right after the ambush that decimated Gromnir's army."

The armored man tilted his helm to one side. "And you naturally blamed me for the ambush?"

"Who else?" Abdel asked with a shrug. "You knew the battle plan, you could have sent a message to the army beyond the walls. And you disappeared during the battle. Why not assume you were the traitor?"

"Your evidence could implicate others as well," Sarevok countered. "Gromnir knew our tactics. In fact, it was the mad general who devised the strategy. And he, too, vanished during the battle."

"No. Gromnir did not arrange this. I saw him die on the battlefield."

"Did you?" Sarevok asked. "Truly? Or did you merely think you saw him die?"

"I was there when Grominr died," Abdel insisted. "I killed . . . I mean, I saw how he was killed. Crushed by his own horse."

"Perhaps you only saw what Gromnir wanted you to see," Sarevok cautioned. "The Calimshite general was a Bhaalspawn, Abdel. Do you truly believe a fall from a horse could so easily end his existence?"

At first Abdel had no reply. The scenario Sarevok painted was improbable but not impossible. Since learning of his own unbelievable parentage, Abdel had come to accept the improbable almost as a matter of course, but he was not yet ready to accept Sarevok's theory without question.

"If Gromnir was a traitor working for the Five, then why was he hiding in Saradush with Melissan and the other Bhaalspawn?"

"Imagine you are a servant of the Five," Sarevok said slowly, "maybe even their leader, the one known only as Bhaal's Anointed. You learn of Saradush—a town where the Bhaalspawn you seek to destroy can seek refuge and sanctuary. Would you not bring your army to the gates of this town?"

When Abdel nodded, Sarevok continued. "And would you not come up with a clever ruse to have them invite you in? Would you not seek some way to infiltrate their ranks?"

Again, Abdel nodded.

"Perhaps Gromnir came to Saradush intent on destroying it, his Calimshite soldiers the vanguard of Yaga Shura's larger force. He convinced the people of Saradush to grant him admittance to their city, then seized power. When the troops of Yaga Shura arrived, Gromnir would then be in control of both sides of the siege."

"But why go through a siege at all?" Abdel protested. "Why not just slaughter the Bhaalspawn as soon as he came to power?"

Sarevok shrugged with the familiar grating shriek of metal on metal. "Maybe he did not expect Melissan to be there. She is powerful, Abdel. Perhaps Gromnir was forced to maintain the charade for fear of retribution from Melissan.

"Or maybe," Sarevok added in the nearest approximation to a whisper his monotone speech could achieve, "Gromnir knew you were coming. Maybe all this was a charade to lure you into Saradush and manipulate you into a battle with Yaga Shura. Unfortunately, you survived, and Gromnir was forced to stage his own death to hide his treachery."

"No, it's all too far-fetched," Abdel declared after a moment's consideration. "The plot is too convoluted, too intricate."

"That is how most Bhaalspawn think," Sarevok reminded him. "Treachery is in our blood. We will go to any lengths to achieve our devious ends."

"Including spinning a fantastic tale of deceptions and deceits to cover your own involvement?"

His half brother made no reply to Abdel's thinly veiled accusation. After several minutes of uncomfortable silence, Sarevok spoke again.

"Do you wish me to go, brother?"

Abdel nodded. "I can't trust you Sarevok. I can't trust anyone but myself. If you are innocent of these crimes, I have no wish to spill your blood. Therefore, I will grant you the benefit of the doubt. But understand this, *brother* . . . if we ever meet again I will know you are responsible for this bloodshed. And I will kill you."

With a series of harsh, grinding noises Sarevok rose to his feet. "I understand."

The armored man turned and left the cave. Abdel could hear the clink of his half brother's armor growing ever fainter until it was lost beneath the soft whistling of the wind.

He whispered a brief prayer, though he knew no living god who would hear his pleas. He prayed he had made the right decision by letting Sarevok live, and he prayed that Jaheira still survived, wherever she might be.

Chapter Fifteen

Imoen had been traveling for nearly seven days, accompanied by Melissan and the small group of soldiers and refugees from Saradush. As far as Imoen could tell, she was the only Bhaalspawn among them. It was hard to imagine that of the dozens and dozens of men and women who shared Bhaal's tainted blood, only she and Abdel had survived the slaughter unleashed upon the city.

The young girl shifted in her saddle. Melissan had managed to find horses for them all, making the trip bearable, but even riding could not make the journey pleasant. They set out each morning before the sun rose, and they rode long past the coming of dusk. After a week, their arduous trek was finally nearing its end.

They had set out for Amkethran the same morning Abdel had left to pursue the dragon that had taken Jaheira. However, while Abdel had gone south, Melissan and her company had ventured west, heading down the well-maintained trade route known as the Ithal Road.

The countless hours she had spent poring over the maps tucked away in the Candlekeep archives while dreaming of a life beyond the stodgy library walls had given Imoen a strong sense of geography even in these unfamiliar lands. She knew the village of Amkethran lay several hundred miles southwest of Saradush. But there was nothing unusual about the much longer route Melissan was leading them on by sticking to the western-running Ithal Road.

A more direct path between Saradush and Amkethran would have led them right through the heart of the Forest of Mir, or, as many of the locals called it, *Khalamjiri*—the place of deadly teeth. Even if it had been possible to somehow survive a journey through the lethal woods the more direct route would have emerged right at the base of the all-but-impassable Marching Mountains. In truth, the route Melissan had chosen was the only route they could have taken.

Melissan had kept to the Ithal Road for the first four days. Only then, a full day's ride past the merchant city of Ithmong and just beyond the western tip of the Forest of Mir, did they turn to the south. Two more day's ride had brought them to the edge of the Calim desert, where the stress and strain of the long forced flight had been made even more torturous by a full day's ride through the burning heat of the endless sea of sand.

Now Imoen's legs were stiff and aching, her muscles unused to clinging to the back of a horse for so many days without a break. Her rump was sore and blistered from rubbing against the saddle. Her fair skin was red and raw, burnt by the wind and the sun that was even now setting beyond the horizon. The meager rations of water they were allotted since entering the desert did nothing to stave off thirst.

Mercifully, the ordeal would end soon. Since early afternoon she had been able to make out a gleaming marble edifice in the distance. That must be the monastery at Amkethran, Imoen thought. Melissan had explained that the monastery was run by a man named Balthazar and his monks. Balthazar, Melissan had promised, would provide the last refuge for Imoen—and Abdel, once he joined up with them.

As the last light of day disappeared and the soothing cool of night settled in, the group at last reached their destination. Amkethran was, to Imoen's eyes, little more than a shantytown, nothing but a number of tents and baked mud homes built around the monastery. A crude two-story building that might have been a temple stood in one corner of the village.

Riding through the dusty streets of the village Imoen couldn't help but notice the browned and leathered faces of those who toiled in the hard-scrabble environment of the desert. The paucity and insignificance of Amkethran was made even more noticeable by the towering white marble walls of the monastery on the eastern edge of the town. Thirty feet high, the perimeter defenses of Balhazar's fortified residence dwarfed the other structures.

Though it threatened to make her legs cramp up, Imoen spurred her horse forward until she rode even with Melissan at the head of the company.

"This Balthazar sure likes to rub his fortune in the noses of these villagers," she whispered, appalled at the ostentatious display so blatantly shoved into the face of the abject poverty of Amkethran itself.

"Hush, child," Melissan cautioned. "Beyond these walls Balthazar and his monks live a sparse, barren existence. These walls are for protection, not for show."

Imoen blushed and turned her eyes to the ground. She admired Melissan. The tall woman was beautiful, strong, and wise. Men and women alike looked up to her. Imoen felt herself drawn to this mysterious woman who had become her protector. She felt herself constantly staring at the imposing figure in black, unable to take her eyes from Melissan's powerful, athletic form. Imoen loved the way Melissan dressed. Her dark clothing covering her entire body not only made her more mysterious, it also seemed to reject the stereotypical flashes of flesh most women used to attract the attentions of men.

Imoen had wanted nothing more than to impress Melissan. That was the sole intent of her comments about Amkethran. Instead, she had stupidly embarrassed herself. Thankfully, Melissan had not noticed Imoen's shame—or at least, she had the decency to pretend not to notice.

Imoen tried to save face by explaining her earlier comment. "I just meant, well, did they have to build the monastery right on the eastern edge of the town? It casts a shadow over all of Amkethran. It must take hours before the first light of the morning sun even touches the villagers."

Melissan tossed her head back and laughed, her raven tresses cascading down her back as she did so "You have the history of Amkethran somewhat backward, dear girl. The monastery has stood here for many generations. It is the town that is new. And it is no accident that those few who choose to live here have built their homes beneath the shadow of the monastery.

"You have spent but one full day beneath the blazing sun of the Empires of the Sands," Melissan continued. "Surely you can appreciate the relief even a few extra hours of shade each day would provide. You should watch what you say in the streets of Amkethran. Balthazar and his monks are held in high esteem by the people of this town."

Chastened by Melissan's words, Imoen could only stammer out a feeble apology. "I . . . I'm sorry, Melissan I meant no disrespect."

Melissan reached over to place her elegant hand reassuringly on Imoen's shoulder. The young girl felt a thrill at the noblewoman's touch. "Your concern for the less fortunate is touching, Imoen. In this case it is misplaced, but you must never apologize for your instincts to help others In my youth, I, too, shared your passions."

Looking up into Melissan's eyes, Imoen saw a genuine and sincere compassion. Imoen wanted to say something else, but she was afraid of ruining the moment, and the moment was gone.

The electric touch of Melissan's hand slipped from her shoulder, and the tall woman spurred her horse forward. "I must go and see that the monks are prepared for our arrival," she called back over her shoulder. "We can speak again inside the safety of the tower."

Imoen watched Melissan gallop off, her eyes drawn to the glorious mane of jet-black hair streaming out behind the woman.

* * * * *

In the comfort of his dragon's den, among the company of his faithful pets, Abazigal fantasized about his future as a pure-blood wyrm. The respect commanded by true dragons, the mere glory of their very existence, would be his once Bhaal had been resurrected. Abazigal, once spurned as a half-breed, would be hailed as a hero by all of dragonkind as he led them to their true destiny as rulers of Faerûn.

He had come far since his humble beginnings. Abazigal remembered nothing of his dragon mother. Did she reject him as the abomination he was, or did she protect him and nurture him? It didn't matter. Her existence was nothing but an idealized concept, his link to the glory of dragonkind, and a way to deny the history of his youth.

Abazigal's earliest memories were of his cruel master, the nameless wizard who had sought to unlock the secrets of dragons through torture and experiments. Abazigal had served as a slave to the sadistic mage, cleaning the laboratory, caring for the dragon's eggs the wizard had managed to steal, feeding the young hatchlings as they were born, and disposing of their mangled, broken bodies when the wizard's experiments went awry.

He was often experimented on by the master, though the mage was careful never to bring about Abazigal's death. Dragon eggs he had by the dozens, but a half-breed, the link between man and wyrm, was a rare beast indeed.

That was exactly how the master had treated Abazigal and the dragons he kept imprisoned in his lab, as beasts. The experiments of the wizard destroyed most of his subjects' minds, the dragons lucky enough to survive his torturous research were left little more than brutes—incapable of speech or spells, stripped of their magnificent intelligence by a sniveling human wizard who dared to use the wyrms for his own twisted purposes.

Abazigal was no mindless brute, though he pretended to be an imbecile in the master's presence. His act resulted in many beatings and painful punishments for failing to follow even the simplest of instructions, but they were a small price to pay for maintaining the ruse. Believing him to be stupid and harmless, the wizard allowed Abazigal free run of the laboratory. While the mage studied the secrets of Abazigal and the dragons, Abazigal studied the wizard's own secrets.

With his dragon mother's innate intelligence, Abazigal mastered the intricacies of sorcery, teaching himself over many, many years—all the while slaving beneath the master's heavy hand. Once he had learned all he could from the wizard, Abazigal turned on his captor.

The mage's death was slow and painful. Abazigal extracted retribution for not only his own sufferings but the sufferings of the pure-blood dragons whose torture he had witnessed over the years. Every shattered egg, every dead hatchling, every wyrm that had been transformed into a dumb beast no longer worthy of the title "dragon" by the master was avenged in the wizard's agonizing end.

Winning his freedom did not end Abazigal's responsibilities to the young dragons the wizard had imprisoned. A dozen wyrms still lived, all too mentally damaged to fend for themselves. Abazigal had adopted them as his own. He tried to restore their minds, to elevate them to their rightful status, but the damage done by the master was irreparable.

Perhaps killing them all, aborting their pathetic existence, would have been the right thing to do, but Abazigal could not bring himself to destroy them, flawed as they were. Instead, they became his pets, his army of quasi-dragons. Fiercely loyal, they served him without question to the best of their limited abilities.

He was careful to hide the existence of his pets. If the true dragons learned of their existence, they might destroy them as an affront to the species. Yet Abazigal had allowed the greatest of his pets, a young but nearly full grown red, to participate in the siege of Saradush.

His pet had done well, slaughtering dozens of the cowering Bhaalspawn during the battle. Part of Abazigal had hoped the battle would help the creature understand its own power. Part of him hoped it would not come back, choosing to try and survive on its own in the world, but instead, the young red had returned bearing a gift: a female half-elf.

Abazigal knew the identity of the half-elf. She was the lover of Gorion's ward, and Abdel Adrian was coming for vengeance. No doubt he was currently trudging across the plains beneath the newly risen sun, following the path of Abazigal's pet toward the Alimir Mountains. Even if his enemy rode a horse, Abazigal knew, he would still be several days away.

The wise course of action was to simply wait, bide his time until Abdel arrived, then unleash his pets on the Bhaalspawn. No single man, not even Bhaalspawn, could withstand the assault of a dozen dragons. Since his meeting with the council of dragons the previous morning, Abazigal was nearly out of patience. He had spent years suffering beneath the master's tyranny, futilely hoping he would learn some way to rid himself of his half-breed status. He had spent years plotting and conspiring with the foul drow Sendai and the rest of the Five to bring back their father.

Now his greatest desire was nearly within his grasp. The sooner Abdel Adrian was dead, the sooner Bhaal would return and grant Abazigal true dragon status. Then Saladrex would support his plan to restore dragons to their rightful place.

With a sharp, hissing whistle Abazigal grabbed the attention of his pets. "Find Abdel," he said slowly so their damaged minds could process his instructions. "Seek him out on the plains to the north. When you find him, kill him."

One by one the dozen young wyrms who served Abazigal leaped from the mouth of his great cavern, eager as ever to do his bidding. Gathering speed, their great bodies rumbled across the plateau where Abazigal had built his lair, charging toward the sheer cliffs that fell away from the mountain peak on all sides. Screaming their hunting cries, their bodies plunged over the precipice, hurtling toward the ground below. At the last second they pulled out of the steep dive and arced high into the early morning sky, their calls still echoing throughout the mountains.

Abazigal watched them go, as magnificent as any true dragons he had ever witnessed. Soon Abazigal himself would be one of them.

* * * * *

Abdel had passed the entire night without sleeping. His body, weary and battered from his battle with Sarevok, felt fresh and energized once again as the first rays of dawn peeked through the mountaintops to illuminate the entrance of his cave. Then he heard them—the unmistakable cries of a dragon in flight.

He burst from the cave, scanning the skies for the beast. To his amazement he saw not one dragon, but nearly a dozen. Their enormous bodies dropped like stones from the top of a nearby peak, then swooped up and away. Abdel, fascinated by the spectacle, could only stand and watch.

The dragons flew off to the north, oblivious to the human standing a short distance to the south watching their progress. When the final wyrm disappeared on the horizon, Abdel set off toward the peak they had launched themselves from, certain he would find Abazigal there, and hopefully Jaheira as well. If he had any hope of saving his lover, he would have to find her and escape before the army of dragons returned.

It took less than an hour for Abdel to reach the base of Abazigal's mountain enclave, but the most difficult part of his journey was still ahead—a thousand feet straight up the sheer rock face. Studying the obstacle before him, Abdel could make out a number of small ledges and jutting rock formations large enough for a man to stand on. These were few and far between. Scaling the mountain would mean free climbing with no chance to stop and rest. Even Abdel's own godlike endurance had limits, and he was about to test them fully.

Hoping his healing abilities could save him should he fall, Abdel began the ascent. Any ordinary man foolish enough to even attempt the climb would have surely plunged to his death long before reaching the first ledge, unable to push his body through the tremendous physical strain of literally crawling up the side of an unassailable mountain. Abdel had the strength necessary to drag himself ever higher.

His powerful hands found holds in the countless tiny cracks and fissures that covered the cliff wall. His boots scrabbled and scratched at the hard surface, seeking and finding footholds in the rough stone. Often he was forced to support his entire weight with a single arm, hauling his massive body up until the sweat-slicked, groping fingers of his free hand were able to fasten onto a tiny outcropping of stone higher up the mountain. Again and again his limbs fought against fatigue as he dangled hundreds of feet above the rocks below, but each time the essence of his immortal father gave him the endurance to press on and up to the next ledge where he could stop and allow his body a few minutes to recuperate.

The higher he climbed, the more difficult the trial became. The atmosphere grew thin, and Abdel found himself gasping for breath. The cold air of the mountain's upper reaches chilled his limbs, making them stiff and heavy. A sheen of icy frost coated everything, seeping into the crevices he used to pull himself along and making his grip slip and slide.

When he finally slung his leg up over the ledge of the plateau at the summit, the sun was at its zenith. The climb had taken him well over three hours, time Abdel was afraid he couldn't spare. Determined as he was to rescue Jaheira, he had no illusions about what would happen if all the dragons returned at once to find him atop their mountain lair. He had barely survived an encounter with a single of the winged monsters—a dozen would shred him to bits.

In the center of the plateau was a great, gaping hole— an entrance to the miles of passages, caves, and caverns descending deep into the mountain's heart. Somewhere in the rock labyrinth, Abdel prayed, he would find Jaheira.

He drew his heavy broadsword from the sheath on his back and marched toward the cavern's entrance. Before he reached his destination, a single figure emerged from the pit and stood to face him.

The thing was shaped like a man, but its skin was patched with multicolored scales. Its head was smooth and hairless, its eyes reptilian in appearance.

"I did not expect you ssso sssoon," it hissed, a serpentine tongue flicking from its mouth as it spoke. "Even now my petsss are out hunting for you in the plainsss to the north."

"I have come for Jaheira," Abdel said, brandishing his sword as he bargained for his lover. "Return her to me and I will leave."

"Your lover isss no more," the monster hissed at him. "I sssaw her lasst breath myssself."

The lizard thing laughed, and Abdel could no longer deny the awful truth. Jaheira was dead. Numb with grief, he could only shake his head in helpless denial. Images of her grisly end came unbidden to his mind, spurred on by

the memory of his last image of Jaheira writhing in the
dragon's grasp.

In his mind's eye he could see her beautiful features
twisted in relentless agony as she was crushed within the
dragon's ruthless grip, her bones snapping like kindling.
He imagined her head thrown back in a soundless scream
as one of the beast's savage talons pierced her armor and
chest, impaling her frail body even as she was frozen by
the icy winds of the dragon's flight.

"No!" Abdel screamed, his mind desperately scrambling
to find some small sliver of hope. "No! I will not accept this!"
He remembered this pain. He had thought Jaheira lost to
him once before, but she had been brought back to life by
the clerics of Gond Wonderbringer.

"Give her to me! She may yet be saved!"

Abazigal sneered, his reptilian lips curling into a disdainful sneer. "What makesss you think I will lisssten to
your pleasss?"

Abdel knew how ludicrous his request seemed. He
understood the lunacy of begging his mortal enemy for
the life of his lover, but he didn't care anymore. All he
wanted was Jaheira back.

"I will give you anything," Abdel promised, his voice
wild. "My essence, my spirit, my soul . . . anything!"

The only response was a scornful hiss. "Ssshe isss
gone, fool! Her blood-soaked, broken body gasssped itsss
lasssst as my pet dropped her at my feet, as an offering
for my approval.

"Ssshe sssuffered, Abdel," Abazigal whispered, his
voice dripping venom. "Ssshe died in pain. And then I
gave her to my petsss. They ripped her apart and
devoured her mangled corpsssse pieccce by pieccce!"

"No!" Abdel's scream ripped the sky, the very mountain
trembled beneath the fury of his outrage. Had he the
words, he would have vowed a million excruciating deaths
upon Abazigal to avenge his fallen lover. But words rarely
came to Abdel. He was a man of actions.

"Your half-elf isss dead, Abdel Adrian," Abazigal replied mockingly. "Asss are you."

The creature's taloned hands began to weave the arcane patterns of sorcery in the air, and he began to recite the words of a spell. Abdel leaped toward the monster, determined to hack the reptilian sorcerer down before he could complete his incantation.

Three bounding strides brought Abdel in range. Spinning to build momentum he slashed his sword at the creature's neck, intending to avenge Jaheira's death by beheading his foe with a single blow. His sword deflected mere inches from the beast's throat, ricocheting harmlessly as it struck some unseen, impregnable sorcerer's shield.

Lightning flared from the creature's clawed fingers and struck the big sellsword square in the chest, blowing Abdel backward through the air and nearly sending him over the plateau's ledge. Abdel landed less than a yard from the cliff's edge, then leaped to his feet and dived out of the path of a second blast of lightning that would have sent him plummeting over the precipice.

He ducked and dodged the onslaught of electrical bolts, slowly working his way ever closer to his enemy. The wizard didn't seem to care that Abdel was steadily closing the distance between them. Just before Abdel got himself within range to try another swipe of his sword, the creature vanished.

Abdel spun around, certain his foe would reappear directly behind him, but the lizardlike mage was now standing on the far side of the plateau, already invoking another spell. Abdel heard a terrible roaring from above and just barely managed to dive clear of the column of flame plunging down on him from the sky. Abdel screamed in pain as the terrible heat blistered and seared his skin. As with the dragon's breath, the injuries inflicted by the fire did not heal.

Badly wounded, Abdel slowly struggled to his feet, only to be knocked to the ground by another lightning blast.

Baldur's Gate II: Throne of Bhaal

"You have no chance, Abdel Adrian," his enemy hissed. "Your crude warrior's skills are no match for my sssorcery."

As he lay on the ground, singed and no longer even able to stand, Abdel knew Abazigal spoke the truth.

Chapter Sixteen

Imoen shifted from side to side on the thin straw mattress that served as her bed. Melissan had not been exaggerating when she claimed the monks within the monastery lived a sparse, barren existence. Apart from the none-too-comfortable sleeping mat, there were no furnishings in Imoen's room. The walls were smooth, bare, white stone—just like every other wall she had seen since entering the sanctuary.

Imoen had been surprised to find the interior of the monastery was nothing more than a collection of single-story stone barracks lining either side of a large, open courtyard. In the center of the courtyard was a single stone tower, just slightly shorter than the thirty foot walls surrounding Balthazar's simple keep.

Melissan had introduced her to two of the order's members, Brother Regund and Brother Lysus. Imoen found herself fascinated by the intricate tattoos covering the shaved heads and faces of the two men. She was dying to ask the significance of the glorious designs, certain they carried some deep religious significance. Remembering how she had embarrassed herself in front of Melissan with her earlier erroneous observations and comments about Balthazar and the monastery, she was willing to let her curiosity go unsatisfied.

Balthazar, the monks had explained after the brief introduction, was temporarily unavailable. They had assured Melissan that they would see to Imoen's comfort and safety to the best of their abilities.

It seemed to Imoen as if Melissan had found Balthazar's absence particularly troubling, but the tall woman had merely nodded her head in acceptance of the news.

"Go with these men," she had reassured Imoen. "They will take you somewhere safe. I have business to attend to, but I will come see to your comfort once I am free."

Though she was reluctant to leave Melissan's side, Imoen had followed the two men without protest into the solitary tower jutting up from the center of the courtyard. They led her through the tower's only door and up a long staircase to the windowless second floor. The floor consisted of nothing but a long, dark hallway and open doors that led into half a dozen rooms—all empty except for a single torch and the straw mats Imoen now struggled to find a comfortable position on.

"Here in the meditation rooms you can rest without fear," Brother Regund had assured her.

"The members of our order will patrol the entrance to the lower floor to ensure your safety," Brother Lysus had added. "We will see that no one disturbs you until Balthazar has returned. Our leader will be most eager to speak with you."

And on that rather ominous note, they had left her alone.

Time passed slowly for Imoen when she was by herself. If the austere surroundings were supposed to inspire peace and contemplation, they weren't working for her. In fact they seemed to have the opposite effect. She was restless and bored, her quick and curious mind anxious to find anything to draw its attention.

Without the benefit of windows to see the passing of the moon outside, Imoen couldn't even estimate how long she had been cooped up here. An hour? Four? She wished again that Melissan would come up to visit her. The taller woman had mentioned something about speaking to Imoen once they were safe inside, but she hadn't come to check on Imoen yet.

Drew Karpyshyn

Perhaps she was busy with more important matters. Or maybe, Imoen suddenly thought, the monks below would not allow Melissan inside the tower until Balthazar had returned.

The idea seemed preposterous at first glance, but the more she considered it the more plausible it seemed. Imoen had assumed that Melissan and she were guests, but the more she thought about the words and actions of the monks who had greeted them upon their arrival the more Imoen began to suspect she might be a prisoner.

Something about the guards had made Imoen nervous. Their strange tattoos had unnerved her, but it was more than that. Their words were spoken without emotion or feeling. Their faces were lined with intense focus and concentration, but Imoen couldn't even began to guess what the object of their attentions might be.

Their eyes didn't roam across her body like those of other men. They didn't even sneak quick peeks at her when they thought she wouldn't notice. When they looked at Imoen, they stared directly into her eyes, as if they were peering into her very soul.

In many ways, Imoen realized, the monks reminded her of Sarevok. Determined, intense, inscrutable, and cold. Not really alive, but merely going through the motions of life. As if the passions and fires of the world could not touch them.

Imoen shivered. The monks were religious fanatics, she decided. That was what bothered her. They served some higher purpose, some unknown code of belief she would never understand, and now she was in their power, trapped inside this inescapable tower until the mysterious Balthazar arrived to . . .

No. Imoen shook her head and laughed. It was preposterous. Bored with the dull surroundings, her mind was working overtime. Fashioning bizarre conspiracies out of the thinnest of threads. Melissan wouldn't have brought them here if she felt there was any danger. No, Imoen decided, she was not a prisoner. Still, she had to admit, the monks were odd.

Her guards' fanatical obedience to some unknown higher authority that had so troubled Imoen only moments before now reassured her. There was no chance one of them would creep up later while she slept to paw at her with filthy hands. More importantly, she knew she didn't have to worry about these men betraying her for gold or out of a mad hunger for power. In her situation— hunted, hated, alone except for Melissan, a woman she didn't even really know—Imoen realized the religious devotion of Regund, Lysus, and their comrades might be the best protection she could hope for.

She shifted once more on her sleeping mat. Her body ached from the long ride across the desert. She felt fatigue in her muscles and joints. Even her bones were tired. Her mind, exhausted by the convoluted track of suspicions and reassurances it had just traversed, finally grew quiet. Lying still, Imoen felt the silence of the tower seeping into her body and spirit. She welcomed the peace it offered, and within seconds Imoen was snoring softly.

* * * * *

With the climbing claws strapped to her hands, Sendai scaled the smooth marble walls of Amkethran's monastery as easily as most women would ascend a gently sloping set of steps. At the top she crouched low and scampered along the edge of wall, oblivious to the thirty-foot drop on either side.

She moved without a sound, silent as a shadow. The courtyard below was bathed in darkness, but the drow's eyes were able to study the layout of the buildings and the placement of the guards.

Several of Balthazar's monks were standing at full attention near the base of a tall tower in the center of the compound. Had her target been a drow matriarch, Sendai would instantly have dismissed the tower as too obvious. That was how the drow mind worked. The guards would be mere bait to lure her into the structure that would then collapse and kill them all. She knew surface dwellers were simple folk, that they were not devious enough to set such a trap. Or perhaps they merely lacked the will to sacrifice dozens of their own followers' lives to catch an assassin.

Whatever the explanation, Sendai could not help but feel her talents were wasted and unappreciated by these pale-skinned amateurs. Back in Ched Nassad, the Underdark city of her birth, the professional assassin had been respected and feared for her talents—not vilified and scorned.

As she studied the movements and positions of the guards, plotting how she would slip past them and into the tower, Sendai couldn't quell the anger stirred up by the recollections of her homeland. Anger for all she had lost.

A daughter in the minor noble house of Kenafin, she had been born with the character traits of most drow females: She was ambitious, ruthless, sadistic. Sendai was also wise enough to see that her chances of political advancement were slim. She lacked the devotion to Lolth required of a priestess. So she had chosen a different path to make her name, though one perfectly acceptable in drow culture.

It hadn't taken long before Sendai's considerable skills in discreetly eliminating her foes and rivals drew the attention of Ched Nassad's more powerful matriarchs. Just barely past her twentieth year, she had already become the darling of the ruling mothers. Each sought to use her for their own purposes. They tried to entice her loyalty with offers of power, slaves, and wealth. In typical drow fashion, Sendai had managed to play the dangerous game of serving no one house in particular, maximizing her opportunities—and her enemies.

Sendai, young as she was by drow standards, had already become a master of the political game. She managed to avoid the pitfalls, forming alliances when necessary and breaking them when it proved advantageous. In Ched Nassad the name of the assassin Sendai was often whispered as a rising star, worthy of both fear and respect.

The priestesses had ruined it all. The Spider Queen was a jealous god, she would brook no rivals in her domination of drow society. Knowing this, Sendai had kept her father's identity secret. Any of her close family who could have exposed her had already tasted the edge of her poisoned blade, including her mother.

In the Underdark secrets are many, and none can stay buried for long. Somehow the Temple learned of her tainted Bhaalspawn blood, and the priestesses came to take her to their interrogation chambers to test her loyalty. Sendai had experienced torture in her young life—it was almost inevitable given the nature of drow society. But she was not about to submit herself to the unimaginable sufferings of the Matron Mothers. Not when their interrogations would likely end with the decision that the offspring of Bhaal was too dangerous to live among them.

So Sendai had fled. She spent a year as a fugitive, moving from Ched Nassad to Menzoberranzan to Ust Natha, seeking some corner of the Underdark where she might find refuge from the priestesses' pursuit. The web of the Spider Queen wove its reach through every city and noble house of drow society, and finally Sendai had been forced to flee the Underdark, exchanging the glorious world of caverns and tunnels for painfully bright and open skies.

There Bhaal's Anointed had found her and offered her the chance to join the Five. The opportunity seemed like a task worthy of Sendai's considerable skill—slay the Bhaalspawn, assassinate the offspring of a god, but the idea was far more grand than the actual act. Most of Sendai's targets were not even aware of their immortal heritage. They lived petty, pointless lives. Ending their existence was almost a favor. Even the nobles and powerful merchants in the surface dwellers' society were easy prey and did little to sate her lust for a challenge.

Sendai fought a never-ending battle against complacency, fearing her skills would atrophy or her technique would become sloppy. She needed to stay in top form, for once the Five had eliminated the last of the Bhaalspawn, she intended to turn her poisoned blade on her co-conspirators. There was a challenge worthy of her, a true test of her abilities. Every assassination until then was nothing but a pale imitation of the artistry she knew she was capable of.

The drow, her dark skin and clothes virtually invisible atop the monastery wall, shook her head in disgust. In the past she would have never let her mind wander while in the middle of a job. More proof she was losing her edge. She refocused on the task at hand and leaped from the wall.

She landed softly on the ground, absorbing the impact by tucking into a ball and rolling through the momentum of the thirty-foot fall. She sprang to her feet to see if any of the guards had heard the faint noise of her unorthodox entrance. For several seconds she stood still, her keen drow ears straining to pick up the sound of an alarm or feet rushing over to investigate.

Hearing nothing, she approached the tower. Sticking to the shadows and dark corners, she crossed the courtyard right beneath the noses of the monks standing guard, invisible as a ghost. She couldn't help but laugh silently at their earnest, ineffective vigilance.

The two monks by the tower's only door were more problematic. Their deaths had to be quick and silent, lest they alert the others. The hooded lanterns the sentries held in each hand complicated her task. Twin beams of ight shot out from the burning lanterns, cutting across he courtyard and clearly visible to all the other guards patrolling the area. If anything happened to those beams of light—if one of the lanterns was dropped, even for an instant—someone was sure to notice and come over to investigate.

Standing motionless in a dark shadow not ten feet from the tower entrance, Sendai briefly considered the best way to eliminate the monks without alerting the entire order to her presence.

Moving slowly so as not to reveal herself, she drew two tiny feathered needles from her belt. From another hidden pouch she produced a small crystal vial. She removed the stopper and cautiously dipped the tip of each needle into the clear liquid. Taking great care to not accidentally prick herself with the poisoned darts, she placed the first needle in her open palm. She brought her hand up to her lips and gave a single soft puff of air, sending the dart silently on its way toward the closest monk.

Another gentle breath sent the next dart on its way toward the second target. Sendai waited for a few seconds to give the poison time to work, then slipped from the concealment of the cloaking shadows and made a quick dash to the cover of the tower door.

Safely hidden from sight once again, she paused and listened. There were no cries of surprise, no shouts of "intruder," nothing to indicate anyone had noticed the slim figure that had infiltrated the monastery. Confident she had not been seen, Sendai turned her attention to the guards standing motionless next to her. This close, she could see her darts had both found their marks. She deftly plucked the tiny weapons from the necks of the paralyzed guards and replaced them in her belt.

The eyes of the monks followed her motions, but every other muscle in their bodies was rigidly locked in position. Their partly extended arms still held the lanterns, their unresponsive fingers still wrapped tightly around the handle. Soon the poison—a derivative of the drow sleeping poison that Sendai had devised herself—would work its way to their heart and lungs. The muscles pumping blood and oxygen through the monks' bodies would seize up, become as rigid as the other muscles in their motionless forms. The guards would slowly suffocate where they stood, unable to call for help, unable to even collapse in a heap once they died. Sendai knew from previous experience that the frozen fingers of their corpses would have to be broken off to make them release their grip on the lanterns. Either that, or the lanterns could be buried with them.

The macabre thought brought a slight smile to Sendai's face, and she slipped silently up the stairs to complete her mission. As she had suspected, Sendai found no guards inside the tower. The lower level was deserted.

Without a sound, dagger drawn, the drow assassin crept to the chamber at the top of the stairs. The doors were all closed, the hallway dark and empty, except for one of the heavy portals. The soft light of a burning torch seeped out from underneath.

Sendai approached the door and listened, her keen ears picking up the distinctive sound of a young woman's soft breath. With a touch so delicate as to be almost imagined, Sendai gently opened the door.

The orange glow of the flickering torch forced the dark elf to avert her eyes, but not before she noticed the young woman resting on the sleeping mat in the center of the room. Shielding her eyes against the firelight, Sendai slipped across the room and extinguished the torch. The darkness was absolute.

* * * * *

Imoen woke with a start, her breath escaping in a terrified gasp. She was surrounded by darkness, and beneath her she felt only a cold, unyielding surface. She had half scrambled to her feet before she remembered where she was, safe in the meditation rooms of the Amkethran monastery. The faintly burning torch must have gone out when she had drifted off to sleep.

The young woman tried to laugh off her momentary panic, but she could only muster a half-hearted, nervous giggle. She had been having a nightmare. That much she remembered. The exact nature of the dream, however, she couldn't recall.

"Fire," she whispered to herself. Most of her nightmares were of fire, the devouring flames of her unholy, immortal father. She wondered if Abdel ever dreamed of such a blaze.

She shook her head to dispel such gloomy musings and tried to get her bearings in the absolute darkness of the room. She took her best guess at the direction of the torch, then took a single hesitant step. Imoen froze.

Someone was in the room with her. Imoen didn't hear anything, there was nothing to hear. She felt someone watching her with great interest. She could feel the heat of her gaze, she could sense the lusting in her eyes. For a brief second her mind conjured up an image of Brothers Regund and Lysus, standing motionless in the dark and leering at her as she stumbled unawares around the room.

"Who's there?" she whispered, as if she could dispel the intruder with her soft words.

"Do not be afraid," a husky female voice whispered. "You will feel no pain."

"Melissan?" Imoen asked, knowing full well the tall woman was not the speaker.

The invisible intruder laughed gently. "No, my pretty Bhaalspawn. She is conveniently absent."

Imoen understood. "You are one of the Five." There was no fear in her voice, no anger. Only weary acceptance. She had not expected it to end like this, but she was ready to face whatever destiny fate held in store.

"I am Sendai," the voice purred, drawing closer.

Drew Karpyshyn

Imoen hesitated a heartbeat, her fingers stealthily wrapping themselves around the hilt of the dagger tucked into her belt. She could try to scream, but what would that accomplish? Even if anyone heard her through the thick stone walls of the room, could they get here in time to save her? No, Imoen decided as she slowly drew her knife. She was on her own. Melissan would not come charging through the door at the last second to save her. Abdel would not suddenly arrive at the monastery and rush to her rescue. She would have to save herself or die in the attempt. Without warning, she lashed out at the darkness with her tiny blade.

"Alas, little one," the throaty voice chuckled. "I am not there."

"You won't gain anything by killing me," Imoen declared, spinning to slash at the blackness behind her. "Whatever part of me belonged to Bhaal has long since vanished." She leaped forward, stabbing blindly at where she guessed her would be assassin might be.

"Do not struggle, child. It will make things more difficult."

"Abdel took Bhaal's taint from me," Imoen said, still vainly flailing away at the impenetrable gloom. Her words were punctuated by the swish of her blade as it sliced only air.

"We have plans for that one," the voice assured her.

It sounded as if the assassin was right in her ear. Imoen swore she could feel the hot breath of her killer tickling her skin. But when she thrust her elbow back there was nothing to connect with.

"You may kill me, but Abdel will avenge me. He'll kill you . . . all of you. You have no idea how strong he is." Imoen warned.

"Yes, my pretty young girl, we do. The news of your death will break his warrior spirit."

Imoen felt the blade plunge into her back, skewering vital organs as the assassin struck with uncanny, lethal accuracy. Her screams of agony were nothing but a silent rush of air and a faint gurgle of blood as Sendai mercifully slit her throat.

Chapter Seventeen

Abdel's entire existence had become a world of pain. Fire rained down on him from the sky. It erupted from the ground to consume him. It arced in jets from the fingers of his tormentor to sear and melt his flesh.

Above the roaring blaze he could hear Abazigal's laughter as the scaly skinned mage fed the conflagration devouring Abdel's body and soul.

Then suddenly the fire stopped, winking out of existence. Abdel, his eyes shut tight against the heat, peeked from beneath his blistered lids. Abazigal's body lay beside him on the hard rock of the plateau. The wizard's reptilian head lay several feet away. Standing over them both was Sarevok, the blades on his forearms dripping with the green blood of the mage.

Abdel tried to speak, though he didn't know what he would say. His scorched throat could only manage a feeble cracking cough.

Hampered by his heavy plate armor, Sarevok crouched down with difficulty beside Abdel. "The dragons are returning," he said simply. "Already I see their mighty forms on the horizon. They will rend us limb from limb if we do not escape."

Unable to reply, Abdel could only shake his head. He could hear the shrieking screams of the enraged dragons reverberating across the mountain plateau, growing steadily louder as the wyrms drew ever closer. But he was too badly injured to even stand, let alone attempt the treacherous descent. Sarevok seemed to understand.

"You can escape into Bhaal's realm," the armored warrior explained. "You have done it before, when you killed lasera and Yaga Shura. You are weaker now, and it will be more difficult. You must allow yourself to be drawn here by the essence of Bhaal as it flees Abazigal's dead body. It will lead you to the plane of our father. There your body will be restored, and the dragons cannot follow you."

Too weak to argue, Abdel closed his eyes and tried to do as Sarevok had instructed. He could feel it, a faint tug on his innermost being like a zephyr of wind on a still summer day. Abdel focused on the sensation, and the zephyr became a breeze. The breeze became a gale, the gale a hurricane. Abdel felt his soul snatched up by the roaring spirit wind and opened his eyes in surprise.

For a brief second he was still lying on the ground, the decapitated remains of Abazigal beside him. Sarevok stood several yards away, his body braced to meet the onslaught of the dragons alighting all around them. A pair of taloned feet struck the ground next to Abdel's head. He could smell the terrible scent of the wyrm's fury as it investigated the corpse of its master.

As one, the assembled dragons screamed, but Abdel never heard the sound. The material world had already begun to dissolve.

* * * * *

Abdel found himself prostrate on cool, brown dirt. His body was still covered in burns, but he could feel it healing. Within seconds he felt strong enough to stand.

He was back in the Abyssal realm of Bhaal. The great empty plains still stretched before him, but somehow they looked less barren. The earth was a dark, fertile brown, and in the sky were wisps of what might have been rain clouds beginning to form. Before him stood the familiar free-standing doors, but now they numbered only three.

187

The big sellsword cared little for the magical or mys
tical, but even he could plainly see what was happenin
to this world. With the death of the Bhaalspawn, th
Lord of Murder's essence was returning to the Abyssa
plane from which it had first been born. The dead worl
was slowly being resurrected—though what hideou
forms of life might sprout up in the accursed realm wa
anyone's guess.

He heard the sound of someone walking behind hir
and spun to face his unknown companion. Abdel didn'
know who or what to expect. Had Sarevok followed him
Perhaps it was the spirit of the recently slain Abaziga
whose spirit had led Abdel here. Maybe it was the othe
star-covered being, waiting to taunt him with more mad
dening prophecies or eager to offer more shrouded, secre
tive, useless advice. Whatever awaited him, Abdel wa
ready for anything. Except what he saw.

"Jaheira!"

The half-elf smile at him. "I prayed to Mielikki yo
would come before it was too late," she whispered.

Abdel pulled her close, clutching her to his chest
relentlessly pressing himself into her body as if h
hoped they would become one and he might never los
her again.

"I thought you were dead," he said, tears of relie
streaming down his face.

The druid clung to him as fiercely as he clung to he
but when she spoke her voice was filled with grief. "I ar
dead, Abdel. That is why I am here."

Reluctantly Abdel loosened his grip so that he coul
look into his lover's eyes and see if she was joking. Wha
he saw was a longing so deep it made his heart want t
rend itself in two.

"You . . . are you a ghost?"

She brushed her long, delicate fingers across hi
brow, smoothing out the wrinkles of confusion on Abdel'
forehead. Her touch was warm and soothing. "This is bu

y spirit, my love. My body is no more, though in this
orld my spirit is as real as my physical self was on the
aterial plane."

"No!" Abdel declared, his voice rising in angry denial as
e pulled Jaheira's taut, muscular form tight against his
wn. "No, this cannot be!"

The half-elf nestled her head against Abdel's powerful
est. The subtle scent of his lover's hair filled the sell-
word's lungs.

"It is true, my love," she whispered. "We must accept
and make the most of my time here. I begged Mielikki
grant me this time, but I cannot stay for long. My link to
ou keeps me here, but soon my soul must become one
ith the whole of nature."

Abdel pushed her away, refusing to give up. "No, it
oesn't have to be like this! I brought Sarevok back to life.
can do the same for you!"

Jaheira gently shook her head. "No, Abdel. That cannot
e. I am not a child of Bhaal, I do not possess the same
ssence you and Sarevok share. You cannot give me a
iece of your soul to make me live again."

"Why not?" Abdel demanded. "It might work. It's worth
try." He turned and marched toward the nearest door,
etermined to return to the material plane and reenact
e ritual that had reincarnated Sarevok.

"I beg you, Abdel, stop this madness." The soft pleas of
aheira caused the big sellsword to freeze in midstride.
art of Abdel knew what she was about to say.

"Even if you can perform the ritual to restore me,
hat will that accomplish? You have seen Sarevok. He
s not truly alive anymore. He is a thing, cold and pas-
ionless, without emotion. Is that what you would wish
r me?"

Abdel dropped his head and turned back to face his
ver, desperate tears burning his eyes. "Maybe Sarevok
as like that to begin with. Maybe you will be as you
lways were."

Drew Karpyshyn

With a wan smile, Jaheira walked slowly over to him.
"No, my love. This is not nature's way. My time on that
world has passed, and my time on this one grows short.
Share this time with me, Abdel. Do not waste it with
frantic plans and foolish wishes that cannot be fulfilled.
Let us just enjoy the little time we have left."

She reached out, and her touch caused Abdel's skin to
tingle. His blood boiled with desire, and he reached out
with trembling hands to peel away the simple tunic
Jaheira wore, exposing his lover's breasts before pulling
her close. Jaheira's fingers slid beneath the scraps of his
charred shirt still hanging from his shoulders and
traced a sensuous path down Abdel's powerful back,
caressing his muscles before tearing away the tattered
remains of his breeches.

Abdel took her there, in the soft brown earth of Bhaal's
realm. Their love making was savage and primal, fuelled
by urgent desire and the fierce longing brought on by the
knowledge of their imminent separation. Above them
lightning crackled, and thunder rolled as the skies burst
dousing them with the shock of chill rains that couldn't
quell their desperate passion.

When they were finished, they lay side by side in the
cool mud, letting the downpour wash their bodies clean.

Jaheira snuggled up against Abdel, pressing herself
into the crook of his arm and drawing on her lover's
heat to ease the shivering of her naked form. Physically
spent, exhausted by their furious copulation, Abdel
held his half-elf lover and pretended they would be
together forever.

The rains ceased, and their soaking bodies slowly dried
beneath the empty night sky of the Abyssal plane. How
many hours they spent together taking comfort in the
simple closeness of each other, Abdel could not say. An
eternity would have seemed but an instant to him, no
length of time would ever be enough to justify the unfair
ness of having to ever let his lover go.

It was Jaheira who finally broke their embrace. "I can stay no longer," she apologized as she tried to get up. "I must leave."

Clutching her firmly but gently by the wrist, Abdel kept her from standing. "How can this be?" he asked, staring up into her violet eyes as she crouched overtop of him. "How can I go on without you?"

The half-elf bent to kiss him deep on the lips, then softly pulled herself away.

"You will find a way, Abdel. You must. Do not let my death poison you against the world," the half-elf warned. "If you let hate and regret consume your mind, the foul essence of Bhaal will swallow your soul."

"I don't want to be alone," he whispered.

"You won't always be alone," she assured him. "There will be others. Other friends. Other lovers."

The big sellsword shook his head. "No. Not like you. Never like you."

The half-elf smiled again, though her eyes were sad. "I loved you Abdel, as I loved no other man. But I also loved my husband Khalid as I loved no other man. Someday I hope you will find another to share your love, as I have, but that will not diminish what we have shared."

With a despondent sigh, Abdel rose to stand beside her. "You are my strength and my wisdom, Jaheira. Without you, I am lost. I cannot face the world alone. Without you I am nothing."

"You are Abdel Adrian: hero of Baldur's Gate, savior of the Tree of Life, son of Bhaal, ward of Gorion, lover of Jaheira," the half-elf replied simply. "You are who you are, Abdel, and nothing will change that. The way before you will be difficult, the tunnel of your future is long and dark. But if you remember who and what you are, I am confident you will emerge in the light on the other side."

"Will I ever see you again?" Abdel asked, frightened at what the answer might be.

Jaheira planted a kiss on his chest. Her lips were cold bringing goose bumps to Abdel's exposed skin. "Suc questions not even the gods can answer, my love."

Her voice sounded distant, as if she was speaking t him across a great chasm.

"No!" Abdel cried out reaching to grab hold of his love "No, not yet! Don't go yet!"

His hands passed through Jaheira as if she was noth ing but mist.

"No!" he screamed as the half-elf began to fade awa before his eyes, vanishing like a column of smoke diss pating on the breeze. Her body was dissolving, whiske away by some force Abdel could neither see nor stop no comprehend.

Just before all trace of her features vanished, Jaheir spoke the last words Abdel would ever hear from her lip

"I love you, Abdel Adrian. Forever."

Abdel clutched one last time at the vanishing wisp wind, then collapsed to his knees. Jaheira was gone, an he was alone in his father's realm, sobbing uncontrollabl and clawing at the damp, dark earth in grief and anger.

Chapter Eighteen

The sun had yet to climb high enough to crest the monastery's marble walls, but Melissan was already up. Balthazar had not yet turned up, despite the many reassurances of his followers that his arrival was imminent. Her own extensive investigation of the premises had not turned up the missing monk either. Melissan was beginning to grow suspicious.

She had learned long ago not to trust anyone. Many times the Bhaalspawn she had chosen to save in the past had betrayed her. She had known Balthazar for many years, ever since the Five had first come into existence. He had been her most powerful ally throughout all her efforts. Because of this she consented to allow Imoen to be separated from her when they arrived at Amkethran's monastery. Now, with Balthazar still absent, Melissan had her doubts.

When she discovered the dead guards at the foot of the tower, still standing rigidly in position, it merely confirmed what she had most feared. The tall woman bounded up the steps two at a time, already knowing what she would find at the top of the stairs.

Imoen's throat had been slit and her heart cut out. The mark of the drow assassin Sendai was carved into her forehead. Looking at the gruesome corpse, Melissan knew not even the most powerful cleric in Tethyr would be able to restore Imoen to life. Sendai had defiled her corpse, she had polluted the remains with foul poisons,

and she had sucked what little immortal essenc
remained from Imoen's soul.

Somehow she had done all this right beneath Melis
san's nose. The tall woman knew Sendai was long gon
The drow would never allow herself to be caught abov
ground during the light of day. A shiver ran down the ta
woman's long spine nonetheless. Melissan had not eve
been aware Sendai was on the prowl. There had been n
warning of the slaughter. Melissan knew that could onl
mean one thing.

Balthazar and Sendai were working together, plottin
against her. She whispered a silent curse at not havin
foreseen this outcome. She had grown careless, allowin
herself to believe of all her allies, Balthazar would be th
last to turn on her. She had foolishly thought the monk
could protect Imoen until Abdel returned from destroyin
Abazigal. Imoen had suffered the ultimate consequenc
for Melissan's naive faith in Balthazar's loyalty.

With Imoen dead, Sendai would go after Abdel nex
Once Gorion's ward was slain, the work of the Five would b
all but complete. Their last task before attempting to rais
Bhaal once again, Melissan realized, would be to kill her.

She heard a commotion from down below. Some of th
other monks had discovered the paralyzed corpses
their brethren. Melissan suddenly realized how muc
immediate danger she was in. It was unlikely Balthaza
would be able to corrupt the entire order. They woul
not willingly aid him if they knew he was allied with
drow assassin.

But the monks would never think to question thei
enlightened brother's leadership without blatant proof
his foul betrayal. If Balthazar lied to them, they woul
simply accept his words as truth. If he told them Melissa
was working with the Five, they would accept it as fac
without considering Balthazar's own role in Imoen's deatl
If the monks found her here now, standing over the mut
lated corpse of the one they had sworn to protect . . .

Melissan could hear the sound of many feet cautiously ascending the steps. She was no longer the only one who had noticed the rigid corpses of Brothers Regund and Lysus.

The monks moved warily, expecting to find the enemy who had slain the guards by the door still within the building. She could hear their plodding progress. They moved without urgency, knowing there were no windows in the upper floor, no way out of the tower but the stairs that were now lined with a dozen of the religious warriors.

Cursing herself for not foreseeing Balthazar's treachery, Melissan muttered a quick incantation. Her form shimmered and disappeared, her body and all her clothes and items becoming ethereal. No longer anchored to the material world, Melissan's incorporeal spirit simply passed through the floor, sinking slowly to the ground below. Invisible and unsubstantial, she drifted across the courtyard and through the marble walls, then wandered unseen through the all-but-deserted streets of Amkethran. She did not allow the spell to end until she found a strong mount capable of carrying her swiftly across the desert.

Sendai and Balthazar were working together now, and Melissan did not have the power to stand against them, but Abdel might, if he yet lived.

Melissan was intent on preserving his life if at all possible. She had to try and warn the big sellsword that Sendai would try to kill him. Even now the drow was probably preparing an ambush somewhere between here and the Alimir Mountains where Abazigal made his lair. If Abdel was still alive he would be heading toward Amkethran and right into Sendai's trap.

Knowing the drow already had half the previous night as a head start, Melissan spurred her steed into a quick gallop, leaving the shoddy tents of Amkethran and the imposing marble walls of the monastery far behind.

Drew Karpyshyn

* * * * *

He felt empty and numb. Abdel's grief slipped into the ground and loam beneath his fists. It poured out of him in tears and wails of anguish, and now there was nothing left inside. His spirit was hollow, his naked body an empty shell.

Abdel filled the void with the only thing he had left—thoughts of vengeance. He no longer cared about the fate of his Bhaalspawn kin. It no longer mattered to him if Bhaal returned and ravaged the land, or if the Lord of Murder stayed dead forever. Jaheira's death had liberated him, freed him from the confusion and moral turmoil that came with being at the center of such epic events. Abdel's life had become very, very simple. He would kill the Five for what they had done to Jaheira. Beyond that nothing mattered.

He couldn't avenge her death here, wallowing in the dirt of Bhaal's realm. Abdel Adrian rose to his feet and stepped through the nearest of the three remaining doors.

He found himself alone on the plateau just outside the entrance to Abazigal's lair. By the position of the sun, Abdel guessed he had been gone for several hours, though an entire night had passed in the Abyssal plane. All around him were the signs of a great battle. Abdel stood in the aftermath of Sarevok's confrontation with Abazigal's hoard.

Along with Abazigal's decapitated form, half a dozen great dragon carcasses were strewn about the blood-soaked battlefield. Their corpses were scarred and disfigured by deep, ragged gashes from the blades forged onto Sarevok's arms and legs, or horribly gouged and gored by the terrible spikes jutting from the dark warrior's knees and elbows.

Sarevok himself was gone. Scattered around the dragons' remains were bits and pieces of his armor, rent asunder by mighty talons, or charred and blackened by the fire and acid spewed forth from the jaws of Sarevok's enemies. At Abdel's feet lay the armored warrior's visored helm, cloven nearly in two. There was no sign of Sarevok's body.

Abdel wasn't surprised. The victorious dragons would have devoured the flesh of their defeated foe—if there was even anything to devour. After his encounter with Jaheira's departing soul, Abdel couldn't help but wonder if Sarevok had been anything more than a suit of armor animated by a disembodied spirit. Whatever Sarevok might have been, man or ghost, the evidence of his grisly end was indisputable.

The many fallen corpses of the serpent horde attested to the legendary battle Sarevok must have fought before he succumbed to their overwhelming numbers. Had Abdel's emotions not been purged from his heart by Jaheira's death, he might have shed a tear for Sarevok's noble sacrifice. His half brother had saved his life, slaying Abazigal and then standing alone against the dragons while Abdel had retreated into the safety of Bhaal's nether world.

But Abdel had no more use for legendary heroics. In the bloody aftermath smeared across the plateau, Sarevok was still dead, and the dragons, bereft of their master, were gone.

Yet Abdel lived. He shivered as a cold blast of wind swept across the plateau, and he realized he was naked, his clothes reduced to ashes by Abazigal's fiery magic. He scoured the battlefield, searching for anything to cover his exposed body. In the end, he was forced to strip the bloodstained robe from Abazigal's headless corpse.

The loose-fitting garment barely came down to his knees, and his arms extended well past the cuffs of the sleeves. The hooded cowl was better than wandering around fully exposed. Armed only with the heavy broadsword he had salvaged from the carnage of Sarevok's final stand, Abdel began the long descent back to the mountain's base.

He rested only briefly at the bottom before setting out toward Amkethran. He had only one goal: Find Melissan and demand she lead him to the rest of the Five so that he could extract gruesome vengeance for Jaheira's death.

Based on the directions Melissan had given him, Abdel calculated that Amkethran was a tenday or more due west of the plateau where Abazigal had fallen. There, in the monastery of a man named Balthazar, Melissan and Imoen awaited his arrival. To get to them, Abdel had to pass through the southern arm of the Forest of Mir. Either that or journey several hundred miles to the north or south to circumvent the far reaching woods. Before they had parted ways at Saradush, Melissan had suggested Abdel take one of the longer, safer, routes and avoid the dangerous forest.

It took Abdel less than a day to reach the eastern edge of the Forest of Mir. Beyond its western border lay Amkethran. Driven by the urgency of his need to spill the blood of the Five, Abdel never even considered taking the long way around. He plunged into the dense growth without a second thought.

By the third day he was already regretting his decision. He had reached the Forest of Mir with no difficulty, but once inside the dark wood his progress had slowed to a crawl. Most of his time was spent ripping and tearing branches or smashing his way through thick, thorny underbrush. Abdel was lucky if he covered ten miles in a day. He was beginning to wonder if it would have been quicker to try and go around the almost impassable forest.

At least the legendary lethal denizens of the Forest of Mir never bothered him. Abdel suspected the reports of their existence were highly exaggerated. Or perhaps Abdel's power had become so great that even the foul creatures hiding within the shadows instinctively knew to avoid a confrontation with the strange intruder to their world.

Cursing his slow progress and his own stupid refusal to follow Melissan's advice, Abdel pressed onward through the dense trees.

* * * * *

Abazigal would fail. Sendai knew this, just as she knew the half-dragon's arrogance was nothing but a front to hide his true self, a simpering mongrel so disgusted with his own existence he sought salvation by trying to become something else entirely. The drow knew of the mage's ludicrous plan to unite the dragons of Faerûn. She knew of his ridiculous dream of becoming a pure-blood wyrm, and she knew such a pathetic creature would be incapable of slaying Bhaal's avatar.

Abdel Adrian would kill Abazigal, then would set off to reunite with his sniveling half sister at Amkethran, unaware that Sendai had already devoured the young woman's still-beating heart. Just as she would devour Abdel's own.

She had ridden fast and far since murdering Imoen, traveling under cover of night and seeking shelter from the accursed sun during the day. She was anxious to reach the cover of the Forest of Mir before Abdel found his way through the dense woods. It was there beneath the comforting darkness of the thick branches that she wanted to set her ambush for the last remaining Bhaalspawn. Even so, it had taken her nearly four nights to reach the eastern edge and find the narrow, overgrown path she sought out.

The road between Abazigal's enclave and Amkethran was little used, but Sendai suspected Abdel would find it. The trail, ill kept and treacherous as it was, provided the only viable path through the Forest of Mir's southern arm. If Abdel was heading directly from Abazigal's enclave in the Alimir Mountains toward Amkethran he was sure to stumble across this path at some point.

Unaware of the events that had transpired at the monastery, Abdel would suspect nothing as he journeyed toward Amkethran. If all went as Sendai planned, he would charge headlong into her ambush. With Gorion's ward disposed of, she and Balthazar could then turn their attention to getting rid of Melissan.

The drow worked quickly, littering the narrow forest path with snares and trip wires and making liberal use of her arsenal of poisons. She had chosen a spot several miles along the path, well within the dark confines of the Forest of Mir. Here the thick shadows cast by the tightly packed trees blocking out the sun made her work easier. Hiding her traps was often as simple as tossing a handful of dirt over the trigger or burying her work beneath a pile of deadfall.

She spent nearly a full day setting her ambush, then retreated into the upper recesses of the branches that overhung the trail to wait for her prey.

* * * * *

Abdel couldn't even see the midday sun through the thick, overlapping growth of the trees that pressed in on him from all sides. The Forest of Mir was every bit as dense, dark, and foreboding as the legends had led Abdel to believe. Yesterday he had been fortunate enough to stumble across a path heading in the general direction of Amkethran.

After three days of slow, plodding progress through the undergrowth, Abdel was determined to make up for lost time, but the pervasive gloom, even here on the path someone had blazed through the wood, still hampered his progress. As he raced along the narrow trail he was constantly tripping over roots hidden in the oppressive gloom.

His eyes straining to pierce the darkness, Abdel never saw the trip wire stretched across his path. He felt the faint tug as his leg tore through the string, he heard the sharp snap of a spring uncoiling, and he felt the stinging bite as a dozen tiny darts pierced the thick cloth of his robe and embedded themselves in his right thigh.

His leg went instantly numb, causing him to fall forward onto the small spikes hidden beneath a pile of leaves. A dozen tiny points jabbed through his cowl and into the flesh of his torso, and he felt the corrosive toxin coating the spikes as it began to dissolve his skin.

He rolled to the side and ended up on his back, his hands frantically swatting at the circles of burning pain slowly spreading out from the puncture wounds in his chest and abdomen. He heard the crack of dry wood, and the ground disappeared beneath him.

Abdel lashed out with a single hand and managed to grab the edge of the pit as he fell. For a second he simply dangled above the unseen bottom, imagining what atrocities lay in wait beneath him. He could faintly hear the clatter of the sticks and dry branches that had camouflaged the yawning trap as they struck the pit floor far below.

He heaved himself up and out of the trap. He tried to stand, but his paralyzed leg gave way, and he staggered forward. The noose tightened around his left ankle, and snatched his good leg out from beneath him. Abdel found himself hanging upside down, the robe draping down to cover his head and face and exposing the rest of his body.

As he struggled to tear the cowl off so he could see, his body was peppered with tiny jolts of pain. Dozens of darts from an unseen assailant buried themselves beneath his skin. Abdel felt his struggles growing weaker, his arms and shoulders growing as numb as his leg. Within seconds, he was unable to move at all. The robe slipped from his head and fell to the forest floor below.

A slim figure in black dropped down from the branches above, landing lightly on the ground a few feet away. Even though he was looking at her upside down, Abdel could clearly see she had the sharp, pointed features of an elf. Her skin was the color of ash. He tried to mouth the word "drow," but the paralyzing poison from the darts still protruding from his body had rendered him completely immobile.

The drow moved toward him and pulled a runed dagger from her belt. Abdel recognized the symbols—he had seen them on the axe of Yaga Shura and the arrows of Illasera. This dark elf was one of the Five.

Abdel tried to swing himself around so he could cut himself down, but his muscles refused to respond. He couldn't even make his fingers twitch, he couldn't even scream out his frustration. One of the Five was less than ten feet away, and he could do nothing.

Images of violence and unbridled savagery filled his mind. He envisioned himself ripping the thin elf limb from limb. He imagined his sword splitting her skull and spraying gray matter across the thick trunks of the nearby trees. He fantasized about slicing open her stomach and watching her clutch feebly at her guts as they spilled out and onto the forest underbrush. His imaginings aside, Abdel simply hung from the noose like meat on a hook, swaying slightly from side to side.

With a quick swipe of her blade Abdel's captor cut him loose. His body dropped like a stone. Unable to even roll his shoulders to absorb his fall, Abdel slammed onto the ground, landing facedown.

The fires of Bhaal's fury began to rise within Abdel's soul. Instead of quelling the flames as he had so often done, Abdel stoked the embers of hatred into an inferno of madness raging inside his impotent body.

Crouching beside Abdel's motionless form, the drow rolled him over to stare into the eyes of her helpless victim.

"Imoen shares your fate," she whispered, determined to deliver a cruel blow to Abdel's heart before she delivered the slash to his throat. "I killed her myself."

Though his throat was frozen in silence, Abdel's mind screamed in protest. Not Imoen, too! Jaheira's death had ripped his soul bare. He thought the pain he felt from his lover's loss was infinite. But the knowledge that Imoen now lay dead as well, shredded new wounds in his spirit. The unbearable suffering—a pain within his heart greater than any physical injury he had ever sustained—grew even worse. Gorion, Jaheira, and Imoen. Their blood was on Abdel's hands.

The drow continued to speak, but Abdel no longer even comprehended her words. Consumed by the burning darkness of Bhaal, the part of his being that was Abdel Adrian was gone. Only the vile essence of the Lord of Murder remained. As it had done once while under the spells of the sorcerer Irenicus, Abdel's body began to change. This time he urged it onward. His bones cracked, and his skin burst apart, unable to contain a skeleton four times the size of Abdel's own. His hands became claws, his head a hideous combination of mandibles and teeth. Two more arms exploded from his chest, their taloned fingers ripping and slashing at the air. His skin formed a hard, chitinous exoskeleton. The Ravager had been unleashed on Faerûn once more.

The transformation was instantaneous. Where Abdel had once been, only an abomination remained, lying prone on its back beneath the twisted branches overhead. Sendai leaped back in horrified surprise, her finely honed instincts for self preservation saving her from a quick and violent death.

The drow didn't wait to see if the creature was mobile but vanished into the trees, fleeing for her life. It was too late for her. The thing that now lay on the forest floor was not a creature of the mortal world, it was not affected by the paralyzing toxins Sendai had pumped into Abdel's body, and it was much, much quicker than the drow.

Sendai's lithe form flitted in and out among the thick trunks and sturdy branches of the trees. Her desperate flight was hampered by the dense woods, but if anything the enormous creature behind her would find its own progress even more difficult. The heavy forest growth would help hide her from the monster's sight as she fled without a sound.

The Ravager didn't need to hear or see her to track her. It could smell her, as it could smell all living things. The great demon leaped up from the forest floor, smashing its head and shoulders through the canopy of leaves and twigs hanging in its path. It caught the drow's scent and bounded off in pursuit.

While the drow was forced to weave in and out between the trees, the Ravager took a more direct route. Crashing through the undergrowth, it left a wide path of shattered stumps, uprooted trees and trampled vegetation in its wake. The horrendous thunder of its pursuit could be heard throughout the Forest of Mir, sending birds, game animals, and far more monstrous beasts scurrying for cover. The terrible din was only cut short by the shrieks of Sendai as the beast ran her down.

The Ravager ripped Sendai apart with its four arms, bathing in her blood and reveling in her suffering as it tore her into tiny bits. The beast gorged itself on her spewing innards, then cast the drow's physical shell aside as it sensed the invisible essence of Bhaal that wafted up from the corpse like the scent of rotting evil.

Abdel Adrian found himself in his human form again, standing once more in the Abyssal realm of Bhaal.

* * * * *

Balthazar sat motionless in the secret uppermost room of the monastery's central tower. It was nothing more than a tiny chamber completely surrounded by the thick marble of the tower's roof. There were no doors or windows, no physical entrances or exits whatsoever. Accessible only through the mystical passages of an enlightened mind, the room was Balthazar's inner sanctum, inviolate and impregnable. Even his own disciples were unable to enter—only he had mastered the mental discipline that enabled him to transport his physical body through solid rock and into the secluded meditation chamber.

He needed no food or water. He did not even require air. His body had reached a state of purity, a state of awareness and existence far beyond the physical consciousness that bound all the world in chains they could not even see.

Balthazar had already been in his hibernation chamber a full day before Melissan had arrived with the girl Imoen, though time had little meaning in his current state. He remained there while Sendai had slit the Bhaalspawn's throat and didn't move when Melissan made her escape. He was still there now, focusing his mind in preparation for the battle to come.

From here, he could see and hear events across the entire continent: the secrets of Waterdeep nobles plotting in their high towers; the clandestine whispers of Amnian adulterers huddling beneath the sheets at a seedy inn; the laughter of Sembian commoners in a tavern; the prayers of a Daleland widower by his wife's grave. The screams of a dying drow in the Forest of Mir.

They were only two now—Abdel and Balthazar, last of the Bhaalspawn. Soon there would be only one. Melissan had become inconsequential to their destiny. Bhaal's Anointed had become irrelevant. Melissan still had her part to play, but it was a minor role. She would send Abdel after Balthazar. They would fight. Balthazar would kill him. And this would all be over.

Chapter Nineteen

As he stood in the plane of the Abyss that had once been the home of Bhaal, Abdel could remember becoming the Ravager. He remembered the sensation of his body transforming, becoming the demon. He remembered rushing through the forest, hunting the fleeing drow. He remembered ripping into Sendai's soft, yielding form with his claws, the glorious taste of death on his teeth and tongue. The memories were distant and faint, as if they were not his own. He had not done those things. Abdel Adrian was not responsible for the bloody slaughter. It had been the Ravager.

"But you unleashed the Ravager." The being that had confronted him in the past materialized before him once more, its infinite voice once again responding to thoughts he had not spoken aloud.

Abdel ignored the creature before him and turned his attention to the doors that would lead him away from this place and back to the material plane where he could resume his quest to avenge Jaheira's death. There were only two doors now.

"As you slay each of the Five, the potential fates of you and your kin become fewer."

Interesting, but not interesting enough to keep Abdel from leaving.

"Beware, Abdel Adrian," the annoying creature warned. "You risk losing yourself to the Ravager. It cannot be controlled. It will devour you from within even as it devours your enemies."

The big sellsword spun to face the being preaching at him. "I don't care!" he spat in anger. "As long as it lets me kill the Five, I don't care what happens to me!"

The being shook its glorious head. "Abdel, I fear for your future—and the future of Abeir-toril. There is so much you do not know. So much I would tell you, were it not forbidden by the power I serve."

"There is nothing you can say that would affect me now," Abdel assured his host with a sneer. "You cannot bring back Jaheira, or Imoen, or even Gorion. My Bhaal blood has brought only suffering and loss. There is no hope for me, no chance for happiness. All I have left is my vengeance."

"Your bitterness is understandable, Abdel. But suffering and loss are a part of existence—mortal or immortal. Your words dishonor the memories of those who have walked by your side down the path of your destiny. Learn from their examples."

"Learn? Learn what?" Abdel made no effort to hide the scorn in his voice.

"Sarevok showed you the potential for redemption."

"And now he is dead."

"Jaheira saved you through the power of her love."

"And now she is dead."

"Gorion sacrificed himself so that you might achieve your destiny."

"And he too is dead. Is that the lesson you would have me learn? Death? I know that lesson all too well, my starry friend, and I intend to share this learning with each and every one of the Five."

His adversary changed tactics. "There is only one of the Five left," it said. "Kill him and the blood of Bhaal will survive only in you."

Abdel shrugged. "So my work is almost done." He turned and stepped through the door.

As the plane of Bhaal dissolved away, he heard the infinite voice call out, "There is more to your destiny than mere vengeance, Abdel. I pray you are ready for what will come."

* * * * *

Melissan found Abdel along the sole path cutting through the southern arm of the Forest of Mir, less than a mile away from the western edge of the woods. The big sell sword was wearing only a hooded cowl that seemed at least two sizes too small for his massive frame. In one hand he carried a heavy broadsword. In the other he held Sendai's dagger, its blade easily recognizable by the arcane symbols etched upon its surface. His body was covered in blood and gore, his feet were bare, and he was traveling on foot.

"Praise the gods you yet live!" the Melissan exclaimed as she pulled up her mount beside him. "I came to warn that an assassin hunts you. One of the Five."

"The drow is dead," Abdel said simply. "And the lizard man."

"Abazigal and Sendai are both . . ." Melissan muttered then seemed to catch herself at the last second and changed topics in midsentence. "We have been betrayed Abdel. Imoen is dead."

"I know." Abdel was surprised at how much the words still hurt, even now. The mere mention of his half sister's demise was like a knife twisting in his heart. "Tell me what happened."

"We sought sanctuary in Amkethran's monastery. The monks welcomed us, invited us in, and promised to protect us. They took Imoen to the central tower to guard her but by morning she was dead."

"The drow assassin," Abdel guessed.

Melissan nodded. "Sendai was her name. But I fear there is a yet more sinister explanation behind Imoen's death. The leader of the monastery—a monk named Balthazar—I believe he was working with Sendai. I think . . . I think he is the last of the Five, Abdel.

"I cannot say if the other monks know of his secret. I doubt they do. They serve their master absolutely, completely oblivious to his true nature."

The big sellsword bit his lip hard enough to draw blood. He felt Melissan wasn't telling him everything. She was still holding something back, she still kept her secrets well guarded. It was obvious she had known about Sendai and failed to warn either Abdel or Imoen about the drow. Abdel didn't care what games Melissan was playing anymore. She had told him more than enough.

"Give me your horse," he demanded. "I want to be fresh when I reach Amkethran."

He thought Melissan would try to dissuade him or suggest some type of plan other than a frontal assault. At the very least he thought she might even offer her help. Instead she only said, "Good luck, Abdel."

* * * * *

Abdel leaped from his horse once he reached the tents and ramshackle mud buildings of Amkethran. He ripped the cowl from his body—he wanted nothing to slow him down when he faced Balthazar. The sight of a naked, seven-foot-tall, heavily muscled man drenched in dried blood and wielding a heavy broadsword in one hand and a cruel, rune covered dagger in the other sent the few people he encountered scurrying for cover.

The great iron doors of the monastery were barred against him, but Abdel ripped them from their hinges. With each death of the Five he had become stronger and more powerful, growing ever closer to his father's immortal existence. Abdel believed he now had the strength to smash right through the marble walls if necessary.

He stepped through the torn gates and was immediately attacked by an army of the monastery's guardians. The warrior monks fought without weapons, delivering lightning-fast kicks to his knees, punching their fists in a blur at his throat, driving their knees to his groin. Their attacks would have shattered the bones of any mortal.

Abdel shrugged off the blows as meaningless. He slashed out with his sword and Sendai's dagger, driving the monks back as they dodged his cuts and stabs or fell injured to the ground. But he didn't follow up his initial attacks. His efforts were merely meant to clear a path through the mob. The deaths of these mindless followers of Balthazar were inconsequential to Abdel, and pursuing the injured to finish them off would only cost him precious time.

Had he wished for slaughter, it would have been a simple task to unleash the Ravager on his enemies. But the demon lusted only for indiscriminate death, it cared nothing for Abdel's desire for revenge. If Abdel set the Ravager free now, Balthazar might escape unnoticed in the ensuing carnage. So Abdel quelled the rising fire of his father's evil, and he pressed on with grim, passionless determination.

The monks threw themselves at him, willing—even eager—to sacrifice themselves to halt his progress, but their adversary was immune to their fists and feet. Despite their overwhelming numbers and despite the fact that Abdel couldn't even be bothered to kill them, they were unable to slow his relentless advance toward the tall tower in the center of the compound.

Somehow Abdel knew Balthazar was inside the tower. He could sense the taint of Bhaal on his quarry glowing like a beacon, calling to the evil taint within his own soul. He continued to swat away the pestering gnats who rained blow after blow down on his invulnerable body, his eyes focused intently on the tower's heavily guarded entrance.

Two figures emerged from the door, their arms weaving strange patterns in the air and their voices chanting unfamiliar sounds that rang out above the din of battle. These mages were sent to stop him where the warriors had failed. The crush of humanity surrounding Abdel fel back, anxious to avoid the effects of the spells about to be unleashed upon him.

Fire erupted all around him, the flames engulfing his body. Lightning flashed down from the sky to split his skull. Clouds of noxious fumes obscured his vision. Walls of ice materialized before him. Enchanted arrows appeared from nowhere to unerringly strike his body, splashing corrosive acid across his skin wherever they hit.

Abdel's stride never faltered. The magic of Abazigal had nearly ended his existence, but with the death of the half-dragon and the drow Sendai, Abdel had evolved yet again. The magically summoned elements of the mages were as ineffective as the physical blows of the warrior monks. Abdel was an unstoppable messenger of death.

The mages stepped aside, and a single, black-skinned figure stood in the tower's entrance. Like Abdel, this man was naked—though it was difficult to tell. His ebony skin was covered head to toe in tattoos. The colors and designs seemed to shift and writhe beneath the man's dark flesh, as if the symbols were alive with power. Though nearly a foot shorter than Abdel, the tattooed man's body similarly rippled with knotted, corded muscle.

The tattooed man called out, "Stop! This is not your battle."

Bowing respectfully, the warrior monks and mages alike stepped back and cleared a path for Abdel to approach. Not even caring if it was a trap, Abdel rushed at the black-skinned man, certain he was none other than Balthazar.

The man disappeared inside the door, and Abdel followed. As he leaped across the threshold he heard the horrible shriek of stone being warped and twisted. Glancing back over his shoulder, Abdel wasn't surprised to find the door had been magically sealed behind him, the rock of the tower walls closing over the opening.

He turned his attention back to the tower's interior. At the far end was a steep staircase leading to the second

Drew Karpyshyn

floor, but otherwise the first floor was empty. It resembled an arena, or perhaps a training ring. In the center of this circle stood the black-skinned Balthazar.

"This must end here," the monk said, his voice neither threatening nor afraid. "This must end now."

Abdel couldn't have agreed more.

Chapter Twenty

Abdel rushed the monk. Balthazar waited until his enemy was nearly on him, then turned to the side. His left hand slapped the tip of the thrusting broadsword down and away from his body. His right forearm smacked the wrist of Abdel's left hand, redirecting the path of Sendai's dagger as it sliced down from above. His leg shot out, tripping Abdel's feet so that the charging sellsword's momentum carried him stumbling past Balthazar to slam into the hard stone of the far wall.

Unharmed but burning with angry embarrassment at his foolishly ineffective attack, Abdel spun around to face his opponent once more. Balthazar still stood in the very center of the room, casually awaiting Abdel's next move.

"You do understand why your death must come to pass?" he asked nonchalantly.

"I know you want to bring Bhaal back to life, but that's not why I'm here."

With that Abdel rushed forward again, crouching low and keeping his feet wide, bringing his center of gravity close to the ground. This time the monk wouldn't be able to redirect his momentum with a simple twist of his body.

Balthazar also crouched down, then sprang up into the air as Abdel approached, flipping and twisting above the head of his surprised opponent. Balthazar's left heel caught Abdel in the back of his skull, momentarily stunning him. The monk's right foot delivered a stiff kick in the middle of Abdel's back, sending him sprawling face down on the hard floor.

Abdel flopped on his stomach gasping for breath. His head and back stung from Balthazar's kicks—he could already feel his body beginning to swell and bruise from the vicious blows. Unlike the army of monks he had waded through in the courtyard, Balthazar was able to inflict real injury.

It was the tattoos, Abdel realized. Like the runes on the weapons of the other members of the Five, the designs and symbols covering the arms and legs of Balthazar gave him the power to harm Abdel's body. Knowing he was vulnerable forced Abdel to change his tactics. He would have to approach with more caution. Slowly Abdel rose and turned to face the monk again.

Balthazar had landed nimbly on his feet after his gravity-defying maneuver and stood once again in the center of the room. He continued the conversation as if nothing had happened.

"I have no intention of bringing Bhaal back to life," the monk explained. "The evil of Bhaal must be purged from Faerûn forever, Abdel. His taint must be wiped from the face of Abeir-toril. That is why you must die."

The sound of Abdel's bitter laugh echoed off the stone walls encircling them. "I know you are one of the Five! You hunted your own Bhaalspawn kin so that you might use their essence to resurrect our father!"

"I was one of the Five," Balthazar admitted as Abdel cautiously approached, his twin blades weaving hypnotic patterns in the air, "though I never shared their vision. They wanted to bring Bhaal back, and I want to ensure he stays dead forever. Killing those who shared our tainted blood was common to both their end and mine, so I aided them in the hunting of the Bhaalspawn. But all along I intended to betray them at the end, Abdel."

Abdel was barely even listening to the lies spilling from his enemy's mouth. He wouldn't let the words distract him from the task at hand. If the monk wanted to jabber away while the sellsword inched ever closer, Abdel would let him speak—until he silenced Balthazar by slitting his throat.

Although he rarely fought with a weapon in each hand, Abdel knew how to use twin blades to maximize his offensive advantage. He led with a series of high offensive thrusts and slashes from the broadsword, designed to drive the monk back and throw him off balance. He'd follow up by stabbing the dagger in toward his foe's kidney, forcing him to turn away from the tiny blade—and right into the heavy edge of the broadsword cutting down from the other side.

Something went wrong, Balthazar did not retreat beneath the first savage assault. He parried the sword with his bare left hand, turning his wrist so that the palm met the flat of the blade and deflected its arc harmlessly away. Abdel's second thrust was similarly met and turned aside. In desperation he tried to bring the dagger up, but a stiff kick from Balthazar's leg caught him in the elbow and knocked the knife from his numb grasp.

Balthazar ducked down and away from what Abdel had expected to be the finishing blow, letting the heavy broadsword slice harmlessly through the air less than an inch above his head. Before Abdel could reverse the momentum of his attack he was doubled over by a knee slamming into his groin. An instant later he was straightened up as the knee slammed into his chin.

Blinded by stars of pain, Abdel never saw the rapid flurry of punches to his midsection, though he did feel several of his ribs crack in quick succession. He felt a pair of firm hands wrap themselves around his wrist and heave on his arm, and Abdel was hurled through the air to land hard on his back.

"As long as even a single drop of Bhaal-tainted blood courses through living veins, there is a chance someone will find a way to bring Bhaal back to life," Balthazar calmly explained, not even breathing heavily after their confrontation. "Like all the other Bhaalspawn, you have the taint of Bhaal within you, and you must be killed for the good of the world."

The ceiling slowly came into focus as Abdel's vision cleared. His left hand was paralyzed. He couldn't even clench his fingers into a fist. Every breath brought agonizing pain as his cracked rib cage was forced to expand and contract. He coughed and choked as a trickle of blood crawled up his throat. He could feel his body struggling to restore itself, fighting to overcome the powerful sorcery contained in every punch and kick Balthazar delivered. His body *was* healing—slowly.

"What about you?" Abdel croaked, stalling for time. "You are also a Bhaalspawn. Must you die for your tainted blood?"

"I have learned to control the evil within me, Abdel," Balthazar replied. "These markings on my body contain my vile essence with powerful magics. I have devoted my entire life to mastering the mental discipline that enables me to keep Bhaal's fury caged within my body and soul. But as long as I live," the monk continued, "there will be those who would seek to release what I have worked so hard to imprison. The chances of them succeeding are infinitesimal, but even that risk is too great. Once you are dead, Abdel, I also must die. We are the last two. With your death and my ritual suicide we will forever free the world from the threat of Bhaal's return."

The bones in Abdel's chest were mending. He could feel sensation and strength returning to the fingers of his left hand. Throughout the savage beating he had managed to hang on to his broadsword, but he still needed a few more seconds.

"You're mad, Balthazar."

"That is an inevitable consequence of who and what we both are," the monk said. "Bhaal's essence brings madness and death. No matter how we try to avoid it, no matter our intentions, we cannot help but manifest the darkest of our father's traits. And all those around us suffer."

His body was whole once more, but Abdel did not leap up to attack right away. Something in Balthazar's words rang true. Had not Abdel always been a harbinger of death and suffering? How many men and women had he slain in his career as a blade for hire? Hundreds? Thousands?

There were those who sought to turn him away from a life of bloodshed. Those who loved him despite his violent nature. Gorion, Jaheira, and what had become of them? Dead, like Imoen, and like Sarevok, like everyone he came in contact with.

"Is there no way to rid ourselves of Bhaal's taint?" Abdel asked, praying Balthazar would give him an answer that offered even the faintest glimmer of hope before he ended the monk's existence.

"The curse of our father cannot be avoided." Balthazar's voice was somber, even regretful. "Many of our kin simply submitted to Bhaal's foulness and let the essence consume them. Sarevok was once one of those. The other members of the Five were also of that kind. Others tried to resist the Lord of Murder's darkness, as you and I have done. But we are doomed to failure. Despite our efforts, death follows in our wake. Our footsteps are left in a trail of blood, Abdel. Even I, with all my training, have not been able to resist the killing urges of Bhaal."

The implications of Balthazar's words were too much for Abdel to bear. If the monk was right, Jaheira's death was his fault. His unholy heritage had doomed her from the start. Abdel wouldn't accept that. He couldn't. How could he avenge her death if he was the one to blame?

He clung to his vengeance like a drowning man to a rope tossed from the shore. It was all he had left, the only thing that could fill the emptiness inside. The Five had killed Jaheira, not he, and the Five would pay.

Abdel leaped to his feet, struggling to keep the inferno inside from overwhelming him. He didn't want to release the Ravager. Not unless he had to. He wanted the pleasure of killing Balthazar himself.

This time Abdel came in slowly, giving his opponent a wide berth as he circled. In their first confrontations Abdel had been the aggressor. Each time he had lunged in Balthazar had countered by using the big sellsword's aggressiveness and momentum against him.

Abdel was about to turn the tables on his enemy, taking away his advantage. This time, Abdel would wait for the monk to make the first move. For several long seconds Abdel held his ground, staying well out of range. Waiting, hoping to lure his opponent in.

Balthazar took the offensive. The monk came straight at him, moving fast. He came in low, trying to sweep Abdel's legs out from under him. Abdel leaped back and brought his sword chopping down with both hands to cleave Balthazar's skull. The monk was already gone, twisting and spinning clear of the blade.

Abdel tried to retreat and reset himself. Balthazar had moved in too close for him to use his weapon effectively. The monk pressed forward, refusing to give Abdel the space he needed. A fist to the jaw, an elbow to the throat, a spinning roundhouse kick to the temple and Abdel collapsed groggily to one knee. A knee to the face, and Abdel's nose exploded in a bloody geyser.

He thrust out blindly with his broadsword, hoping to get lucky. Balthazar seized his wrist, braced Abdel's arm and snapped it backward at the elbow, shattering the joint. Abdel screamed in pain and tried to roll clear. He came to his feet just in time to feel Balthazar's foot driving through the side of his knee, dislocating it and ripping the ligaments and tendons from the bone now protruding just beneath Abdel's thigh.

Balthazar stepped back, leaving his crippled opponent writhing on the floor. "Even now I relish the pain I am inflicting," he said, almost by way of apology. "We cannot deny what we are Abdel, no matter how much we try. I suppose that is why Bhaal's Anointed recruited you to eliminate the Five. No matter which side eventually triumphed, Bhaal's evil would still reign supreme in the victor's soul. When this is all over, Bhaal's Anointed can use that evil to resurrect the Lord of Murder."

Abdel shook his head, trying to ignore the all consuming agony of his two mangled limbs while he struggled to follow the words of Balthazar. "Bhaal's Anointed?" he asked, gritting his teeth against the pain.

The monk gave him a sympathetic smile. "You have no idea, do you? You are a pawn, Abdel. A puppet on a string. Melissan has been manipulating you this whole time."

Chapter Twenty-One

Melissan breathed deep of the dank, musty air as she slowly walked toward the abandoned temple. It smelled of empty decay and rotting death—a smell she had become all too familiar with over the last thirty years. Beneath the stale, fetid stench she caught a hint of something else: smoke and fire. The scent of burning hatred, the perfume of violent, living, palpable fury. She smiled.

After giving Abdel her horse, she had been forced to journey here on foot. The trip had taken many days, but that was a minor inconvenience when compared to the decades she had been patiently waiting, and now her patience was about to be rewarded. The hot glow of the flames bathed her body as she entered the door and gazed up at the grinning skull that was the symbol of her god. She felt the heat from the flames lick her skin, caressing her tingling flesh as Bhaal himself had done while he had walked the land before the Time of Troubles.

The inferno in the pit flared up as she approached, as if the collected essence of the dead god burning within recognized her: Melissan, High Priestess of the Lord of Murder, Bhaal's Anointed. Long ago, Melissan had enacted the sacrifices and gruesome rituals that fed her god's hungers. She had led Bhaal's followers in bloody devotion, slaying enemies and victims alike and tossing their bodies and souls onto the evil, eternal fire at the center of the temple.

For her faith, Bhaal had rewarded her with the secrets of ascension so that she might bring the Lord of Murder back to life after his inevitable death. The time for the ritual had come, the essence of Bhaal's offspring had been collected through the Five's war of bloody sacrifice. All was ripe for the dead god's return.

But Melissan now had other plans. The tall woman slowly removed the fine chain mesh she wore over her clothes and let it drop to the floor. She removed her silver gloves and boots and peeled off her long black sleeves and her tight leggings. She stripped away the tight black cloth undergarments that clung to the curves of her shapely form, revealing the horribly disfigured skin beneath. Thirty years ago, Bhaal's anointing baptism of fire had burned his mark onto every inch of her body, except her face, leaving her flesh a mass of ugly, twisted scar tissue that would never heal.

She had undergone the transformation willingly, knowing the rewards would be well worth the suffering when the time for retribution came, and that time was nearly at hand.

Melissan, naked and exposed, stepped into the roaring blaze at the center of Bhaal's temple. The torment was bearable. Temperatures beyond the scope of mortal fathoming incinerated her spirit, though her mutilated, repulsive body was unharmed. The shrieks of tortured souls, the Bhaalspawn trapped within the conflagration, flooded her ears, splitting her eardrums and piercing her brain.

She welcomed the pain. She embraced it, and the hellish fire embraced her in return. Orange fingers crept up her skin, crawling inside her mouth and nostrils like a living entity seeking to devour her from the inside out. The flames engulfed her, slowly and painfully purging her mortal existence and opening the way for Melissan's own ascension to immortality.

"This must stop!"

Instinctively, Melissan had closed her eyes as she had entered the sacred fire. At the sound of a seeming multitude of voices speaking in unison, they popped open.

Through the hazy orange veil of dancing flames she saw an enormous figure towering over her, its head nearly scraping against the roof of Bhaal's temple. It spread its massive black, celestial robe, dwarfing the naked woman. Melissan recognized this being—a solar, servant and messenger of Ao, the strange being that ruled over even the gods themselves.

Despite the all-consuming heat, Melissan trembled.

"This is not permitted!" the being warned. "You cannot do this." But the creature made no move to intercede. It stood motionless while the ascension ritual progressed, taking no action to disrupt the sacrament.

Melissan's fear slowly vanished as the truth dawned on her. This was no divine guardian of fate and destiny, no all-powerful entity sent to smite her down. This was a mere projection, a harmless spirit from another plane.

"You have no place here!" she screamed above the roaring conflagration. "And you have no power here!"

"A mortal may not ascend in Bhaal's place," the creature stated ominously. "Only one of Bhaal's lineage must be permitted to fulfill this destiny."

"What of Cyric?" Melissan challenged. "Was he not a mortal who ascended to the pantheon?"

"Cyric was a mistake," the entity admitted, "an exception that will not be permitted a second time."

"Then unleash the wrath of your master upon me," Melissan dared, made bold by her knowledge of the history of Faerûn. Only once in recorded memory had Ao ever intervened in the events of Abeir-toril, during the Time of Troubles. But that era was over, and Ao had long since retreated once more into the mists of philosophical legend.

When nothing happened Melissan cackled with mad relief. She had called the solar's bluff and she had won.

"Your master is as disinterested as ever. Soon Balthazar will kill Abdel, or perhaps the other way around. It makes no matter. With either death I will gain access to enough of Bhaal's immortal essence to begin my transformation."

222

Powerless to intervene, unable to even dispute Melissan's bold words, the solar simply vanished.

The triumphant laugh of Melissan reverberated off the walls of the abandoned temple. The sacred fire intensified, and Melissan felt her flesh begin to melt. Her laughter turned to screams as her body turned to ash.

Melissan found herself standing in Bhaal's Abyssal realm. Her physical body was gone, devoured by the flames raging in the center of Bhaal's temple back on the material plane. Here in this nether realm she had form once again. She was beautiful once more, the scars and disfigurements of her initiation as Bhaal's Anointed had been cleansed from her body. She ran her fingers in wonder over her now-smooth, unblemished skin, marveling at her own perfection.

The heavy rumble of thunder drew her attention skyward. Above her dark clouds roiled and churned, riding the chill wind. Stretching as far as she could see in every direction was dark, rich earth. The gathering essence of Bhaal had brought malevolent life back to the sterile void. The Abyssal plane was now ripe with potential, simply waiting for a powerful hand to shape its growth.

Closing her eyes and tilting her head back, Melissan raised her arms and began a soft chant. In response the ground began to tremble, and the soil began to bubble and burst as tendrils of diseased vegetation struggled into existence, crawling across the dirt to fawn at the feet of Bhaal's Anointed. Mountains of stone erupted like jagged teeth on the horizon, encircling the realm with a forbidding, impassable border.

Melissan opened her eyes to witness the rapid terra-forming of what she already considered her domain. This world obeyed her every whim and desire, yet something was lacking. Melissan felt the power of Bhaal's immortal essence pulsing through the ground at her feet. It hung like a static charge in the air. She was able to bend that essence to her will, but she herself was not yet part of that essence. She was still a mortal in a god's realm.

It was only then that she noticed the single door, standing without walls or frame in the middle of the world. Cautious and curious, the mortal who would be a god approached the odd portal.

Chapter Twenty-Two

"Melissan has been using you, Abdel," Balthazar patiently explained to his helpless opponent. "Perhaps she suspected the Five now saw her as no longer necessary and were plotting against her. Perhaps she learned of my desire to betray her cause. Or perhaps she simply realized the Five were becoming too powerful for her to control.

"Whatever the reason, she played us off against each other. When you came to Saradush she manipulated you into killing Yaga Shura, and she tricked Gromnir into opening the gates of the besieged town. In one fell swoop she slaughtered nearly all the remaining Bhaalspawn and managed to turn you against the Five."

Balthazar paused to gauge Abdel's reaction. The crippled warrior shook his head in denial. "No," he said through gritted teeth, "I don't believe you."

"What you believe does not matter. Once we are both dead there will be none of Bhaal's offspring left for Melissan to manipulate, no one to listen to her promises of glory, and no way for Melissan to bring the Lord of Murder back to life."

The pain from his demolished joints made cogent thought difficult for Abdel. Balthazar had to be lying, but why? What could the monk possibly gain by spinning such a web of deceit? The big sellsword shook his head, trying to clear away the indecision. Unraveling Melissan's role in the events of his recent life would have to wait.

Abdel pushed his confusion down, burying it beneath simpler, purer thoughts.

The Five had killed Jaheira. Balthazar was one of the Five. Balthazar must die.

Abdel knew he was overmatched. The monk was too skilled for the warrior to defeat in combat. He had wanted to avenge Jaheira himself, but looking at his horribly mangled sword arm and the bone jutting from his lower leg Abdel now knew that was not to be. Yet vengeance was still possible.

The fires of Bhaal flared up within him, and Abdel abandoned himself to his father's evil. His body exploded, sending bits of flesh spewing around the room as the Ravager broke free.

The roof of the building wasn't tall enough for the demon to stand to its full height, but the beast simply hunched forward and braced itself by placing two of its arms on the stone floor. The other pair of clawed limbs extended out before the creature as it scuttled toward the doomed monk.

* * * * *

The sight of Abdel's transformation into the hideous manifestation of Bhaal's evil did not surprise Balthazar. He had expected this. He was prepared.

Balthazar ducked beneath the swiping talons of his enemy. He spun away from the gnashing, snapping jaws and delivered a series of hard kicks and punches to one of the abomination's back legs. His blows bounced harmlessly off the hard exoskeleton of the monster.

The Ravager kicked out its leg, moving so fast Balthazar never even saw the attack coming. A gigantic foot caught the monk in the chest with enough force to turn his bones to dust. But Balthazar's body was able to absorb the force and roll backward with the blow. Instead of shattering every bone in the monk's torso, the kick simply sent him tumbling backward in a series of backward somersaults that stopped just short of the stone wall.

The Ravager spun toward the monk again, its immense size effectively cornering Balthazar against the wall. The beast lunged in with all four claws this time, each hand slashing in at a different height and from a different angle.

Balthazar ducked and dodged, his body bending and twisting in ways that would have snapped the spine of an ordinary man. The Ravager was relentless in its attacks. Its claws were nothing but blurs of horrible, grasping, gashing death. Yet somehow the monk continued to evade the lethal talons, deflecting, parrying, and redirecting a half dozen attacks in a single second.

The Ravager was faster and stronger than any creature that Balthazar had encountered, but he knew it was but a beast, an untrained animal. It attacked with simple brute force and fury, it had no concept of tactics or strategy. Decades of study in the arts of combat allowed Balthazar to anticipate and defend against each and every attack.

As Balthazar learned the rhythms and patterns of the monster's assaults, he slowly began to take the offensive. Mixed in with the dodges and parries were vicious counterthrusts, punches, and kicks to the bulging, faceted, insect eyes of the demon. The beast seemed oblivious to the damage Balthazar was inflicting. It was as if pain had no meaning for this monster.

But as the monk continued to gouge and brutalize the demon's ocular organs, the Ravager's attacks became wilder and more frenzied, and less and less accurate. Soon the creature was thrashing madly, swinging blind in the fervent hope it could somehow find its opponent by touch alone and rip him to shreds.

The mad, chaotic efforts of the sightless Ravager were as ineffective as its previous attempts to destroy the monk. In desperation, the beast slammed its entire body against the wall in a wild effort to crush its elusive foe.

Balthazar sensed the desperate move and easily ducked under the Ravager's widespread legs as it coiled itself for the leap. The demon threw itself against the magically reinforced stone, sending great cracks through the very foundation of the indestructible tower.

The monster was up an instant after slamming into the stone, turning and flailing around with its arms as it tried to locate the monk. Balthazar stood calmly at the far side of the room, gathering all of his power into a single hand.

The blind beast smelled or heard or simply sensed where the tattooed man stood and charged forward. Balthazar held his ground, letting the monster come to him. He crouched beneath the Ravager's talon grasping for his throat. He leaped over a claw that slashed at his legs. Balthazar calmly stepped toward the beast and thrust his open palm into the beast's massive chest.

The Ravager reeled backward, screaming in frustration and confusion. It stumbled back, waving its four arms in futile attempt to regain its balance. Halfway across the room it collapsed to the floor, its entire body trembling with vibrations from Balthazar's quivering touch like a tuning fork struck with a hammer.

Still shrieking its impotent rage, the demon struggled to its feet. It stood unsteadily, its body quaking and shuddering as the vibrations intensified. There was a horrendous crack as a million spiderweb thin fissures appeared all at once in the chitinous shell that was the Ravager's skin. The trembling continued, wracking the monster's form with violent convulsions. The hairline cracks spread and widened, and a viscous green liquid oozed out.

The Ravager screeched one final time, then collapsed in silence on its back as great chunks of its body began to shake free, dropping to the earth with sticky thuds. A single crack wound its way up the entire length of the demon's torso, and the two halves split wide apart.

The massive body of Abdel Adrian crawled free of the mucous and slime that encased him. Balthazar could see the man's injured arm and leg had been restored during the transformation, but the big warrior seemed oblivious to his healed limbs. He flailed his hands and feet in primal revulsion, struggling to break free of the crumbling shell and the sticky, oozing substance that clung to his body like foul syrup.

Balthazar watched in curious fascination as Abdel emerged naked from the husk that had been the Ravager. Then he stepped forward and delivered a savage kick to Abdel's chest as the sellsword was wiping the repulsive slime from his eyes. The monk's blow lifted Abdel from the ground and sent the sellsword sailing through the air to slam into the stone walls of the tower, crushing the back of his skull and pulverizing his brain.

The monk walked purposefully forward to deliver the killing blow to Abdel's twitching, brain-dead corpse. He pulled up short when a tall, ethereal form materialized in his path.

"Balthazar, I am here to warn you of Melissan's plans." The creature's voice seemed to come from everywhere at once, as if an invisible chorus spoke in unison with its voice.

Wary of further treachery from Melissan, Balthazar took a step backward. "I will thwart Bhaal's Anointed," he assured the entity, not certain if it was friend or foe. "Once Abdel is slain I shall end my own life and forever remove the threat of Bhaal's return."

Much to Balthazar's surprise, the glorious being suddenly appeared nervous. "I should not tell you this . . . I should not even be here. The Hidden One disapproves of this. . . . But Melissan has gone far beyond the bounds of what was foreseen. She has made it necessary for me to break my oath of noninterference."

The monk shook his head. "I do not understand you, creature."

"Melissan does not seek to restore Bhaal—she seeks to supplant him. Even now she walks Bhaal's Abyssal plane. If she learns how to become one with Bhaal's immortal essence she will ascend to godhood."

There was silence as Balthazar mulled over the implications of the messenger's words. He had sworn himself to preventing the return of Bhaal, but to allow Melissan to become the Lord of Murder herself was an equally reprehensible solution.

"I will stop her," Balthazar declared. "Take me to her."

"I can open the path to Bhaal's realm," the magnificent being explained, "but once there you must follow Melissan through the final door yourself."

Balthazar nodded in understanding, then waited for the way to become clear. After nearly a minute the angelic being spoke again.

"Why do you hesitate, Balthazar? Time is of the essence."

"I am ready," Balthazar replied, slightly confused. "Show me the path and I shall begin the journey."

"The gate is open." There was deep concern in the entity's infinite voice. "Simply pass through to enter Bhaal's Abyssal plane. Once there, you must follow Melissan through the final door."

Balthazar turned his head from side to side. "Where? I see no gate. I see no door. I see nothing."

The shadowy being was beginning to dissolve.

"Melissan is within Bhaal's realm. She has passed through the final door. Enter the realm and follow her through the door. I will keep the gate open as long as I am able." And the creature was gone.

Knowing time was short, Balthazar rushed back and forth around the obviously empty room, trying to find the gate that was supposedly there. The inner peace Balthazar had cultivated with a lifetime of study and contemplation was rapidly disintegrating, lost in the frantic, futile search for a gate he could not see. He could feel the purpose of his very existence slipping from his grasp. Melissan was about to become the Lord of Murder, and his life's work to prevent Bhaal's return would be meaningless if he did not stop her, but he still could not see the way to his father's Abyssal realm.

Understanding dawned slowly on the monk. His mind resisted the truth, and tried to bury it in an inescapable fortress of mental will and discipline. Just as it had resisted and buried the essence of Bhaal for so many years. Balthazar could no longer deny the truth, not if he wanted to stop Melissan. Forced to accept his own impotence, he turned his attention back to the comatose Bhaalspawn on the floor.

* * * * *

The empty, gray existence of unconsciousness slipped away as Abdel's awareness returned. He felt the warmth of magical healing spreading throughout his body, bolstering his own regenerative powers with their tingling touch. Someone cradled his head in his lap, chanting the soft words of the restoring spell.

He opened his eyes, expecting to see Jaheira. Instead, he found himself staring up into the tattooed face of the black-skinned Balthazar.

Before he could react, the monk jabbed the fingers of his right hand into the side of Abdel's neck, just below the line of his jaw. Balthazar's left hand had a firm grip on the other side of Abdel's jaw, almost as if the monk was about to twist his head clean off his spine.

"If you move, Abdel, I will be forced to kill you."

Abdel knew this was no idle threat. He was unfamiliar with the particular nuances of the maneuver Balthazar seemed poised to unleash, but Abdel had no doubt it would be instantly fatal.

"Why not just kill me now and end this?" he asked. Even the slight movement caused by speaking sent jolts of pain through Abdel's neck and skull. Balthazar must have sensed the sellsword's discomfort because he loosened his grip ever so slightly.

"I must speak with you, Abdel," Balthazar said, still cradling the sellsword's head in his lap even as his hands maintained a firm and ominous pressure. "I must know if you see a gate or a door in this room."

Realizing he was at the mercy of his foe, Abdel could do little but answer honestly. Though he was unable to turn his head, Abdel cast his eyes around the circular first floor of the tower. The entrance to the building was still sealed, the only exit was the stairway to the second floor.

"I see no gate. I see no door."

"It is as I feared," the monk muttered, "I have waited too long. The messenger's power has waned, and the path is no longer open."

Balthazar sighed, a sound of despondent resignation. Almost as an afterthought he asked, "Have you ever visited the plane of our father?"

Still uncertain what the monk was insinuating, Abdel could see no reason to lie. "I have seen Bhaal's Abyssal realm."

The pressure on his neck increased momentarily, causing Abdel to wince in pain.

"How?" the monk demanded, his voice unable to mask his excitement. "How do you enter this realm?"

Abdel hesitated before answering. If Balthazar knew the secret to reaching Bhaal's world, he might very well end Abdel's life in an effort to open the passage. However, if Abdel didn't answer, Balthazar would kill him for sure. And in the end it didn't matter. Even if he could somehow break free from his current compromising position, Abdel realized he would never be able to avenge Jaheira's death. Balthazar was too great an opponent. Abdel could never defeat the tattooed warrior.

"I cannot control it," the big sellsword said carefully, resigned to his inevitable fate. "It has happened whenever

I have killed one of the Five. As they die, I suddenly find myself in the plane once ruled by Bhaal."

"Of course," Balthazar whispered. "The essence of Bhaal would return to its planar home. If the essence was great, as it was in each of the Five, your own essence would be drawn with it."

The monk's hands suddenly shifted, and Abdel braced himself for his own death. But instead of wrenching his neck, the monk's hands released their grip. Abdel felt something cold and hard slap into the palm of his right hand. He glanced down and saw he was holding Sendai's dagger. Instinctively his fingers wrapped around the grip.

"You must kill me, Abdel," Balthazar demanded. "Kill me and enter our father's world."

Abdel hesitated, unsure if this was some type of trick or test.

"Why?"

"Melissan has entered the Abyssal plane," the monk explained hastily. "She seeks to become the new Lord of Murder. You must enter the plane and pass through the final door to stop her."

Still on his back with his head on Balthazar's lap, Abdel pressed the point of Sendai's blade against the monk's throat. He didn't know if Balthazar was telling him the truth about Melissan, but he couldn't see any reason for the monk to lie. Abdel finally had his chance to avenge Jaheira. But for some reason, his hand still refused to draw the rune-covered edge across Balthazar's neck.

"Why me?" Abdel asked. "Why not just kill me and do this yourself?"

"I cannot," Balthazar replied, his voice sounding almost ashamed. "I have caged the Bhaal essence within me so thoroughly that I am no longer able to enter the realm of our father. The enchanted markings on my body keep the foul essence contained, the years of mental discipline reinforce the bars of the prison within my soul so that I am unable to access the power of my own tainted blood.

"It must be you, Abdel. You are the last of our kind. You are the only one who can follow Melissan now."

The monk tilted his head back, exposing his throat to Abdel's blade. Earlier the sellsword had lusted for just such an opportunity, but now he found he was unwilling to deliver the final cut.

"Time is of the essence," Balthazar reminded him, his voice placid and serene.

Abdel sliced the knife across the monk's neck. The warm blood rained down from the jagged wound to coat Abdel's hand and wrist. It pumped forth, splashing across the sellsword's face and chest. Balthazar's body slumped forward across Abdel's own.

Chapter Twenty-Three

Abdel recognized the Abyssal home of Bhaal through some innate feeling of familiarity. Perhaps it was his own immortal essence that drew him to this place, perhaps it was simply the fact that he had been here so many times before. Whatever the explanation, Abdel instinctively knew he was once again in his father's realm.

But he couldn't tell by looking at the surroundings. Each time he had visited Bhaal's corner of the Abyss Abdel had noticed the subtle changes. From empty void, to parched desert, to fertile, rain-soaked earth Abdel had been witness to the evolution of a dead, forgotten world. What he saw now, however, boggled his mind.

He was standing in a jungle—diseased, rotting, moribund—but a jungle nonetheless. Gnarled trees the color of deadwood arced up to disappear in the canopy of wide, yellow-splotched leaves overhead. Sickly gray vines hung down from the trees, putrid brown flowers bloomed among the infected flora.

There was no sound in the plague-filled tangle of trees and foliage, merely a heavy, oppressive silence that seemed to press in on Abdel from all sides with an almost physical presence. Even more overpowering was the pungent, cloying odor of gangrenous growth that hung in the air like a noxious cloud. With every breath Abdel was forced to fight against the urge to disgorge his last meal.

The moldering jungle grew so thick around him, Abdel could barely see five feet in front of him, but he knew the door he sought was somewhere in the murky, mildewed forest. Despite his revulsion to even touch the diseased plant life, he would have to hack his way through the growth to find the door.

Abdel took a hesitant step forward, and his bare foot sank an inch deep into the dark lichens and fungi that carpeted the ground. The decomposing moss squelched up between his toes in a dark green mush of liquid and vegetable matter. As if reacting to his movements, slime coated vines dropped down from overhead to wrap themselves around his head and bare shoulders.

He shrugged them off in disgust only to discover thick, deformed weeds had sprouted up from the earth beneath his feet and were entwining themselves around his naked legs. Abdel kicked them loose, their malnourished, sickly stalks far too feeble to offer much resistance. Gagging at the fetid stench of decomposition wafting up from the mulch beneath his feet, Abdel pressed onward.

Shuddering at the mucky feel of the vegetation against every inch of his exposed skin, Abdel snapped off branches and tore through thick jungle leaves. A blade would have made his progress far less distasteful, but Abdel was completely weaponless. Again and again he reached out with his bare hands to rip his way through the dense growth. His fingers became discolored and sticky with the foul-smelling sap leaking from the plants surrounding him.

It didn't take him long to realize that the plants were pressing in on all sides—literally. The foliage reached out to brush against him like the begging hands of lepers huddled in front of Ilmater's temple. The vines continued to drop down from above, coating him with their stringy, tangled tendrils. Roots and weeds hounded his every step, writhing in and about his legs and feet as if they would trip him up.

The clutching, grasping forest of living disease quickly became more than mere inconvenience. Abdel found himself struggling to maintain his balance beneath the heavy net of sickly, wet vines from above. The malevolent undergrowth became more insistent, tugging and yanking at his feet and ankles and quickly wrapping itself up as high as his knees if Abdel kept his foot in place for more than a few seconds.

The realm of Bhaal was opposing him, trying to prevent him from blazing through the jungle in his search for the door through which Melissan herself had passed. It was succeeding. Abdel became frantic, swatting and kicking furiously in his efforts to dislodge the aggressive plants, but no matter how much he struggled he could not break free.

Abdel reached down deep inside himself, trying to summon the Ravager once more. Balthazar might have bested the gigantic beast, but Abdel knew his demonic form could easily tear a savage path through the vegetation. The fires of his father's fury began to rise, and Abdel braced himself for the terrible transformation.

It never came. Abdel could feel the inferno blazing within his soul, but it had no effect on him. The jungle, however, responded emphatically. Like some enormous spider spinning a cocoon, the plant life wrapped itself in spirals around him. The trees bent down to entwine their branches around Abdel's limbs, caressing and clinging to him like a long-abandoned lover.

Abdel realized Bhaal's world was indeed alive, but it wasn't attacking him or impeding him. It was drawn to him. It recognized the immortal essence within Abdel, and it wanted to fawn and fondle him. In trying to summon the Ravager, Abdel had only intensified the yearning of the jungle.

With awareness came mastery. Abdel stopped resisting the plants and instead focused his will on shaping them. He imagined the thick vegetation retreating, drawing away like respectful servants retreating after their master had dismissed them. The vines, roots, and branches encasing his body receded in response to the will of one of Bhaal's children.

Abdel envisioned the jungle parting before him, clearing a path to the hidden door that led to Melissan, and again his mere desire made it so. The way before him was obvious now, a narrow corridor knifing through the dense growth that led straight to a single wooden door standing untouched by the forest.

The leaves rustled as he walked past, like subjects waving at the procession of a new king's coronation. Unimpeded, Abdel marched to the door and opened it without hesitating.

The realm of Bhaal vanished, and Abdel found himself in the void once again. But this void was already occupied. Melissan hovered in the emptiness, her body encased in a pillar of glowing power. The ends of the shining column stretched to infinity in every direction, but its width was barely enough for a single person.

At least, Abdel assumed it was Melissan in the light. The tall, attractive woman he remembered from previous meetings was gone. In her place floated a hairless, smooth skinned being who was neither male nor female. Melissan had become both ageless and sexless. She had shed all previous identities, and was in the process of being reborn, remade, and rebuilt as an immortal.

The new Melissan noticed Abdel hovering in the void beside her. When she spoke Abdel was not surprised to discover her voice had already begun to adopt the infinite depth of an immortal.

"So the Avatar of Bhaal has triumphed over Balthazar. I am impressed." Despite her words, Abdel knew she was mocking him.

"Have you come to stop me, Abdel? Come to strip me of my destiny?"

Abdel said nothing, but simply nodded. Melissan drifted free from the column of power, gasping slightly for air as if she had been taking a long drink.

"If you want Bhaal's power, all you have to do is come and get it," she taunted.

Angry, vengeful thoughts propelled Abdel through the void as he flew at her throat. His outstretched hands clasped themselves around the entity's neck and squeezed. Melissan disintegrated into sparkling dust, then reformed a few feet away.

"Your ignorance is amusing," she chuckled. "You cannot kill me here, Abdel. This is Bhaal's world, and I am now a part of it. Not just a part of it, Abdel. I *am* this world! This world is me! I have become one with the immortal essence!"

Abdel recalled how his encounter with Sarevok in the Abyss had been similarly ineffective. He realized it might truly be impossible to kill Melissan in this world, but somehow, he vowed, he would make her pay for Jaheira's and Imoen's deaths.

He hurtled toward her again, but Melissan simply raised a smooth hand and repelled his assault with a flick of her wrist. Abdel felt himself spiraling toward the glowing column in the center of the empty universe.

Melissan watched with interest as the big sellsword was sucked into the pillar. Abdel felt the euphoria of infinite power washing over him. He felt the endless possibilities of immortality, the unlimited potential of being a god. He was drowning in the essence of Bhaal.

His euphoria turned to panic. Abdel could feel himself dissolving. He was becoming incorporeal, his form washing away in the river of energy raging through him. His physical manifestation was being wiped away, buried beneath the all-consuming identity of the immortal. Like Melissan he was becoming one with the sum of Bhaal's essence. Unlike Melissan, Abdel was not prepared for it.

"Good," Melissan cooed, "give yourself over to Bhaal's power. Mingle your essence with that of your father and your siblings that I may devour you all."

Abdel tried to break free of the glowing pillar. It was like swimming from the center of a whirlpool. The currents drawing him back to the center were too strong to resist.

"Do not struggle, Abdel," Melissan advised. "This is what must be. From Bhaal's common seed all the Children were born, and to a single pool you must all return. You are all one and the same. Bhaalspawn, offspring of the Lord of Murder. It is what you are. It is what defines you."

"No," Abdel said weakly, his very will to resist vanishing beneath the onslaught, his identity and sense of self eroding. His memories were vanishing despite his efforts to hang on to them, spilling through his clenched fists like grains of sand.

Imoen, Gorion. The names meant nothing to him now, and then even the names were gone, swept away by the irresistible currents of the collective infinite identity surrounding him. Everything he had been was being stripped away, until only the essence of his father remained. Even his own name was lost now. All he had left was the face of a woman, her slightly pointed ears and violet eyes hinting at the elf side of her parentage.

Jaheira. He clung to her memory, refusing to lose the last spark of his individuality. He drew strength from her name. Jaheira. He managed to conjure up recollections of not just her face but her voice. Jaheira. Abdel could feel substance returning to his body. He could hear his lover's laugh, he could feel her warm touch. Jaheira.

"Your submission to the collective essence is inevitable," Melissan declared. "You are a Bhaalspawn."

Jaheira. He could remember her clearly now, the half-elf druid who had stood by him during his darkest times. The lover who had even resisted the call of death to spend one last night by his side. He remembered everything about her: the feel of her soft touch, the smell of her long hair, the sound of her laugh.

And he remembered what she had told him. *Remember who you are.* At last he understood. They were all wrong—

Gorion, Sarevok, Melissan, the Five, Balthazar. Even Jaheira had been wrong, though it was her words and love that had saved him and led him to true understanding.

"No!" Abdel's voice resonated with renewed strength. "I am not just some speck floating in this infinite whole! I am not just a Bhaalspawn!

"I am Abdel Adrian! Hero of Baldur's Gate! Savior of the Tree of Life! Son of Bhaal, ward of Gorion, lover of Jaheira!"

Abdel finally understood.

He stopped trying to deny the part of him that was his father's legacy. The taint of Bhaal was within him, it was a part of who he was. Gorion and Jaheira had tried to suppress that part of him, and to please them Abdel had tried to separate himself from it. Balthazar had succeeded in accomplishing what Abdel could not. He had cut himself completely off from his immortal taint, caging it so completely that he was not able to call upon it when he needed it. That was not the answer. By denying that part of his soul, Abdel left a hole in his own identity.

But Sarevok, the Five and even Melissan had gone too far in acknowledging the essence of the Lord of Murder within the Bhaalspawn. They had fed and nurtured the small bit of evil within them, until it became consuming and they lost themselves to their father's fury. That was not the answer either.

He was a Child of Bhaal. It was a part of him. But only a part, nothing more. It did not define him—he would not let it define him. He was who he was, nothing more, nothing less. He was Abdel Adrian.

"I am Abdel Adrian." he declared once more, affirming his individuality against the force drawing him in toward a single, collective existence.

The current sucking him down toward the center of the pillar was suddenly gone, and Abdel was able to float back out into the void to confront Melissan again.

Surprised, she watched him emerge from the glowing column of divinity. Abdel casually swung his fist at

Melissan's face. As before, her form simply dissolved and reformed, completely unharmed by his punch.

"Your fortitude and persistence surprise me, Bhaalspawn," she admitted. "But no matter. I have no need of your essence to complete my ascension. And once I am a god I will crush you without a second thought."

"You are no god," Abdel said simply. "You are Melissan, nothing more."

He reached out again and swung his fist through his foe's insubstantial form. But this time he felt a hint of resistance as he made contact. From the expression on her face as her spirit reformed, he knew Melissan felt it too.

"You are Melissan, Bhaal's Anointed," he insisted, "False protector of the Bhaalspawn. Betrayer of the Five. Manipulator. Liar. Deceiver. But you, Melissan, are no god. You are an invader in this realm. You are not a part of this world. You do not belong!"

Abdel's fist caught Melissan beneath a suddenly solid chin, and he felt the jaw bone crack beneath the force of his blow. Her hairless head snapped back, and her mouth twisted into an O of shock and pain.

Long before he had met Melissan or even Jaheira, long before he had any hint of his immortal heritage, Abdel had been a brawler. A blade for hire. A mercenary and a sellsword. He settled his disputes with fists and weapons, and all his problems could be solved with simple brute force.

With the knowledge of who and what he truly was, Abdel's life had become much more complicated. The responsibilities and challenges facing the son of a god were convoluted and complex, and required more than mere fisticuffs to solve. But now, on the cusp of immortality, facing the greatest challenge of his life, Abdel had returned to his simple roots.

"I am Abdel Adrian," he declared, slamming his heavy hands into Melissan again and again, "and you are no god."

He pummeled the suddenly all too physically real spirit of Melissan with his bare hands, pounding her body into submission as it feebly tried to ward off his fists. He beat the woman who had betrayed and manipulated him since Saradush until she was nothing but a bloody, bruised pulp of physical, mortal existence. Then he grabbed the thing that would be a god by its shoulders and hurled it into the glowing, pulsating pillar.

The column flared momentarily as Melissan's screaming form was consumed by the light. The essence of Bhaal that she had already managed to steal became one with the greater whole. The insignificant physical shell that remained—the part of Melissan that was still Melissan—was instantly and totally obliterated by the divine power.

Abdel waited for an eternity to be sure his enemy was truly gone. Once he was confident Melissan's existence had been completely annihilated, he willed himself back through the door between the void of Bhaal's true essence and the realm of the Abyss Bhaal had chosen to make his own.

Epilogue

He emerged from the door and found himself amid the thick, decaying vegetation once again. Abdel waved his hand, dispelling the entire jungle with a single thought. In the distance he could see a ring of sharp, forbidding mountains. These also vanished on nothing more than a whim.

"You have done well, Abdel Adrian."

Hearing the infinite voice of the celestial entity did not surprise Abdel. He doubted anything would surprise him for a very, very long time.

"Now what?" he asked, his voice betraying the weariness he felt in his very soul.

"You stand on the edge of godhood," the creature explained. "You are the last heir to Bhaal's immortality. It is yours to take."

Abdel shook his head. "It's not mine. It never was."

The creature tilted its head slightly. "There is much you can do with this power," it reminded him. "Your greatest desires can be achieved in an instant."

"Can I bring Jaheira back? Or Imoen? Or Gorion?"

"No," the being admitted. "Even a god must accept certain events as things that cannot be undone. But there is much you might accomplish as an immortal, Abdel."

"There is still much I can accomplish as a mere mortal," Abdel pointed out.

"Your wisdom is most unexpected in a Child of Bhaal."

Abdel shrugged. "There is more to me than my bloodline."

"You understand that if you reject this destiny you will lose the essence of those you have absorbed within you. You will cease to be an avatar, and you will become a normal human male, with all the vulnerabilities and weaknesses of other men."

"I understand." With a rueful smile, Abdel added, "I'm looking forward to it. I was not meant to be a god, or even an avatar. It is not who I am."

"Then I shall free you from this burden."

Deep within his body Abdel felt the faintest pull. It lasted but a moment, and was completely painless. He peered into his soul and discovered only the tiniest ember of Bhaal's spirit within himself. This miniscule portion of immortal essence was his to keep. It had been a part of him at his birth and it would be a part of him when he died. But it was simply that. A part of him. A small, virtually insignificant piece of a much greater puzzle.

The big warrior turned his attention back to the celestial being who had guided him through this bizarre journey. Abdel couldn't read any emotion on the face of the man, but he sensed this was not the end the entity had anticipated.

"You seem disappointed."

"Not disappointed, merely surprised. This possible destiny was foreseen by the one I serve, but certainly it was not expected."

"What happens now?"

"I shall disperse the essence of Bhaal throughout the world," the celestial entity promised. "The Lord of Murder will disappear forever."

The words should have filled Abdel with joy, but he had lost too much, paid too dearly, to feel any happiness within his soul. Gorion, his foster father. Imoen, his sister. Jaheira, his true love. Even the death of the reborn Sarevok added to the seemingly infinite list of those who had stood by Abdel, and fallen.

"You are not responsible for those deaths, Abdel," the

divine messenger assured him. "You cannot carry the guilt of their blood on your shoulders."

"And what of the pain?" Abdel asked. "Regardless of guilt, the pain is still there."

"Your wounds go deep," the being admitted, "but in time even your scars will heal, Abdel Adrian."

Abdel nodded, knowing it was true. But there was still something he needed to know.

"So what happens to me? What is my destiny now?"

The great figure standing before him vanished. The Abyssal realm of Bhaal dissolved, and Abdel found himself standing on a trail he had crossed many times before. A half mile to the north the road led to his childhood home of Candlekeep. To the south it met up with the trade routes that wound throughout the width and breadth of the Sword Coast, down into the Southlands and across the entire continent of Faerûn.

Your destiny, the infinite voice said inside Abdel's head in answer to his question, *is whatever you choose to make it.*

Realizing he was once again wandering around completely naked, Abdel could only sigh. He hesitated a brief second, then started up the path toward the mountaintop silhouette of Candlekeep, just barely visible in the rapidly fading sun.

Venture into the
FORGOTTEN REALMS
with these two new series!

Sembia
GET A NEW PERSPECTIVE ON THE FORGOTTEN REALMS FROM
THESE TALES OF THE USKEVREN CLAN OF SELGAUNT.

Shadow's Witness
Paul Kemp

Erevis Cale has a secret. When a ruthless evil is unleashed on Selgaunt,
the loyal butler of the Uskevren family must come to terms with his own
dark past if he is to save the family he dearly loves.

The Shattered Mask
Richard Lee Byers

Shamur Uskevren is duped into making an assassination attempt on her husband
Thamalon. Soon, however, the dame of House Uskevren realizes that all is not
as it seems and that her family is in grave danger.

JUNE 2001

Black Wolf
Dave Gross

The young Talbot Uskevren was the only one to survive a horrible
"hunting accident." Now, infected with lycanthropy, the second son
of the Uskevren clan must learn to control what he has become.

NOVEMBER 2001

The Cities
A NEW SERIES OF STAND-ALONE NOVELS,
EACH SET IN ONE OF THE MIGHTY CITIES OF FAERÛN.

The City of Ravens
Richard Baker

Raven's Bluff — a viper pit of schemes, swindles, wizardry, and
fools masquerading as heroes.

Temple Hill
Drew Karpyshyn

Elversult — fashionable and comfortable, this shining city of the heartlands
harbors an unknown evil beneath its streets.

SEPTEMBER 2001

FORGOTTEN REALMS

COLLECT THE ADVENTURES OF
DRIZZT DO'URDEN AS WRITTEN BY
BEST-SELLING AUTHOR
R.A. SALVATORE

FOR THE FIRST TIME IN ONE VOLUME!

Legacy of the Drow Collector's Edition

Now together in an attractive hardcover edition, follow Drizzt's battles against the drow through the four-volume collection of

THE LEGACY, STARLESS NIGHT, SIEGE OF DARKNESS, and PASSAGE TO DAWN.

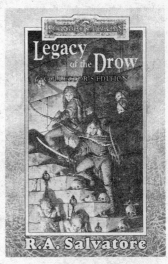

The Icewind Dale Trilogy
Collector's Edition

Read the tales that introduced the world to Drizzt Do'Urden in this collector's edition containing *The Crystal Shard, Streams of Silver,* and *The Halfling's Gem.*

NOW AVAILABLE IN PAPERBACK!

The Dark Elf Trilogy
Collector's Edition

Learn the story of Drizzt's tortured beginnings in the evil city of Menzoberranzan in the best-selling novels *Homeland, Exile,* and *Sojourn.*

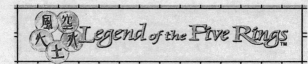

The Phoenix
Stephen D. Sullivan

The five Elemental Masters—
the greatest magic-wielders of
Rokugan—seek to turn back the
demons of the Shadowlands. To do
so, they must harness the power of
the Black Scrolls, and perhaps
become demons themselves.

March 2001

The Dragon
Ree Soesbee

The most mysterious of all the clans
of Rokugan, the Dragon had long
stayed elusive in their mountain
stronghold. When at last they
emerge into the Clan War, they
unleash a power that could well save
the empire . . . or doom it.

September 2001

The Crab
Stan Brown

For a thousand years, the Crab have
guarded the Emerald Empire against
demon hordes—but when the greatest
threat comes from within, the Crab
must ally with their fiendish foes and
march to take the capital city.

June 2001

The Lion
Stephen D. Sullivan

Since the Scorpion Coup, the Clans
of Rokugan have made war upon
each other. Now, in the face of Fu
Leng and his endless armies of
demons, the Seven Thunders must
band together to battle their
immortal foe . . . or die!

November 2001